This Angel on My Chest

This Angel
on My Chest

Stories

∾

Leslie Pietrzyk

UNIVERSITY OF PITTSBURGH PRESS

The following stories have been previously published:
"Ten Things," *The Sun,* and reprinted in *The Mysterious Life of the Heart,* edited by Sy Safransky (North Carolina: The Sun Publishing Company, 2009); "Acquiescence," *Shenandoah;* "Slut," *Cimarron Review;* "I Am the Widow," *r.kv.r.y;* "One True Thing," *The Collagist;* "Someone in Nebraska," *Potomac Review;* "What I Could Buy," *Hobart;* "The Circle," *Gettysburg Review.* A section of "One Art" was performed at Story League: Sophomore Outing, May 2011, Washington, DC.

Published by the University of Pittsburgh Press, Pittsburgh, PA, 15260
Copyright © 2015, Leslie Pietrzyk
All rights reserved
Manufactured in the United State of America
Printed on acid-free paper
10 9 8 7 6 5 4 3 2 1

Library of Congress Cataloging-in-Publication Data

Pietrzyk, Leslie, 1961–
[Short stories. Selections]
This Angel on My Chest: Stories / Leslie Pietrzyk.
    pages ; cm — (Drue Heinz Literature Prize)
    ISBN 978-0-8229-4442-3 (hardcover: alk. paper)
I. Title.
PS3566.I428A6 2015
813'.54—dc23

2015025366

We tell ourselves stories in order to live.

Joan Didion, *The White Album*

Contents

This Angel on My Chest

TEN THINGS

These are ten things that only you know now:

ONE

He joked that he would die young. You imagined ninety-nine to your hundred. But by "young" he meant sixty-five, fifty-five. What "young" ended up meaning was thirty-five.

In the memory book the funeral home gave you (actually, that you paid for; nothing there was free, not even delivering the flowers to a nursing home the next day, which cost sixty-five dollars, but you were too used up to care), there was a page to record his exact age in years, months, and days. You added hours; you even added minutes, because you had that information. You were there when he had the heart attack.

Now, when thinking about his life, it seemed to you that minutes were so very important. There was that moment in the emergency room when you begged for ten more minutes. You would've traded anything, everything, for one more second, for the speck of time it would take to say his name, to hear him say your name.

Later, when you thought about it (because suddenly there was so much time to think; too little time, too much—time was just one more thing you couldn't make sense of anymore), you wondered why he'd told you he was going to die young. The first time he said it, you punched his arm. "Don't say that," you said. "Don't ever say that again, ever." But he said it another day and another and lots of days after that. And you punched his shoulder every time, because it was bad luck, bad mental energy, but you knew he'd say it again. You knew then that there would always be one more time for everything.

TWO

He once compared you to an avocado. He was never good at saying what he meant in fancy ways. (You had a boyfriend in college who dedicated poems to you, one of which won a contest in the student literary magazine, but that boyfriend never compared you to anything as simple and real as an avocado.)

You were sitting on the patio in the backyard. It was the day the dog got loose and ran out onto Route 50, and you found him by the side of the road—two legs mangled and blood everywhere—and you pulled off your windbreaker and wrapped the dog in it while your husband stood next to you whispering, "Oh God, oh God," because there was so much blood. He drove to the vet, catching every red light, while you held the dog close and murmured dog secrets in his ear, feeling his warm blood soak your clothes. And when the vet said she was sorry, that it was too late, you were the one who cupped the dog's head in both hands while she slipped in the needle, and you were the one who remembered to take off the dog's collar, unbuckling it slowly and looping it twice around your wrist, and you were the one whose face the dog tried to lick but couldn't quite reach.

So, that night, out on the patio, the two of you were sitting close, thinking about the dog. It was really too cold to be on the patio, but the dog had loved the backyard; every tree was a personal friend, each squirrel or bird an encroaching enemy. It was just cold enough that you felt him shiver, and he felt you shiver, but neither of you suggested going inside just yet. That's when he said, "I've decided you're like an avocado."

You almost didn't ask why, you were so busy thinking about the dog's tongue trying to reach your face and failing, even when you leaned right down next to his mouth. But then you asked anyway.

He looked up at the dark sky. "You're sort of tough on the outside," he said. "A little intimidating."

"Maybe," you said, but you knew he was right. In photos, you always looked as if you didn't want to be there. Lost tourists never asked you for directions; they asked your husband. It was something you'd become used to and no longer thought about or wondered why anymore.

He continued: "But inside, you're soft and creamy. Luscious, just like a perfectly ripe avocado. That's the part of you I get. And underneath that is the hardest, strongest core of anyone I know. Like how you were today at the vet. Like how you are with everything. An avocado."

At the time, you smiled and mumbled, but could only think about the dog, the poor dog. That was five years ago. What you remember now is not so much the dog's tongue but being compared to an avocado.

THREE

He predicted a grand slam at a baseball game. It was the Orioles versus the Red Sox, a sellout game up in Baltimore, on a bright, sunny June day, the kind of day when you look out the window and think, *Baseball.* But in Baltimore it wasn't possible to go to a game just because it was a sunny day; they were sold out months and months in advance—especially against teams like Boston, which had fans whose fathers had been Red Sox fans, whose kids were Red Sox fans, and whose grandkids would be Red Sox fans. He'd actually bought the tickets way back in December, not knowing what kind of day it would be, and it just happened to be that perfect kind of baseball day.

He'd grown up listening to games on the radio, sprawled sideways across his bed in the dark listening to A.M. stations from faraway Chicago, New York, St. Louis. He still remembered the call letters and could reel them off like a secret code. Now he brought his radio to the game in Baltimore and balanced it on the armrest between your seats, and the announcers' voices drifted up in bits and snatches, and part of him was sitting next to you eating a hot dog and cheering and part of him was that child sprawled in the dark listening to distant voices.

The bases were loaded, and Cal Ripken came up to bat. Cal was your favorite player. You'd once seen him pick up a piece of litter that was blowing around the field and tuck it into his back pocket. Something about that impressed you as much as all those consecutive games he'd played.

"What's Cal going to do?" he asked.

You looked at your score card. (He'd taught you how to keep score; you liked the organization and had developed a special system, with filled-in diamonds for home runs, a K for a strikeout, and squiggly lines to indicate a pitching change.) Cal wasn't batting especially well lately—the beginnings of a slump, you thought. "Hit into a double play," you said. Cal had hit into a lot of double plays that season, ended a lot of innings.

He shook his head. "He's knocking the grand salami"—meaning a home run bringing in all four runners. You'd never seen one in person before.

"Cal doesn't have many grand slams," you said—not to be mean (after all, Cal was your favorite player), but because it was true. You knew Cal's stats, and his grand-slam total was four at the time, after all those years in the majors.

"Well, he's getting one now," he said.

After Cal fouled twice for two strikes, you glanced over at him. "It'll come," he said.

On the next pitch, Cal whacked the ball all the way across that blue sky.

Everyone stood and cheered and screamed and stomped their feet, and he held the radio in his hand and flung his arm around your shoulders and squeezed tight. From the radio by your ear, you heard the echo of everyone cheering, and you thought about a boy alone in the dark listening to that sound.

FOUR

He was afraid of bugs: outdoor bugs and indoor bugs; bugs big enough to cast shadows and little bugs that could be pieces of lint. Not "afraid" as in running screaming from the room, but "afraid" as in watching TV and pretending not to see the fat cricket in the corner or walking into the bathroom first thing in the morning and ignoring the spider frantically zigzagging across the sink.

"There's a bug on the wall," you might say, pointing, hand out-stretched, forcing him finally to look up and follow to see where your hand was pointing. You'd repeat: "There's a bug on the wall."

Still he'd say nothing.

"Do you see it?" you'd ask.

He'd nod.

So you'd grab a tissue and squish the bug, maybe letting out a sharp sigh, as if you knew you weren't the one who should be doing this. Or, if it were a big, messy bug like a cricket, you might scoop it up and drop it out the window. Sometimes, if you waited too long, the bug (silverfish, in particular) would scurry into the crack between the wall and carpet, and you'd imagine it reemerging in the future: bigger, stronger, braver, meaner. Bugs in the bathtub were easiest, because you could run water and wash them down the drain. You learned many different ways to get rid of bugs.

He never said, "Thank you for killing the bugs." He never said that he was afraid of bugs. You never accused him of being afraid of bugs.

FIVE

He kept his books separate from yours. Certain shelves on certain bookcases were his; others were yours.

Maybe it made sense when you were living together, before you were married. If one of you had to move out, it would only be a matter of scooping armloads of books off the shelves, rather than sorting through, picking over each volume, having to think. It would allow you to get out fast. Plus, with separate shelves, he could stare at his long, tidy line of hardcovers, undisturbed by the scandalous disarray of your used paperbacks. He liked to stare at his books with his head cocked to the right—not necessarily reading the titles, just staring at the shelf of books, at their length and breadth and bulk. You never knew what he was thinking when he did this.

After your wedding, when you moved into the new house, you said something about combining the books, maybe putting all the novels in one place and all the history books in another and all the travel books together and so on, like that.

He was looking out the window at the new backyard, at the grass no one had cut for weeks and weeks. Finally, he said, "We own every last damn blade of grass."

"What about the books?" you asked. You were trying to get some unpacking done. There were boxes everywhere. The only way to walk through rooms was to wind along narrow paths between stacked boxes. There were built-in bookcases in the living room by the fireplace—two features the realtor had mentioned again and again, as if she knew that you were imagining sitting in front of a fire, reading books, sipping wine, letting the machine take the calls. As if she knew exactly the kind of life you had planned.

"I'll do the books," he said. But he didn't step away from the window.

It was a nice backyard, with a brick patio, and when you'd stood out there for the first time, during the open house, you'd thought about summer nights with the baseball game on the radio and the coals dying down in the grill and the lingering scent of medium-rare steak and a couple of stars squeezing through the glare of the city to find the two of you.

Again you offered to do the books; you *wanted* to do the books. You wanted all those books organized on the shelves; his and yours, yours and his.

"I never thought I'd own anything I couldn't pack into a car," he said.

You felt so bad you started to cry, certain only you wanted the house, only you wanted the wedding. "Is it so awful?" you asked.

He reached over some boxes to touch your arm. "No, it's not awful at all," he said, and it turned out that this was what you really wanted—not the patio, not the built-in shelves next to the fireplace, not the grass in the backyard, but the touch of his hand on your arm.

You did the books together, and suddenly something about keeping them separate felt right, as if now you realized that the books would be fine on separate shelves of the same bookcase, in the house you'd bought for the life you had.

SIX

He once saw a ghost. He was mowing the lawn in front, and you were in back clipping the honeysuckle that grew over the fence. Your neighbor—an original owner who'd bought his house for seven thousand dollars in 1959—wanted to spray kerosene and set the vines on fire, but you said no. You liked the smell of honeysuckle on June nights. You liked the hummingbirds flitting among the flowers in August. You even liked all that clipping, letting your mind go blank as you wrestled with the vines, cutting and tugging, yanking and twisting and pulling—knowing that whatever you cut would grow back by the end of the summer, that in the end the honeysuckle would always come back, maybe even if your neighbor burned down the vines.

It was that time of the early evening when the shadows were long and cool and the dew was rising on the grass; that time when, as a barefoot child, you would start getting damp toes. You half heard the lawn mower whining back and forth, back and forth, and you were thinking ahead to sitting on the patio and watching the fireflies float up out of the long, weedy grass under the apple tree. Then the lawn mower stopped abruptly; it needed more gas, you thought, or maybe there was a plastic bag in the way. When the silence lingered, you walked around to the front yard, curious, and found him leaning up against the car in the driveway, the silent lawn mower in front of him. The streetlight flicked on as you reached him; he held out his arms for a hug, and you felt his sweat, tacky against your skin.

"I saw a ghost," he said.

You pushed the hair back from his forehead and blew lightly on it to cool him down. His forehead was pale compared to the rest of his face.

He pointed over toward the big maple tree, the one that was so pretty each autumn. But nothing was there.

"What kind of ghost?" you asked. You still had your hand on top of his head, and when you removed it, his hair stayed back where you'd pushed it.

"Like a soldier from the Civil War," he said. "He was leaning against that tree, and then he was gone."

"Confederate or Union?" you asked.

He looked annoyed, as if you'd asked the wrong thing, but it seemed a logical question.

"It was a ghost," he said. "I saw a ghost."

"Did he do anything?"

"Maybe it was the heat," he said.

"Maybe it was a real ghost," you said. "Confederate encampments were along here." There was a silence. A car went by too fast, music spilling from its open window. "That tree's big enough to have been here then."

"This is stupid," he said, and he leaned down and pulled the cord on the lawn mower. The engine roared, and he couldn't hear you anymore, and you watched him push the mower across the yard. You saw nothing under the maple tree, just newly cut grass spit into lines and shadows stretching slowly into the dark.

Now you're the one who cuts the grass. People tell you to hire a service, but you don't. When you're done mowing in the evening, you lean against the car and wait, but all you ever see are fireflies rising from the damp grass where you leave it long under the maple tree.

SEVEN

When he ate malted milk balls, he sucked the chocolate off first. Thinking you weren't watching, he'd roll the candies from one side of his mouth to the other, making the sort of tiny noises you'd imagine a chipmunk would make, or a small bird, or something else tiny and cute. If he caught you watching him, he'd instantly stop. Sometimes, just to tease, you'd ask a question to make him talk, and his words would come out lumpy and garbled, pushed around the sides of the candy. "What?" you'd say, still teasing. "I don't understand." But no matter how much you teased, he never chewed.

That's the way he was. He had a special way of doing everything. He developed a method of eating watermelon with a knife, cutting slices so thin the seeds would slither out, and setting aside the juiciest fillet from the middle to eat last. There was an order in which to read the newspaper (sports, business, style, metro, front page). The two of you never left a football or a baseball game until the last second had ticked off the clock, regardless of a lopsided score or a ten-below wind chill or being late to meet someone for dinner. He always carried a pen in his pocket and kept long lists of things to do and places to see on little yellow sticky notes inside his wallet.

If someone had told you about a person who did all these things, who imposed these rules on himself, you would've thought he was odd, annoying. But you found out piece by piece—like putting together a puzzle—and now you couldn't imagine your husband being any other way.

You watched him eat malted milk balls one Easter morning (you'd made two little Easter baskets, setting them up on the kitch- en table, each different because you liked different kinds of candy), reading the Sunday paper in his usual order. You were about to tease him, to make him talk around that gob of candy, to see if he'd bite down just this one time, but before you could say anything, he mumbled something to you, and you didn't say, "What?" because you knew exactly what he'd said; there were always more ways to say, "I love you," and through a mouthful of malted milk balls on Easter morning was only one.

EIGHT

He hated his job for years. You lay in bed and listened to him grinding his teeth at night, unsure whether to wake him. You fan- tasized about waking him: "Let's talk," you'd say, and he would tell you all the things he was thinking, tell you exactly why he hated his job and how he really felt about the long, endless reports he wrote that no one ever read. You would offer sympathy, advice, kindness; you'd tell him to quit his job, offer to do his résumé on the computer; or maybe the two of you would just cry and hold each other tight.

But that's not what happened the times you did wake him. He told you he was fine, told you he was tired of complaining about his stupid job, told you to go to sleep. He used kinder words than these, but his voice was expressionless, like a machine that runs on and on by itself. And then you both pretended to be asleep, and then he really was asleep, because he was grinding his teeth again.

You tried to bring up the subject during the day. "No job is worth this," you said when you called him at his office.

"I can't talk now," he whispered.

"Then when?" you asked.

There was a pause, and you heard his boss being paged in the background. He said, "My father worked for forty years on the line at Chrysler. You think every day was great?"

"This is different," you said.

And he said, "Nothing's different."

The conversation never went farther than that. It was his boss; it was the nature of the business; it was turning thirty; it was stress; it was long hours; it was making enough money that most other jobs would be a step down; it was too much overseas travel; it was overly ambitious coworkers and unambitious secretaries; it was rush-hour traffic; it was sucking up taxpayer money to fund projects that improved nothing except the bottom line of the firm; it was living in an expensive neighborhood in an expensive city on the East Coast; it was a wife who wanted to be a writer and consequently was earning no money; it was needing his health-insurance plan because that was when you still thought you could have a baby together; it was being the oldest child, the responsible one; it was being raised in the Midwest; it was trying to prove he was as tough as his father and his grandfather—tougher; it was being brought up to despise weakness and whiners. You knew it was all those things, but you suspected there was something more that he didn't want to or couldn't explain but that you could help with . . . if only he would talk.

This is what you thought about on those nights when you pretended to sleep: You prayed for him to talk, even though you hadn't been to church in ten years. It felt strange to ask God to make a man talk. You thought about numbers: How many Monday mornings are there in a year? How many Fridays when he had to work late? How many quick lunches at a desk? What do you get if you divide X amount of dollars in his paycheck by Y amount of unhappiness and multiply the result by a year, two years? How many times can one man grind his teeth in a single night?

"It doesn't have to be me," you told him. "Talk to anyone. A friend, your dad, a therapist, a bartender. Just talk. Please."

"There's nothing to say" was all you got from him.

The silence was thick and hard and invisible, like air before a storm. You waited and waited.

One night, you woke up and he wasn't next to you. When he didn't come back to bed, you got up and found him downstairs at the kitchen table writing on a yellow legal pad. A tiny moth circled the overhead light; you watched it instead of him. You asked, "Working late?"

He shook his head, kept writing, flipped the page over, wrote some more, and finally said, "I'm writing a movie."

He might as well have said he was being beheaded in the morning; it was that surprising.

The moth flew too close to the light bulb then dropped onto the table next to him. You leaned in, brushed the dead moth into your cupped hand, threw it in the garbage, and went back to bed.

The next day, he told you the plot of his movie: a guy who hates his job goes to baseball camp to relive his childhood fantasies and wins the big game—not by blasting in a home run, but by bunting.

It took him months to write the screenplay. He thought he was going to sell it in Hollywood and buy a house with a pool and retire. By the time he realized that wasn't going to happen, it didn't matter, because there were changes at his job, new projects that he'd developed and was implementing, ideas that made sense, that made people pay attention. It wasn't the same old story.

You liked that he was happy at work. He talked to you about what he was doing, about his projects, about the results of his work.

The handwritten manuscript of his movie stayed on your night-stand.

NINE

The combination to the lock on the garden shed (0–14–5), where you keep the lawn mower, the rake, the snow shovel, the garden hose.

Every fall, mice took over the shed; you never actually saw them, only the traces they left behind—dry droppings like caraway seeds; a corner chewed out of the box of grass seed; footprints crisscrossing the dust. He looked into poison. A neighbor across the street told him the right kind. "It shrivels their body from the inside," the neighbor explained, "so they dry up: no smell, no mess in a trap, no nothing. Clean and easy."

You didn't like mice. No one likes mice. But what kind of way to die was that, leaving nothing behind?

He set out the poison anyway.

Now, when you open the shed to drag out the lawn mower, you look for some sign of the mice, but he cleaned out the shed in the early spring, swept up all the droppings, hosed away the dust. You think that maybe you thanked him, but maybe not. After he was gone, faced with so much more to do than anyone could imagine, as if the world's to-do list had ended up on your own, you were relieved that cleaning out the shed wasn't on the list.

Now you're somehow disappointed that there are no mice, no

way to know they were once here. You think, *They'll be back in the fall*. And you know that during the winter you'll keep the shed locked, that you won't look. Then you can think, *The mice are there*, never checking to see if you're right or wrong.

TEN

You cheated on him. Once. Barely. Not enough to count, not really. But it was with his best friend, the one he'd grown up with, the one with the odd nickname you never quite understood, the one who met you at the emergency room and cried as hard as you did.

It happened in your kitchen at a party one night when you were drinking too much and your husband was drinking even more than you and, even though it was his birthday, you weren't talking to him, and he wasn't talking to you, but no one knew this except for his best friend, because you both acted how you were supposed to act at a birthday party. You were telling his friend your side of the story, why you were right, and he was agreeing, and the next thing you knew, you were kissing the friend, not a quick, simple kiss, not an embarrassed kiss, but a real kiss, lingering.

It was that sudden.

You thought about that kiss for a long time afterward. You remembered every detail—and that, as much as the kiss, was the cheating part, wasn't it?

The friend said he wouldn't tell, but he did. You didn't find this out until a couple of weeks after the funeral, when you were talking to him on the phone late one night because neither of you could sleep. (There were a lot of long, late nights; each time, you thought, *There couldn't be a longer night*, but it seemed the next one was always longer.)

"Yeah, I told him," the friend said. "It seemed like the right thing to do."

"What did he say?" you asked.

"He broke my nose," the friend said.

You remembered the broken nose, the funny story about walking into a ladder.

"I thought things were pretty much fine between us after that," the friend said, "because we were talking and joking again. But now I think there was something different. I can't say what." There was a pause. Then he said, "What'd he say to you about it?"

There were so many ways to answer that question, so many lies you could've told this friend, but you picked the easiest: "He was furious. Absolutely furious." Then you faked a yawn, said you were getting tired and wanted to grab some sleep while you could. But you didn't go to sleep for a long time—OK, not at all—because you were trying to remember a time, any time, a minute, a second, anything, when there was something different between you and him. But there was nothing to remember, nothing.

That's how much he loved you.

And that's the thing you know most of all.

ACQUIESCENCE

The body flew on a different plane, arriving in Detroit two days ago, at 7:37 A.M. She tracked its arrival online. Not a soldier or a famous politician, just her husband, age thirty, suddenly dead.

His mother wanted him buried in Detroit. Did it matter where someone's dead body was? Did it matter that someone's dead body ended up in the place they had fled?

Now she was in suburban Detroit, being carried along an anonymous highway in his mother's Lincoln. People drove as if they were tense, feeling the crush of that low, gray sky she remembered from their visit two Christmases ago. The graveside service was in an hour, followed by a "celebration of life" at a country club. There would probably be balloons released outside, heartfelt notes tied to them with ribbon. She stared at the parade of silver-paned office buildings out the window. His mother's voice was something broken that wouldn't stop making noise.

Finally they reached the cemetery, that modern kind, with stones flat in the ground to make mowing easy. The spot his mother selected seemed exposed, exactly in the center. She was taller than any of the slender trees.

People pressed her hand, clutched limp tissues. There were old high school girlfriends, all pretty. Though it was cold, no hats. The box with the body in front, blanketed with white roses. A stand displaying his smiling graduation photo. A CD of songs he wrote for his college band, The Elements. The scene felt arranged, like a movie set of a sad funeral. She imagined everyone at home afterward, sponging off makeup, peeling away costumes, slipping into bathrobes to relax after this hard day of work.

A minister with a square head spoke. God this, heaven that. She'd heard it all before.

His mother wept so loudly the crows looping overhead were startled.

When she exhaled, frost clouded the air.

Later, his mother pulled up to the airport curb and said, "Promise you'll come visit," and they both knew she wouldn't. She watched people wheeling black suitcases, in a hurry to leave Detroit. Though she didn't believe in God or heaven or worshipping a flat stone, she half-envied those who did, those who thought it could be so simple. She said to her former mother-in-law, "Maybe spring."

"The marker will be in then," his mother said.

"It was a beautiful ceremony," she said. "I'm so glad. All those Mylar balloons in the sky."

"Did you get a photo?" his mother asked.

She nodded, patting her coat pocket as if a phone was in there. "There's just one last thing." She hadn't cried today, and it was important that she not cry as she said, "It was bugging me the whole time that maybe they'd put him in upside down."

"Upside down?"

"That his head was where his feet should be."

"They wouldn't do that," his mother said. "They don't make those kinds of mistakes. There's hinges on one side."

"I kept thinking about it," she said, which was true. "I couldn't get it out of my head."

His mother spoke urgently: "It doesn't happen like that."

"Don't lots of things happen that we think won't happen?"

His mother tightened her face. "Have a safe trip."

The sound of the car door opening, then closing, was loud. Strange not to have luggage, to float so lightly.

On the flight home, she knew there'd be a time she might wish she hadn't acquiesced to the anger nudging her to speak those un-forgiveable words to her former mother-in-law. But that wasn't today.

A QUIZ

The following questions are multiple choice. Please select the option that best reflects the correct answer. Do not make more than one choice.

1.

You are at a housewarming party. You're wearing a new skirt that you bought half-price earlier in the day because you went to the mall because you thought you shouldn't want to be alone. You don't know the hosts of the housewarming party but your friend does and she's supposed to be meeting you but she's late, so you're standing in a corner holding a plastic cup of pinot grigio, discreetly trying to rip out the tacking threads you forgot to remove from the back slit of the skirt. A man approaches you. You know that most women your age—not quite forty—would find this also-not-quite-forty man attractive enough with his product-bristled hair and loose smile, but you're annoyed that his front teeth are too big. You're annoyed that the tacking thread is stubborn and still there. You're annoyed that you're drinking pinot grigio at a party instead of Maker's Mark bourbon at your house, alone. You're annoyed that your friend is late, that she's always late even when she promises not to be late.

The man says, "Hello, I'm Vince." You say:

A. "Nice to meet you, Vince."

B. "I'm not going to ask you what you do, because everyone in DC asks that, and isn't that so annoying?" and then laugh in a throaty, flirty, fetching way, as you confess that you're a lawyer and wait for him to laugh and tell you that he is too.

C. "Can you see this tacking thread in my skirt?" and then spin around, arching your back a bit as you point down to the thread, knowing he'll be happily confused by this sanctioned opportunity to stare at your ass. Laugh in a throaty, flirty, fetching way. Later, follow him to his place in your own car.

D. "Hi, Vince, you're probably a nice guy, but you should know that my husband died of a brain aneurysm six months ago and he was only forty-two."

The correct answer is D. Choose D. Vince will slither away, and when your friend hears what you've done, she'll threaten never to take you to another party. When you get home, you will pour bourbon into a tall glass and sip it slowly in front of the dark fireplace, obsessively rattling the ice cubes every couple of minutes.

2.

You're at the grocery store, eyes scanning rows of canned tomatoes—diced, petite diced, whole, stewed, crushed, sauce, sauce with basil, sauce with garlic, diced with basil, diced with garlic, fire roasted, low sodium, no sodium, paste. In another aisle, there is also tomato juice. But you've forgotten what you're looking for, what you might have planned to cook with tomatoes. It's a breathless amount of choices and forms for just a tomato. Your cart is empty. You have stared at yogurt, at cereal, at detergent and frozen vegetables and soup, but how is it possible to pick one, you wonder, terrified that you will make the wrong choice, that you will bring home the wrong form of tomato, the wrong cereal, that what you do will be wrong in some ill-defined way. "Excuse me." It's a woman wearing black yoga pants and a too-tight ponytail. "Do you happen to know where the barley is? It's one of those things I can never seem to find." She smiles, the kind of woman skilled at netting people into her life, the kind of woman unafraid to ask for help or call for directions or beg for a favor or show need.

Do you:

A. Smile back, and say, "Aisle 4, near the rice, on the bottom shelf."
B. Smile back, and say, "Aisle 6, near the oatmeal," even though you know barley is actually in Aisle 4, near the rice.
C. Not smile, but speak sincerely: "I'm sorry. I don't know."
D. Smile back and say, "Check near the rice, though you should know that my husband ate a lot of whole grains, but he died anyway, of a brain aneurysm, six months ago when he was only forty-two. You might as well eat Pop-Tarts every day." Keep smiling until your skin feels tight enough to snap off your face.

The correct answer is D. Choose D. She will swing her cart around and barrel back up the aisle, ponytail sawing side to side. You will not buy tomatoes. You will abandon the cart in Aisle 5 and slink out to the parking lot and sit in your car for ten minutes in chilly silence, watching people load bags of groceries into the backs of their SUVs. You'll decide that maybe you wanted petite diced tomatoes for a jambalaya casserole that you used to make for Super Bowl parties and potlucks. At home for dinner you'll eat the last can of the black beans from the "emergency" cupboard in the basement and chuckle bitterly when you see that the expiration date stamped on the top was six months ago. You will not bother heating the beans and you'll eat them straight from the can and you'll tell yourself they actually taste better that way.

3.

You are at a therapist's office. This is not your therapist, not yet, but this is the person who has been recommended by a friend. The walls of the office are gray, the color of mist cloaking a mid-Atlantic beach town in late January, and the upholstery is that same gray. The furniture is comfortable but also business-like, clearly office furniture and not furniture that would be in a house. You are seated exactly in the center of the three-cushion sofa. There is not a coffee table in front of you the way there would be in a house. This is not a house. It is a therapist's office. You have never been to a therapist. Everyone has been telling you to go. Your friend made the appointment. Your friend drove you here. Your friend is at the Starbucks on the corner, waiting for you, drinking an eggnog latte and flipping pages of the free *City Paper* that was left at the table where she is seated. You wish you were seated at that table. You wish you liked eggnog lattes. You wish you were good at asking for help and accepting favors and spilling your guts and finding closure and making progress and crying in front of strangers and wringing your hands and looking on the bright side and keeping a gratitude journal. The therapist, a woman, could be fifty years old or she could be sixty-five. She sits in a gray leather chair directly across from you, about five feet away. Her black shoes are thick-soled, sturdy, very functional, Velcro instead of laces or buckles. You would hate yourself if you ever wore those shoes unless it was to complete a Frankenstein costume on Halloween. You can't stop staring at her shoes, at her ugly, ugly shoes. You are the shallowest person on all of planet Earth.

The therapist says, "Why don't you tell me what brings you here today?" You say:

A. "My friend in her Volvo, haha."
B. Nothing, but you burst into messy, sloppy, choking sobs.

C. "I have insurance, if that's what you're worried about."

D. "My husband died of a brain aneurysm six months ago when he was only forty-two." Speak calmly, speak coldly. Speak as if you don't care if she hears you or not. Speak as though this is a test you are giving her and she is not passing. Speak as if you are a difficult person to deal with, as if you are a bitch.

The correct answer is D. Choose D. She will nod and scribble on a legal pad and she'll say, "Go on," and you will say, "This isn't going to work." Stare uncomfortably at her shoes, and she will explain why and how it will all work, and in the end, you smile and shake her hand and say, "This has been wonderful, thank you. I'll see you next week," and you will go find your friend at Starbucks who has ripped out an article about an art gallery opening she wants to take you to, and next week, you will call the therapist's voicemail to say you have the flu and the week after that you'll tell the voicemail that you're heading out of town unexpectedly and the next week you'll inform the voicemail that you have opera tickets and then one time, the next week or another week, you will call and tell the voicemail that you're sorry, that therapy just isn't right for you though you know that it can do many wonderful things for many people. You will say, "Good luck," into the voicemail and wonder what you mean.

4.

You are at your friend's wedding shower. She is one of your friends from college who you don't see very often and you have driven two hours to another city to attend this wedding shower. You don't really want to be here, but you had nowhere else to be and you didn't want to be alone. You drove twenty miles over the speed limit the whole way, but there were no cops to pull you over and give you a warning, to tell you to slow down. You have bought your friend a gift off a registry, but you worry that the clerk at the store in the mall looked up the wrong registry because you can't imagine what your friend wants with a Moroccan tagine but it comes in an impressively big box that the clerk gift-wrapped for you. Your box is the biggest one on the table. The other boxes are flat and look as though they contain towels and sheets. Your friend is also three months pregnant—she has only started telling people, so this news surprises you when she greets you at the door, announcing in a loud voice: "I'm so glad you made it! Guess what? I'm pregnant!" There is lemonade at the wedding shower, but no wine. You find out that it's a shower for couples, and the men gather in the cold backyard, huddled over a barbecue smoker, watching football on a small TV set that's hooked up through utility extension cords snaking through the house and onto the patio. The favored team is losing by a lot. The men have a cooler full of beer in their part of the shower, but no one says, "Go get some beer if you want," and no one in the women's part of the shower is drinking beer. You're wearing the half-price skirt with the tacking thread finally removed, and the other women are wearing jeans. You're sitting on the center cushion in a three-seat couch with two women you don't know on either side of you. You don't know anyone. The people you know who should be here all called with last-minute excuses as to why they aren't here. There are a lot of cookies, but none homemade, and a lot of tiny cupcakes with inch-thick pink frosting. You are on your second glass of lemonade when one of the women sitting on the couch asks, "Do you have children?"

Do you:

A. Recognize that she wants to talk about herself and pertly ask, "Do you?" and admire the flow of pictures and YouTubes cascading off her phone and murmur "so cute" and "adorable" over and over, a hundred to a thousand times.

B. Remark, "Yes, that's what I heard too, rain for tomorrow and probably the sleet will miss us."

C. Answer calmly: "Not yet."
D. Say, "No, I don't, because my husband died of a brain aneurysm six months ago and he was only forty-two." Stare hard at her, to convey that you were trying to get pregnant but you hadn't yet. Stare very hard, so she understands that you had names for these children who will never exist, two of them, the boy and the girl. Understand that no matter how hard you stare she will never imagine that such a thing could happen to her.

The correct answer is D. Choose D. The woman you don't know will mumble, "I'm so sorry; how awful," and she will work to be sincere and kind. She will rest her hand on your arm, long enough so her fingertips feel seared into your skin. You will have to thank her, you will have to say something to put her at ease, you will have to laugh and stare at her hand still touching your arm—a simple thing, touch—and then you will have to watch her run to the bathroom a minute later or go for more lemonade or it doesn't matter where she goes because when she returns from the bathroom or the kitchen or outside where she's gone to check on her husband—still alive—because when she returns, she will sit in a folding chair opposite the room from you, showing pictures of her kids to someone else, talking about nannies and preschools and car seats. At the end of the party, you will be sitting on the center cushion of the big couch, surrounded by no one. You will be alone. You will be alone in the middle of this party eating barbecue the husbands made, finally with a can of beer, steely cold in your hand, finally, finally, toasting your friend's wedding that you will not attend, toasting your friend's baby that you hope will be quite colicky.

5.

Your friends and some friends of theirs and one friend of the friends—a group, a big group that you don't want to see—suggest meeting for dinner at a sushi restaurant tucked down a Georgetown side street. You know the place. You used to go there when you were in college. You don't know why your friends want to meet there except that maybe because it has a parking lot. They've never talked much about sushi but now some of them gave up gluten. Some of them also gave up dairy. Some of them are trying to lose twenty pounds. Some of them won't eat beef. One of the friends' friends is a vegan who loves seaweed salad. Apparently, the only intersection of what everyone will eat is sushi, just as the only intersection of where everyone will drive is Georgetown (with a parking lot). Friends and their friends live in Bethesda, Rosslyn, Foggy Bottom, Tenleytown, Spring Valley . . . and you, alone in distant Fairfax, which is like another, possibly imaginary, land to them. You have nothing against sushi, or Georgetown, or these friends, or their friends, but you used to go to this sushi restaurant in college at Georgetown. You haven't been back for a long time. In college. College. When you were meeting people. People. Meeting. People. You shouldn't have to explain all this to them, you think. That you want to remember the sushi restaurant in one, singular way—not also as a place you sit with friends and their friends, a noisy, cackling group of "on the side, please," and someone spills sake and someone else confesses to being in an affair with her married boss and someone else tells a funny story about head lice. Not all that, all those stories, covering up what you want to remember, who you want to remember sitting across from you in the back booth, all this other stuff blanketing over this very pure place, this very perfect place in your past. But they keep emailing: "What about the 17th? Or 18th, if it's after 7:30 P.M.?"

You answer by emailing in response:

A. "Let's pick another sushi place, if that's okay with everyone. Of all the gin joints in all the towns in all the world, she walks into mine, LOL—will explain later. ☺ "

B. "17/18 won't work—I'm so busy lately that please, just meet w/o me. ☹ "

C. "17 is fine . . . see you then!!! ☺ "

D. "My husband died of a brain aneurysm six months ago and HE WAS ONLY 42." Type in all caps at first, delete, then retype in part caps to create the perfect emphasis. Push "reply all" then snap shut your laptop and stare angrily out your office window at a stupid pigeon because now the sushi restaurant *is* ruined.

The correct answer is D. Choose D. They will meet without you on the 17th. Someone will spill sake, but the boss story will only be the confession of a crush, which they will decide is harmless enough, and they will share stories from their pasts about all the married men they had crushes on, and then debate whether it's possible that anyone at their husbands' offices has crushes on their husbands and laugh uproariously trying to imagine it. Then they will talk about you. They will say things like, "Well, I drove her to the therapist's office that first time," and, "Well, I invited her to some parties so she'd get out," and, "Well, I sent that spa certificate," and, "Well, I said she could call me anytime, even if it's late at night," and, "Well, we all went to the funeral, right?" and, "Well, I never even met the guy." Then they will fall silent, and their friends will jab chopsticks at the tablecloth. On the 17th you will watch *Dirty Dancing* on cable and think about how Patrick Swayze is dead, and so is Baby's father, and how no one else watching the movie is thinking about that and even if they are, it will not be for the same reason you are.

6.

You're sitting in your living room. It's four thirty. Today you've cleaned out the front closet and packed up a number of old hats and scarves and coats into black garbage bags to donate. You've sorted through the kitchen drawer with all the junk—tiny wrenches from

Ikea furniture that you no longer own, manuals for coffeepots and irons you no longer own, three half-used rolls of duct tape, spools of thread, and all the rest—and you've thrown away the takeout menus that are more than a year old and you've Magic Markered dates on the remaining menus and you ripped up the menus for Indian places because you've decided you don't like Indian food anymore. You've found a folder for the takeout menus. You've scrubbed out both bathtubs, even though no one has used the tub in the guestroom for several months, and there's a woman who comes in to clean every other week anyway. You've finally moved the sundresses and summer blouses to another closet. You've resewn the hidden button that popped off the half-price skirt. You've thrown away the dirty rubber bands from produce and have saved only the clean ones from bundles of mail and you found a small tin to store them in. You organized the wine rack into rows of red and rows of white and one row that holds rosé, prosecco, and champagne. Now you sit in your living room, on the middle cushion of the big couch, and you think about sliding over to sit on the edge, but you don't, and you think about turning on a lamp, but you don't, and you think about getting up to pour a glass of bourbon, but you don't, and so you just sit there.

It's Thanksgiving Day. The phone rings. Do you:

A. Answer cheerfully: "Mom, it's so nice of you to call. I'm doing fine, I really am."
B. Answer cheerfully: "Mom, I've only got a minute because I'm headed out the door to have pumpkin pie with some friends, but thanks for calling me. I'm doing fine, I really am."
C. Answer tearfully: "Mom, I'm so sad right now and tired and all I want to do is crawl into bed and yank the covers up over my head. I'm not doing fine, I'm really not."

D. Answer. Simultaneously mumble and sigh, "Hello," then
listen for a moment, then say, "Mom, my husband died of a
brain aneurysm six months ago and he was forty-two and it's
Thanks-fucking-giving, so how the fuck do you think I'm
doing?"

The correct answer is D. Choose D. You will feel bad for using
swear words with your mother, but she will not be surprised. She
will not be angry. She will not be judgmental. She will not tell you
to shut up and count your blessings; nor will she tell you that you
should see a therapist. She will not suggest that you get out more.
She will not cry. Also, she will not understand, because her husband is still right there in the house with her, downstairs watching
the football game, with a blanket tucked around his legs to keep
out the chill.

7.

You're a writer. You're trying to solve a problem. You want to show
a reader the single-minded obsession of a woman whose husband
has died. You want to show that such a woman has a powerful
need to tell her story over and over because she needs to hear it—a
woman like that needs to hear it, must speak the words again and
again. They cannot be true. They cannot. You want to show that
this woman can't believe that this thing has happened. To her, it has
happened to her.

It has.
Happened.
To her.

This thing has happened to you. This thing has sliced your life into
two parts—the before and the after and no one can understand—

you are certain no one can understand, you are afraid no one can understand—you don't know how to understand. That is the problem.

So you read lots of books: the literary type—*A Grief Observed, Widow, The Year of Magical Thinking, What the Living Know, Without*—and an armload of the self-help, therapeutic type, each implying that it will explain "how to survive." You read and you write. You're a writer. That's how you solve problems: you write about them. That's what you know how to do, that's what you believe in: the power of words. You read books and you write stories, and your stories are pretty good, about women named Vanessa and Kathy and Nicole and women who don't have names. You write your stories, over and over and over. You write a lot of stories.

But that isn't working.

So you think about what's *more* than a story. What have other writers done? (All you know is writing; you're not going to suddenly film a movie or sculpt or knit.) Other writers have written chapters of PowerPoint presentations or included a flipbook figure along the page margins or splashed the page with tangential footnotes or left empty white pages or given to the narrator the author's exact name or interspersed quietly horrific interludes about World War One between the stories about a boy growing up in Michigan or invented the nonfiction novel. James Agee said in his preface to *Let Us Now Praise Famous Men*, "It's only a *book* by necessity," frustrated at having to tell a story that was more than a book.

Flaubert said, "Madame Bovary, c'est moi."

You write more and more, clicking sentences and paragraphs into your computer. People have written about far greater tragedies than yours: World War One, World War Two, 9/11, the Holocaust, slavery, Vietnam, the Civil War, any war, all wars, all evil, all massacres, poverty, incest, rape, murder, genocide, patricide, infanticide, starvation, reeducation camps, atomic bombs, mustard gas, nerve gas, land mines, torture, all the millions and millions and millions and millions and millions of deaths and vast tragedies and horrors that can happen to absolutely any person on Earth at absolutely any moment, and thinking of this, you are left with:

A. Shame.
B. Guilt.
C. Fear.
D. My husband, Robert K. Rauth, Jr., died of a heart attack when he was only thirty-seven.

There is no correct answer.

Choose D. You will write a book. You will tell the same story again and again, until you know it is true.

HEAT

He's the one who wanted the thermostat turned down at night. "What, are we saving like fifty cents?" I teased. He just laughed. I went on: "So, like, over the course of the winter that's maybe what, thirty bucks?" After a pause he said, "Seventy-five." He could do math in his head like that. "That's real money," he said. I guess I agreed because I let him do it. I didn't care. The blanket was big and fluffy, the bed small. We slept tumbled and entwined together like puppies from the same litter, the two no one can bear to separate.

The funeral was in April, so it wasn't until November that I had to turn on the heat for the first time. It was a windy night; the house rattled. My fingers were numb from a day inside, letting the phone ring, pacing through the cold house, not seeing the stacks of mail and magazines, the dirty dishes, piles of laundry—not seeing anything but knowing exactly what was there. I wore two thick sweaters, big woolly socks, and jeans lined with plaid flannel, living as long as I could in the cold because that's the way it was where we'd both grown up—you put off turning on the heat because once it was on it was on and it wouldn't come off until spring.

It was an easy thing to do, to slide the switch from OFF to HEAT, to listen to the rush of invisible air painlessly warming and blowing its way into my house as the wind pushed from the outside.

I didn't even think of turning down the heat that night or any of the nights. In fact, the next day I bought more blankets.

IN A DREAM

Like me, you would have remarried. I know it.

We swore that we wouldn't, if one of us were to die. We were twenty-five when we made that promise in Nogales, Mexico—a three-hour drive from where we lived in Phoenix, in a patched-to-gether grad student life that involved lots of rice, beans, and books. Nogales was a cheap day-trip, and you weren't afraid of anyone's culture; wherever you went, you slid beyond the tourist zone, look-ing for local restaurants and shops, needing an experience, a story, a ping of danger. Most Americans wandered the blocks fanning Nogales's official border point, with their cheap blankets and garish piñatas for sale, maybe climbing onto an ancient burro for a five-dollar photo before loading up on cut-rate pharmaceuticals and returning home.

Not you, and I followed you.

We wound through tight, snaky streets, on dusty uneven ce-ment, passing open doors and inky puddles, catching lacy Spanish and whiffs of cooking oil and diesel, shards of bold colors with ev-ery turn of our heads. Above us the same measureless, pure blue sky from our own side of the border, the same sun and its panting heat. You stopped outside a restaurant on a corner, trickling two fingers over the blue stucco and the sweeping mural of a herd of horses wreathed in flowers, pointed to the curly script proclaiming, *No Hay Otro Mejor,* and your eyes glowed bright. We passed through the propped door, and a man with a walrus moustache and gray snakeskin cowboy boots leapt up from a table in the back, greeting us like best friends. "Amigos! Welcome!" and he reached to the tiled bar, grabbing the neck of an open bottle of tequila. He shot more Spanish through his smile and hurried us to a tiled table at the front picture window, letting us settle into the vinyl chairs—sticky against the backs of my thighs—before splashing a good, solid pour of tequila into each of two juice glasses there on the table, as if he had set them up especially for us and he'd been wondering why we were late but was too polite to ask. It was ten thirty on a Sunday morning, and the only other people around were three silent Mexican men at a back table, rhythmically spooning soup, their faces shadowed by the brims of their cowboy hats. Flies buzzed against the thick glass of the window, and at least a dozen dead ones were sprinkled legs-up on the ledge.

You eyed the glass of tequila: I knew you planned to drink it, a straight shot, and I knew that I would follow even though I also knew that we shouldn't. We shouldn't be in this strange part of a strange city drinking out of these filmy glasses, surrounded by dead flies, about to eat strange food cooked in a strange, foreign kitchen. I shifted my legs, already a slick of sweat under them. The owner kept smiling—one tooth rimmed with a thin line of gold— his hand upraised in the international signal for "hang on"—and a young girl, twelve or so, scurried from the kitchen carrying a chipped plastic plate of lime chunks and a small bowl of salt, which she presented to us, placing them on the table before us with ritualistic precision, as if this were the lost component of the Catholic Masses I'd grown up attending. The owner's hand whooshed forward, meaning, Go, meaning, Now.

You pinched up salt to dribble onto the V of your loose fist, between your thumb and your forefinger, then you wrapped your other hand around the glass, raising one eyebrow at me in that way you had—did you really think I would not follow; did you really? You knew I would. I copied: salt, my palm on the juice glass, warm from a shaft of sunlight hitting it exactly so.

I was afraid, so I jumped first: a smooth lick of salt, sour liquid rolling over my tongue and plunging down my throat, spreading a familiar fiery scorch, and at last, the stab of the lime, its acidic flesh shredding under my teeth.

You laughed, and then you followed me.

The owner clapped his hands—"Amigo, muy bueno, muy bueno!"—speaking the kind of childish Spanish he thought we might understand. Then he tilted us each a second shot from the bottle, and another. You kicked out the third chair, motioning for him to sit down and join us. Instead, he patted your back and winked, suddenly fatherly, and the young girl appeared with tattered, salsa-stained menus.

The world spun through me: I wasn't much of a drinker back then, and neither were you. At ten thirty, the day was already burning through the nineties, and the burr of a few flapping fans wasn't keeping us cool. Neither of us had eaten breakfast, and the morning turned exhilarating and shiny with tequila firing my nerves.

We ordered—*chilaquiles* for you and tamales for me—and just as the owner said again, "Amigos, muy bueno," I jumped in to ask for two bowls of menudo, the traditional Mexican tripe soup rumored to cure weekend hangovers: "Dos menudos rojos, por favor," and to be clear, I pointed to the men in the corner, empty soup bowls and beer bottles a clutter in front of them.

You reached for my hand and squeezed "yes," and I silently hoped we wouldn't be up all night racing each other to the bathroom, hoped this wasn't a foolish thing to do or an embarrassing way to be, hoped that the man was genuinely kind and not mocking us and our American life that we could never shrug off no matter how many blocks we walked beyond the border checkpoint.

Tequila kills the bacteria, you whispered—always seeming to know what I was thinking—and then the lime kills what the tequila doesn't get.

I love you, I whispered back.

I love *you*.

Better soup couldn't exist, more flavor couldn't overflow a single bowl. Red chile-spiked, meaty broth thick with spongy strips of tripe and marble-sized globes of hominy. Handfuls of cilantro and onions to fling on top, ragged flakes of chile for more spice, another heap of lime chunks. I hadn't thought I could or would eat cow's stomach ever in my life, and not in a Mexican border town, and not in a random restaurant we stumbled into because you liked the painted horses on the wall, because you had a "feeling."

The owner plunked the bottle of tequila on the table. Again, you gestured for him to join us, and he sat, the three of us downing shots of tequila in unison, licking sweat and salt and lime from our lips. I tried my ancient high school Spanish, creaky at best, and he went on a rapid-fire tear, sweeping one arm in circles from time to time, calling for the girl to bring more tortillas, to get him a Coke, and we nodded and smiled, and somehow we came to understand his story: how his grandfather had started this restaurant with money he won gambling, and the man had worked here every day since he was eight, missing only for weddings and funerals; it was his restaurant now, and one day it would pass to his three daughters. The menudo was his great-grandmother's exact recipe: days to soak and scrub the tripe, a pig's foot making the broth richer. He paid an artist to paint the mural of the horses because his wife grew up on a ranch and liked horses. He told us he was a lucky man, the luckiest man alive. He pressed one palm flat onto the picture window, stared at his hand for a long moment.

An extended family of a dozen or so people and three strollers piled in, and a couple just out of church, fanning themselves with paper funeral home fans, and a man with two little girls with floppy sky-blue bows at the back of their dresses, and the rush was on: the owner jumped up, bustling everyone about, pushing tables, sliding chairs, smiling and pinching cheeks, calling for the girl, flipping on the boom box to a burst of horns. We were the only non-Mexicans.

You leaned in close and whispered, I'm the luckiest man alive.

I whispered, Then I'm the luckiest woman alive.

I'll remember today forever.

Me too.

Even when I'm dead, you whispered. Exotic, whispering through the noise, in this place where no one understood us or wanted to, because we were passing through in a quick dip out of our little life in America.

Me too, I whispered back. Even when I'm dead. But that won't be for a long time, right?

A hundred years.

A hundred and seventeen years.

A hundred years plus infinity.

A hundred years plus infinity plus one.

You were so happy, with your tequila and your menudo and your chilaquiles and me. Later, we walked around town. We bought a silly piñata shaped like a red chile pepper and a yellow painted enamel parrot the size of a football that I named Sammy and a couple of striped blankets to throw on top of our futon back at our apartment in Phoenix.

Now, I can't remember why the parrot got named Sammy. Also, whatever happened to that piñata?

Now, I'm the only one who remembers that day, unless the man or his daughter or the Mexican men slouching in the corner slurping menudo remember us—and why would they? Our happiness was special only to us.

I've got one of the blankets in the trunk of my car, but the other one vanished in a move or a cleaning purge or truly into thin air.

So it wasn't the restaurant in Nogales where we promised not to remarry if one of us died, but during the drive home from the restaurant in Nogales. The darkness of the desert folded around us—the sizzle of the day's heat easing to a smolder—as the straight shot of interstate carried us north to Phoenix. You always drove fast, the assumption being that where you were going next would be even more fascinating than where you were now. You were edgy whenever I drove, picking at me—I was too slow, why didn't I pass that truck—so I preferred playing passenger, keeping us alert in the dark with conversation and questions.

I asked about your high school hockey team in Michigan and its good luck rituals, and you told me stories about kissing Alan Preysler's collie on the lips before every game, and his mom sneaking the dog into the locker room and driving the dog to away games because the school wouldn't let animals ride on the bus.

I asked what the dorm room looked like when you were teaching geography in a Jamaican high school, and you described the shimmering white cinderblock walls with pencil sketches of race cars that someone before you had drawn, the tile floor with the worn spot near the single window, the way the sheets on the iron-barred bed smelled like bleach and scratched at night.

I asked what your five favorite foods were when you were a teenager, and you told me pizza, Coke with crushed ice but not cubes, your mother's flank steak, yellow cake with an inch of chocolate frosting, and pizza again because that's how much you loved pizza.

I asked how you thought the world would end if it was going to end, and you said nuclear annihilation but then changed to the outbreak of a contagious virus and then you said no that it would be a meteor like the one that wiped out the dinosaurs and you wondered if it would be the meteor killing us all or the aftermath.

I was staring out the car window then, watching the darkness, feeling it. I pressed my palm tight against the glass and stared at the shape of my fingers spread out, traveling the ups and downs with my eyes. The glass was warm, almost something alive. Driving through night often gave me a sense of being whisked too fast through something, the sense that I was missing the important thing. I was aware of the unseen: coyotes loping through brush, owls swooping lethally for mice, jackrabbits hunched along a rock. That churn of life and death while we were safely ensconced in this car, with its air conditioning and upholstery, though statistically a car on a highway wasn't safe at all. Abruptly, nothing seemed safe, and I yanked my hand off the glass, and even though the world wasn't about to end and even though you were a very fine driver, I interrupted as you changed your mind again, suggesting the world would end because God—ironically it would turn out there was one—because God would smite everyone down the way He'd been promising to.

I said, What happens when we die?

You said, We die.

No, I said. What happens?

It was a stupid question, as stupid as naming a yellow parrot Sammy, as stupid as buying a yellow parrot in a border town in Mexico—bargaining over a stupid yellow parrot, getting down to five dollars after ten minutes of round and round and threats to walk away—as stupid as drinking too much tequila and ending up hungover at seven o'clock on Sunday night.

You explained what you knew about decay and maggots. I let you go on, not because I especially wanted to hear about maggots, but because my voice would shake if I spoke. I let you go on because though you were talking about maggots, you understood my real question. You just didn't want to think about it. You did that sometimes, switched the focus to facts, as if only facts existed.

I sucked in a deep breath. One spot in my head ached more than the rest, a round place the size of a dime at the back-center of my skull.

You talked about a law of science, that no matter is created nor destroyed.

Finally, I said, No, no. What happens when *I* die?

We were doing eighty. So was everyone else on the road. We weren't close to the fastest, even at eighty. I imagined the conversations in the cars around us, the personal mix of maggots and pizza and kissing dogs on the lips and yellow parrots. I worried that no one in those cars was having conversations they would remember. I worried that it was all going too fast, whatever "it" was.

Maggots, you said. Same as everyone else. I wish we were special, but we're not, you said. You weren't mean saying it, just factual. A fact, it was a fact.

I hate that I ask that question and you say "maggots," I said.

You said, I hate that about me too.

Silence. Only the tires cutting the road, the radio suddenly jumping forward into that open space—Fleetwood Mac—and you said, I can't stand this song, though I knew that wasn't true, so I didn't twirl the dial. This all was back when people listened to Fleetwood Mac, when cheap cars like ours only had radios, when radio stations weren't all owned by one watered-down behemoth of a conglomerate. This station had a real DJ, a human being behind the music pulsing out of the dark; I imagined this man selecting this Fleetwood Mac song, imagined him wondering who was listening to it, who would be singing along, who would be breaking up while this song played, who would be having sex, who would be washing dishes, who would be driving home after getting fired for mouthing off to a customer. Who would remember this song and this moment of hearing this song?

Stevie Nicks sang about another lonely day.

It's just a question, I said.

I don't like thinking about it, you said, if you were dead.

You prefer thinking about my body covered in maggots? I asked.

Haha, you said. Sometimes you did that, when something wasn't funny, but was me trying to joke us somewhere. Haha, you'd say, just like that, just the way it's spelled. I miss that. I never met anyone else who did that.

We had a great day, you said. Ask me another question. Ask me what color I see in every one of my dreams.

Blue, I said. I already know that. Of course I also already knew about the hockey players kissing the dog on the lips. I knew lots of things about you, but I never thought that what I knew was everything. I expected that we had infinity plus one for all the questions and stories.

Blue, you said. I'm always inside some big blue sky in my dreams. What does that mean, do you think?

That you're happy, I said, that you see unlimited possibilities.

I do, you said, I truly do.

So, well. It wasn't on the drive after the time at the restaurant at Nogales when we promised we would never remarry. It was when we got home that night, back to our cheap apartment. Before we lived in Arizona, we lived in New York City, grubbing at various artsy pursuits, and moving to Arizona was being dropped into the Garden of Eden: our apartment walk-in closet was the size of my first Manhattan sublet. Sure, the place was hideous: gold carpet, cheap painted wallboard, the light fixtures glued to the ceiling, brown refrigerator and matching brown stove. But so big! Two bedrooms and two bathrooms and a tiny balcony overlooking an old tennis court with a crack running parallel to the center line; players aimed for the crack, so the ball bounced askew. The complex included two swimming pools and two hot tubs, and from our tiny balcony was a straight-on view of one of these swimming pools, glowing like a blue jewel all night long. It was a marvel to us, but to anyone living in Phoenix this was nothing extraordinary; most apartment complexes had these amenities, and often we were the only people at the pool or in the hot tub. Everyone else was inside watching TV in air conditioning. People in Phoenix never asked about pools and tennis courts; they knew to want covered parking, which this complex did *not* have. The sun beat into our black car, baking the black vinyl seats. The steering wheel was like a blacksmith's forge until we bought a polyester sheepskin cover from a guy in a grocery store parking lot selling "skins and kins" from his pickup. We've gone native, you said.

The electric bill was so high that whenever we left for more than an hour, we pushed the AC thermostat to eighty. There were discussions about whether holding steady or going on-off was cheaper in the long run—but this is what we did, which meant that when walking in, the apartment would slam up a wall of heat.

We had only been in Arizona three months but that seemed like forever. We complained that there were no good bagels and no good Chinese, but New York was a distant landscape—the moon, maybe; maybe even the dark side—and we weren't staying in Arizona always. It was the in-between place for grad school, and we would step into another life the way we'd stepped into and then out of the restaurant in Nogales, the way we'd stepped through the gate from America to Mexico and back.

Because something needed to feel definitive and certain, I had insisted that we get married before moving to Arizona. We took the subway downtown to City Hall on a Wednesday, waited for about fifteen minutes, and there we were, married. Parents were furious, especially yours, because they liked throwing parties as a competitive sport, and my mother didn't talk to me for two months, which I only noticed after ten days. My father sent a big check from Chicago. It was a relaxing way to get married. You called me Mrs. for a week.

That night, the night I'm remembering, the night after the drive from that time at the restaurant in Nogales, I carried the blankets, and you carried Sammy the parrot and the piñata. We lived on the second floor, and we tried to walk up the cement steps as quietly as possible because the lady on the first floor liked any excuse to poke her head out her door and squawk. She accused us of cooking stinky food, even when it was grilled cheese for dinner. Peering through the cracks between the floorboards of our tiny balcony, we could see that her patio below was stacked wall to wall with shoeboxes. What the hell's inside them, you asked, and wondering was a fun guessing game. She and the shoeboxes were still there when we moved out two years later, and she yelled the whole time we tramped up and down, carrying stuff to the U-Haul. I thought about sending her a letter to tell her you died, but didn't. She might remember that day we brought home the yellow parrot named Sammy because even though we were tiptoeing, her door popped open and she launched into a lecture that if we walked on the balls of our feet, we'd have better posture and be quieter besides.

You were halfway up the stairs, and you stopped to listen, parrot in one hand, chili pepper piñata in the other, and she interrupted herself to say, "No pets allowed means no birds. I'm going to the office tomorrow and I'm filing a report."

Only tonight, you said, we're keeping him for a friend.

"Better not be a talking bird," she screeched.

No, no, you assured her, it's not, not at all. He's more of a thinking bird, a bird who thinks.

She slammed her door and spun the deadbolts, click-clack. When we moved in she warned us that management would snoop if we didn't install our own locks. She had a P.O. box because she didn't want anyone seeing her mail. Arizona was loaded with crazies who were fun at first.

I repeated to the closed door, Only for tonight.

Inside, we pushed through the wall of hot, stuffy air. That achy spot in my head was half-dollar size now. I lifted my hair off the back of my neck, but there was nowhere for it to go, so I just let it drop back down. I tried not to think about it, but I was thinking about it.

There was a hook in the ceiling, where someone before us maybe hung a spider plant, and that's where you decided to put Sammy. He perched on a metal ring that no one had bothered to paint or prettify. Why did we buy such a silly thing? Was that why the tequila flowed, so gringos would end up with junky yellow parrots and chile piñatas? All that tequila had been on the house, by the way, so you left a big tip. Maybe that's why free tequila, for looser tips.

To reach the hook, you stood on one of our rickety metal folding chairs that we used at our dining room table. The apartment had vaulted ceilings, which is also why it was so expensive to keep cool. Another thing to think about when renting an apartment in Arizona, instead of how many hot tubs. Think about covered parking, or if there's a ceiling fan to push around your piled-up, hot, heavy air.

He looks good, you said.

Kind of tacky, I said, but maybe in an okay way?

Don't call our new pet tacky, you said, jumping down off the chair. I rolled my eyes, knowing the lady would bang her cane against the ceiling, which she did so fast it was as if she'd been waiting, locked and loaded. Boom, boom. For someone who wanted quiet, she was noisy.

Sammy the Mexican parrot, I said.

When he wants a cracker we won't understand because he speaks Spanish, you said.

The thinking bird, I said.

We laughed. Nothing we said right then was funny, but laughing seemed important anyway. I miss your laugh, the slow roll of it. Who would think to record a laugh? Who would think it wouldn't always be there?

You stood at the sliding glass door to our tiny balcony and looked out. Let's go swimming, you said.

The pool closed at ten, but plenty of people ignored that rule. If you were quiet, no one cared. Even the lady downstairs didn't fuss over swimmers at night. That shimmer of blue dropped into the dark lured all of us. On hot nights, the water was barely cooler than the soupy air, but it was an escape, that sensation of stepping in and disappearing, inch by inch, melting down to liquid. A luxury in a place like New York, and here, only a matter of tiptoeing down some stairs and walking across the tennis court, pulling open an unlocked iron gate, hoping it didn't creak.

I shrugged. Maybe tomorrow night, I said, I'm kind of tired. All that tequila.

Tomorrow, you said. Tomorrow's fine.

But you kept staring at the blue pool, at the darkness beyond. The rustle of the palm trees. The flowers we didn't know the names of, the orange ones, the purple ones. The glass between you and the pool. I watched the fuzzy reflection of your face in the window, and I tensed, expecting you to say something surprising. I don't know why, but that's what I thought was going to happen. I thought about your dreams, your blue dreams, and maybe that was why you were so drawn to the pool right then, because being in the pool would feel like being inside one of your dreams.

We should remember today, you said.

We will, I said, promise. Then I crossed my heart, which was corny, but felt like a gesture that might not seem corny at this exact moment, and might be significant, like the way we had laughed at the jokes that weren't funny.

I was wrong, and you made fun of me: We're not the girl scouts, you said, too sharply.

I know, I know.

It's just one night, you said, one day. There are lots of days, there are infinity plus one days, and how can we know we'll remember this one over any of the others? What if this day, as good as it was, isn't even the best day?

I know, I know.

Maybe if we went swimming . . . your voice trailed off suggestively.

Go swim by yourself if you want to go swimming so bad, I said, you don't need me holding your hand down there.

I wanted to ask, What if this *is* the best day? What if it is? That's what I should have said. Instead, I kept picking, waiting for the fight: Plus, I have to get up early to go to work. It's not like you, class at one.

Work, you said.

It was typing up classifieds at the alternative newspaper, back in the days when there were classifieds in a paper newspaper. I was terrible at this job because I made typos that ended up in the newspaper, selling a "care" instead of a "car" or a "car" instead of a "cat," and I hated it. But the boss liked me for reasons he shouldn't have, so I knew he'd never fire me though I would have been relieved if he did. But this job paid our rent, which when I was tired and scared and the apartment was stifling hot, I reminded you of, not in a pleasant way. That, and that your dad paid your tuition.

This fight ended where the others ended: Fuck you, fuck you, fuck you, and I ran off to cry in the bedroom, and you slammed the door—bang-bang—and pounded down the stairs—shrieks from the lady—"didn't I tell you already about them stairs; didn't I tell you?"—then silence. I wished Sammy was a real parrot because there was too much quiet in the room once I stopped crying, which I did immediately after you left because I was embarrassed to keep carrying on. Besides, you were gone, which was what I wanted; hadn't I just screamed so several times, inventing several ways to say one thing: *get out?* (The lady downstairs didn't mind our fights; you speculated she preferred them to her TV soap operas.)

These fights were what our parents did, not us. Not you. You were different. I was different. That's how we got married in that room in New York, making those promises, because we knew we were different.

I lay on the futon in our bedroom, still in my clothes, my tennis shoes, thinking that neither of the blankets we got in Nogales was very pretty, and instead we should have bought the other two we had looked at, or gone to more stores because surely in all of Nogales there were prettier, better blankets than these, and I wondered if the cotton would give us a peculiar rash or if there were fleas, and I scratched my suddenly itchy calf, and I started to feel sick to my stomach from the soup that had been cooked with scary Mexican water, the limes and cilantro that had been washed in scary Mexican water—and I thought about eating a pig's foot and a cow's stomach—and all that tequila, and the never-ending heat, and I had to think harder, really hard, to convince myself that I was only psychosomatic. Everything I was feeling was psychosomatic. I loved you, I did, and this marriage wasn't a colossally huge fuck-up and I did not want to jump in the car and race back to New York City to bagels and a closet-size sublet.

I would love you forever. That's what we promised.

I fell asleep, an hour or so according to the glowing digital clock, and I swept my arm along your side of the futon, but no you, and I jumped up and ran into the other room, flipping on every light switch, but you also weren't in the living room watching our tiny black-and-white TV or at the table studying or in the kitchen poking through the brown refrigerator, and I was thinking the worst, without even knowing then what the worst might be, but I had that tendency, didn't I, to find the single thing to worry about that didn't need worrying about, and I hated that about myself. But right then, it was only that you were gone. That was all I knew, that single fact.

I pressed up against the sliding glass door, and you and I had agreed that we weren't praying people, but I thought a little prayer anyway, something simple that was only the word *please,* which didn't have to mean I was no longer an atheist, and I took a deep breath, and you were sitting on the edge of the shimmering blue pool, kicking your feet one at a time in the water, droplets a quick flicker, your hair sleek, wet and slicked back, like seal fur—you had just emerged from that restful water, there it was, there it was, you and the blue water, like one of your own dreams. I was immediately angry, and I said, Goddamnit, and looked guiltily at the parrot as if it would tattle.

Then you saw me: you saw me looking at you, saw the lights of the apartment behind my silhouette, and you waved. You jumped up and motioned me forward; your hand beckoning me; you were telling me to come in, telling me to follow you, that you hadn't gone anywhere except to cool off. I kicked off my shoes and peeled away my socks, and I ran down the cement steps, across the tennis court, still warm from the day of sun, rough against my bare feet, and I ran out there to you: I ran out there to you, to where you stood, waiting for me.

When I think back, I see that it all passed so quickly.

Now that you're dead, now that I'm remarried, now that I live in Chicago, now that I'm getting the baby I wanted, now that years are stacked like bricks between that day at the restaurant in Nogales and the drive and the fight, and now that the parrot named Sammy is packed in a box in the attic and one blanket is missing—now that I can think about these days and those times, now that I can speak in stories and words, now . . . now I can't remember when it was that we promised to each other that we would never get remarried. A drive to somewhere? A lunch? Whispers during a late night? Did we really speak those words? It's the promise of the impossibly young, of people who don't know many things, certain they know everything.

Like me, you would have gotten remarried if I had been the one to die first and young, if the maggots got to my body before yours. You would know—as I know—that in the end, whether there is a god or isn't, no matter if the world ends or if only we each do, you would know, know absolutely, that in a dream, in a blue-drenched dream, there I would always be, always: running to find you.

ONE ART

Experiment: Tell a true story to an audience gathered in a bar. Tell something so personal and so true that you're spattering your ripped-out guts on the dirty floor, so personal and so true that your naked, beating heart lies exposed for everyone to gawk at and poke. Tell the truth. Tell the truth for real. Put it out there. You can do it. That's what you tell yourself, because you're pretty sure you *can't* do it.

WHERE: Story League, Washington, DC, May 2011

WATCH: https://www.youtube.com/watch?v=eavvO3BoKn4.

READ: "You know how people sometimes worry about saying or doing the wrong thing with a bereaved person? I became a bereaved person when my thirty-seven-year-old husband suddenly died, so I know that one wrong thing is to buy a bereaved young woman an expensive flowering dogwood tree and have it unexpectedly delivered a week after the funeral while she's out of the house dealing with lawyers.

"At first I didn't realize that this tree was a 'wrong thing.' At first it was, 'Oh, how thoughtful, a tree to commemorate Robb.' Then I tried to move the damn thing off my porch—six feet tall, a burlap-wrapped rootball the size of a tire. The thing weighed a ton. So I dragged it down the stairs, realizing that this would be a little trickier than the peace lilies people had sent—which were already wilting under my quote—'care.'

"Instructions on the tree were crystal clear, 'Plant immediately. Do not let roots dry out.' Other demands: Shady spot. Acid loam soil. Lots of water. But the real issue was that this tree was supposed to symbolize my husband, flowering every spring and providing beauty in the world for decades to come. God forbid this tree died . . . too.

"It was early April, so not the dead of winter, but honestly, the last thing I wanted was to dig a hole three times as big as the root-ball, dump in a forty-pound bag of soil conditioner—whatever that was—and find the tangled-up garden hose somewhere in the shed. Digging holes was a boy job, not a girl job. And damn the woman who sent me a tree without also sending along her husband to plant it for me.

"I'm not someone who is comfortable with untidy emotions like anger and, well, grief. No, I'm dutiful and responsible and orga-nized. I washed and returned casserole dishes after the funeral; I wrote thank you notes for every last flower arrangement. I knew what I was supposed to do about that tree. Still, I stared at that tree for a few days, at its big, dumb rootball.

"Was I someone who could purposely leave a symbolic tree to die? Was I a woman who 'needed' a man? Since I didn't have a man anymore, I guess the question answered itself. I could do this. I didn't need help. It was the responsible thing to do.

"So, Saturday—cold, windy—I dragged out some shovels, un-tangled the hose, and lugged the tree to a spot in the front yard. Dozens of dead leaves fluttered off the branches, which I tried to ignore.

"The ground was like cement. My shovels were cheap, like beach shovels. I was weak, with spindly arms. The rootball was actually the size of a Volkswagen. My husband was dead and I had to dig a hole three times the size of a Volkswagen for this goddamn tree that would symbolically flower every spring to remind me that my husband was dead.

"Crying. Cursing. Flinging dirt. Chopping worms in half with my cheap shovel. The worst moment was when I realized that because I'd hacked up the yard so much it was too late to go back. I could only dig.

"'Hello, ma'am.'

"I looked up. Mormons. Two of them, boys, with white shirts, black ties, black pants, windbreakers. Bikes. All acne and peach fuzz. You know the uniform.

"Stating the obvious, I said, 'This isn't a good time.' Then I added, 'My husband died last week.'

"To me, that was the get-out-of-jail-free card, and I expected them to back off the way the telemarketers did when I told them Mr. Rauth couldn't come to the phone because he was DEAD.

"But to these Mormons, my response was hitting the jackpot, and they exchanged meaningful looks. One of them—the smart one—dropped his bike and edged over to me the way you approach a wild animal you don't want to startle, saying, 'You know, I could help you dig that hole. Looks like the ground is pretty hard.'

"They'd seen that I was crying and I certainly couldn't pretend everything was fine. Seriously, the wind picked up right then and blew off a hundred more leaves.

"'I don't know,' I said.

"The smart one smiled. Such a bright smile, those big, white Donny Osmond teeth.

"He cautiously reached for the cheaper of my cheap shovels. 'We'll help,' he said.

"Then the other one—the dumb one—said, 'Yes, let us help. If you want to see your husband again, you'd better talk to us right now.'

"Oh. My. God. My husband was dead, I was all alone in the world, the rootball was as dry as dust, and these preachy children with their heaven or second coming or afterlife or whatever the fuck it was, were claiming the only way to 'see my husband' again was to let them save my soul. Oh my God.

"I channeled my inner crone and I stood up, waved my cheap shovel like a pitchfork, and shouted, 'Get off my property!'

"Off they pedaled—dooming me to hell and eternal loneliness.

"With new strength, I ripped through the earth and dug the damn hole. I planted the tree. Watered it all summer.

"Next spring, there were maybe two or three flowers on it. What was I to make of these blooms? So, my husband's life added up to two or three flowers? About then, I realized that I had hated the tree all along, and it must have started feeling my hatred because then it started to look sickly. Oh, I still watered it—I wasn't going to KILL it. Not on my watch, not responsible me. But dogwoods are fragile, and this one was definitely fading.

"The tree couldn't ever be just a random tree in my yard. No, it was a tree that someone else had told me should be symbolic and should make me feel better.

"But you know what I thought of every time I looked at that tree? I thought about how bad shit happens to people all the time, and that finding a god or planting a tree wasn't ever going to stop that. When I was yelling 'get off my property,' I wasn't only angry with the Mormons.

"A few months later the tree finally died. By that time it was totally dried out. I was able to pull it out of the ground with my bare hands, rootball and all. I planted bleeding heart there instead."

THE TRUTH: This story is true and everything in it happened to me. It's what we like to call the truth. But I could tell this story all day long. It's nothing personal. People think my guts were quivering on the floor. People in the audience tell me they watched my naked, beating heart. Not so. No way. I would never really do that. I hide, I hide the truth from everyone, from friends, family, readers, and most of all from (*Write* it!) myself. Those stories I imagine I won't ever tell: those are the personal ones.

DO YOU BELIEVE IN GHOSTS?

Let's stop by the bar that I always think of as Schultz's, though the name on the sign says Burke's. It's an old-time Baltimore place downtown, bordering the tourist zone of the Inner Harbor. Schultz's is "real Balwmer, hon," as the saying goes. Dark, dark, dark, as if light bulbs ran a hundred bucks apiece. The only natural light comes through the glass door in front. Some fake stained-glass windows above the booths let in yellowy glow, but not much, and you can't see in or out. Roomy booths line the walls, benchbacks about five feet high. Everything is heavy wood: tables, barstools, floor. This is where people come to disappear.

There's always a crows' line of men hunchbacked at the bar, staring into Crown Royal and Cokes or 7&7s. The O's on TV or the Ravens, soundless. Some husky-voiced, beehived, sixtyish woman with impeccable makeup inevitably makes her entrance, wearing leopard print something—shoes, scarf, purse—bellowing, "Johnnie Walker Red, rocks, with a splash of Drambuie," her signature drink, her drink of a thousand and one memories. If there's no room at the bar, someone gives up his seat.

Tanqueray martini's good enough for me. That's what I recommend. Martinis here are made with care and attention—no ice chips from over-shaking. I wouldn't suggest asking for vodka. Always trust a woman who orders herself a martini, someone told me. Maybe it was never trust. I forget which.

There's an old cigarette machine in the corner by the front door, the kind with a knob under each pack that you pull straight out with a tooth-grinding screech. It's there for nostalgia or because they forgot about it. No smokes inside, just the empty machine next to an aquarium with purple lights and slow-moving fish dipping in and out of a tiny castle.

Go ahead and order off the restaurant menu. There's German food—schnitzel and sauerbraten—alongside old-fashioned dishes —chopped steak, chef salad, cottage cheese plate—and of course, being Baltimore, there's seafood. Oyster stew is good in winter. Crabcakes are maybe not the best in town but more than respectable, served the right way, on crackers. I recommend steamed shrimp. Get a half pound, then order another half pound when you finish those. You want them so hot they scald your fingers when you peel them. Something about the pain makes them taste better. Steamed over Natty Boh beer, buried in drifts of Old Bay. I can't get enough.

Anywhere else my ghost story would sound crazy, but not at Schultz's. We've got a good booth, here's the martini and its one perfect olive nestled in the bottom of the glass, and the waitress is walking the shrimp order to the kitchen. Are you ready?

When my husband died—. Yeah, that's a shitty place to start. No one knows what to do with a story about a dead person. It won't end with a punch line that gets everyone howling, not like a story that starts, "So, it's pouring rain, I'm locked out of my rental on the Champs-Elysees, and this man with a pregnant poodle walks up. . . ." When a story jumps straight to a dead husband, you know you're going to squirm, unless the teller is maybe eighty years old and this is numero uno in a collection of dead husbands—and I'm not eighty, thank you very much, I'm forty-five-ish (let's say), and I have only the one husband, now dead. Adjust your expectations. Anyway, as I hope you get, Schultz's doesn't make the martinis strong so we can slouch around, laughing our asses off like underage kids. Come to Schultz's with the story you're terrified to tell, the confession of that "thing" you did "that one time" in 1987. And be careful. These martinis will pry it out of you. Don't drink more than two or three—don't drink as many as I do.

Okay, new beginning: Meet cute. That's how it goes in the movies, and this isn't a movie, but it's a story, and I've definitely told the "meet cute" before by itself. I won tickets to a Springsteen concert on the radio with it.

We met in college. He was a sophomore, and I was fringe in a pack of sweetly naïve freshmen girls, and we were all drunk at a frat party, and someone's idea was to catch the sun rising up out of Lake Michigan. He and I were the only two who actually watched— the others occupied themselves by jumping naked into the frigid water—so he walked me back to the dorm afterward, claiming it was dangerous on campus because of the rampaging wild boar. (Not really! We're talking suburban Chicago.) He was singing Springsteen. *Born in the U.S.A.* had come out that summer, and everyone was all about Springsteen, but this guy was into the early, great stuff, "New York City Serenade" and "Sandy," hitting each word, every inflection. Anyone else, and this would have been crazy overboard, but he had these blue-green eyes and passion— not copycatting Bruce's passion, but his own, pulling me like an undercurrent, like the waves pulling at the lake.

Then he jumped into "Backstreets"—off *Born to Run*—every line, every word—and we were at my dorm lobby, and abruptly he stopped before the last verse and said, "So, who are you? Are you Terry, going to break my heart, like in the song?"

"I just met you." I didn't know how to flirt or what to say except for what I thought was true. I was from a small town in Iowa and now I was at this fancy college on the shore of a lake so big you couldn't see the other side.

His eyes kaleidoscoped from blue-green to gray and back to blue. They made me dizzy. The thought of kissing him made me dizzy.

He said, "I got screwed by my girlfriend this summer. She dumped me for my brother."

"Then really I think you got screwed by your brother," I said.

I waited a moment, unsure if I should stay or walk into the dorm lobby, dingy and banged-up already at week two of the semester. I had no previous boyfriend to compare this guy to. His eyes locked onto mine. Streaks of sun haloed rosy and hopeful around us. I was tired and had to pee. My roommate and I planned to go to the Catholic student center for free doughnuts after the ten fifteen Mass. Thoughts collided in my brain. What time did the library open? Whose black Porsche was in the dorm lot?

"Maybe I'll be the angel on your chest," I ventured. A garbled line from "Backstreets," and I'd never exactly understood what it meant—or what the song meant—or who betrayed who—and was Terry a boy or a girl—though I'd listened alone to the lyrics on repeat on my record player many long, late, unsettled nights. In the songs, Bruce always pulled up to the house: "Rosalita," "Born to Run," "Thunder Road."

"I bet you are," he said, and there was the kiss. Remember this forever, I thought right then.

I'm rambling. It's going to be that kind of story, the rambling kind, not the kind you spit right out like a watermelon seed that travels straight and true down the driveway. Also, this martini is so damn good, I bet I need another.

He should have a name, this dead husband, so I'll call him D. H. Appropriate for an Orioles fan who kept score at games. If you don't know, D. H. equals "designated hitter." Pure fans despise the designated hitter, but in the end, the D. H. gives an old guy another chance at making the team, lets a guy prolong his career when he can't field but can still swing away. My dead husband gave people chances. He constantly forked out five bucks to tattered men who needed money for a "cab" or to retrieve their "car" that had been "towed." He liked being liked.

So we were on-off-on-off—dramatic fights, weepy reunions, a campus soap opera—but he delayed grad school a year and worked entry level at Leo Burnett in Chicago, waiting while I finished my senior year, and then it was off to our grad school lives, the cruddy jobs and cruddy sublets in New York, the less cruddy apartment in Washington, the townhouse in Maryland, the house in Baltimore. Fast forward through all that ascension and acquisition. An affair (his) that I never forgave him for; a retaliation affair (mine) that he never knew about. (I can just slip that in, can't I?) A cat that got feline leukemia and a dog that was hit by a car. A new used car, and later, a new new car. Vacations to Arizona, Puerto Rico, Santa Fe, San Francisco. Christmas presents, birthday presents, valentines, St. Paddy's Day hangovers. Kids someday, maybe, maybe not. (Now, not.) A life together shouldn't be easily summed up in a paragraph, but when you're telling a story, no one cares that it was a fluffy black cat named Carlos or that we stayed at the Biltmore in Phoenix or that the woman he cheated with was his boss.

A careful listener like you might observe, "She never said wedding."

Yes, well. I've taken the liberty of marrying us after he died.

So, my dead husband who wasn't a husband and I moved to Baltimore and that's how we found Schultz's, stopping by after the Orioles games, liking it so much we started coming when the O's were away or when it wasn't even baseball season. We often sat at this same booth, third from the door, muttering about carving our initials into the wood, but you can see this isn't the kind of place where people haul out knives to mark territory.

After the affair with his boss, his career was seriously derailed. (No, duh—really?) He had to move to another company and it's not as though anyone would *know*, because how could they?— yet they somehow did or seemed to, so that he got the problem accounts, and the gossipy, lazy assistants, and the chair with the squeaky wheel. His biggest client went bankrupt. His best team member flipped out and held guests hostage with a rifle at a Christmas party and that was all over the news. The CEO caught him not washing his hands in the men's room. He was in charge of the sheet cake for the office potluck, and everyone who ate it was food poisoned. It was his computer that brought in the virus. Karma or coincidence: either way, they got to know us pretty well at Schultz's.

I was pissed off about [Evil Name], the boss/lover who went on to a pretty sweet job. I scheduled appointments with a Google-search couples counselor and bought a bag of self-help books. I was interviewed by a journalist for a magazine article about women who'd been cheated on, though the piece never ran. Plus, of course, the retaliation affair.

Betrayed. As Bruce put it on "Backstreets": "I hated him, and I hated you when you went away." But he didn't go away, and neither did I. We weren't married. We weren't even fucking married, and we stayed together.

We had to say love, otherwise there was no explanation. Or if there was an explanation, it would have been wrong: that we were afraid or comfortable or lazy. Maybe the explanation was that by staying with him, I was punishing him, and he was punishing himself. Because—and here's what I would never say out loud, but Schultz's is where you whisper these things—he loved his boss. He loved her. He loved her more than he loved me.

How did I know this? He told me. He told the counselor. He told the boss. He kept seeing her (he didn't know I knew).

"Sometimes people cheat on a partner to force the issue," the Google-search counselor told us. "To put someone in the position of—to make the other party the bad guy." She was very careful right then not to look at me or at him. She stared at her shoes with the pointy toes. "Because they're unable to find a healthier way of addressing problems in the relationship."

I said, "Isn't an affair about sex?"

He looked out the window, not listening. He was thinking about [Evil Name]. The counselor saw and sighed sharply, ripped a piece of paper off her notepad. She seemed not to know what to do with it; she crumpled it and let it drop to her lap. A lot of noise.

"I don't love you," he said, eyes locked on the window. "That's what it's about."

I'll spare you the details.

Once when the counselor and I were alone, waiting for him to decide to show up or not—this time disguised as a "meeting running late"—she asked, "Where's your anger?"

I shook my head. "I'm very angry." But I smiled, I don't know why.

"I would want to kill him," she muttered, again looking at her shoes. These were brown alligator boots. She was fascinated by her feet. I'm pretty sure she was a lousy therapist. Too fresh, too new. Our sloppy, disorganized emotions weren't following the textbooks and class lectures.

"I do," I assured her. "I do want to kill him." Maybe this was where I was supposed to mention the retaliation affair to get her approval. "But I love him," I said. "Even when I hate him, I love him."

"You have to be lying," she said. Something we both knew she wasn't supposed to say.

Again, I smiled. I don't usually smile much, but it seemed I was smiling all the fucking time around her. It was my only weapon. I was thinking about weapons that whole year. It felt like I was at war that whole year before he died. I dreamed about nuclear bombs more than a dozen times. I wasn't the one dropping them, but I was the one watching as bodies incinerated into black dust, and buildings shuddered and collapsed, and birds plummeted dead from the sky. You know who was there holding me when I woke up crying from those shitty dreams? He was.

I know you think you would do everything better, and I'll go along with that. Sure you would, sure. The story is very clear when you're not the center of it.

My affair was nothing. I wasn't in love with—let's find the right name—Johnny. Who doesn't remember a Johnny who was a solid guy, maybe back in grade school or the mechanic you trust at the garage? This Johnny worked in the cubicle kitty-corner from me and got laid off the same Friday I did. That night, we all met for drinks at McCormick & Schmick's, all of us traumatized, all of us on edge and acting angry and dangerous—that's when. Told me he'd had a crush on me for a year, and I said me too. He probably got that I was lying, but we drove back to his condo anyway.

Being unemployed, we had all this free time, so messing around was a good time filler, except that I got bored without the sneaking and lying. Wasn't the best part of cheating thinking ten steps ahead of your spouse? Tracking mileage? Remembering cover stories? I excelled at detail work, so this too-easy affair with Johnny wasted my skills.

One afternoon when I was at his place, Johnny asked if I thought I could ever love him. The question unsettled me: Not *did* I love him (yeah, yeah, of course, honey-bunny), but did the possibility of my loving him even *exist* in my imagination; if we landed in a different time or place or dimension, might I love him then? Too much thinking. We were on a blanket on the floor because with all this meaningless time we had, one thing we liked to do was sprawl on the floor as squares of sunlight moved across the carpet and onto our bodies. He'd ramp up some blurry, faux-jazz playlist—or maybe it was the same song for the whole eight weeks of our affair—and we'd close our eyes, waiting for the sun to slide its warmth across us. Like we were cats. It doesn't translate to a story, but trust me that we loved doing this. We'd crack and eat pistachios. It was sexy in its low-key way. Obviously we were naked.

"Could I love you?" I asked. I was big on repetition. People mostly want to hear their own words parroted back rather than getting original material. Try it sometime.

"I'm realizing that no one has truly loved me," he said.

I snorted. "Now you're crazy," I said. "For example, your mother is devoted to you. And you've had girlfriends." I'd accidentally get their calls in my voice mail at work because our extensions were a digit off. Before the rise of smartphones, of course. Now, with everyone tethered to one phone number for eternity, I could conduct a secret life in my sleep.

"Lots of girlfriends," he said. "Some told me they loved me."

"Then probably you should believe them," I said.

He shook his head. "Don't you feel that way?" he asked. "Like they're all just saying they love you, even your mother? But it's really a big fucking lie."

My mother died when I was three, but never mind. I got the gist.

Yeah. When you're telling a story, it's easy to slip in a dead mother, and no one will think it's important. Save some of those shrimp for me. Told you they were good.

Johnny was busy feeling sorry for himself, all puppy dog eyes and winging pistachio shells at a worn leather chair.

I said, "This conversation is like being trapped in a college dorm room at three A.M. without pot to make it bearable." Thinking about a dorm room sent me spiraling through thoughts of D. H. and how yesterday, again, he had announced to our counselor that he didn't love me anymore. "I'm sitting right here," I had said, and he nodded. "I used to, I think," he'd said. "Maybe. But [Evil Name] and I are just. . . ." Long sigh. Beyond words. I wanted to slap him. So did the counselor. "Let's back up a little bit," she said. Let's back up a truck, I thought, right on top of all of us. See, anger!

Johnny might have been thinking the same thing about me right at this moment.

So I slipped him the lie: "I do love you." So easy to say, so god-damn EASY to SAY.

"You're just like everyone else," he said. He aimed the pistachio shells at me, not meanly, but not cutely, either. Irrelevantly, he said, "God, I need a job."

Boom, the phone rang, and some kick-ass start-up that had put him through a couple rounds of interviews was on the line with a job offer. Major spine chill. You'd never believe this is how it happened, except that this is a true story and this literally *is* how it happened. Two seconds later, still clenched in the congratulatory hug, I dumped Johnny, and that was the end of my retaliation affair and of squares of sunlight crossing my afternoons.

Back in the beginning, it was like D. H. and I were stitched together. That close, that sickening. We were our own walking romance novel, we thought, in love, so dangerously in love. Even the inevitable fights felt glamorous and crucial, testing our bond: Who promised to buy toothpaste but didn't? Who thought *Caddyshack* was moronic and who thought it was hilarious? Who slept with that gloomy-eyed brunette in the Victorian novels class while who was studying at the library that night?

Yeah, that was his pattern. I got it. He always came back to me. I always let him come back. We trusted each other that way. It would have been crazy except that we considered it romantic.

We'd been together the whole school year when he told me his dad had moved out when he was ten. We were eating ice cream cones, sitting on the flat quarry rocks piled along the shore of the lake. Students painted their names on these rocks; until this moment, we'd been plotting to do the same before summer break, when he let it out about his dad. He bit into the cone part. He ate too fast.

"You didn't tell me your parents are divorced." It seemed like something you say early.

"She's too embarrassed to get divorced," he said. "So they're still married, but these days my dad's shacking up with a stewardess in Boston."

"What about your mom?"

"In love with my old pediatrician." He shook his head. "It's not important."

"It is," I whispered. "At least kind of. Why didn't you tell me?"

He finished his cone and spoke loudly through a too-full mouth: "Don't define me by who they are. I'm not them. I won't be."

Remember how back in those silly college days, people could believe that we could go up against the gods and create our own destiny? I was convinced I'd die at the same age my mother did, and when I didn't, there was relief but mostly confusion. Something promised felt messed up.

D. H. and I shared a dorm room, unofficially. He lived in the nerd and loser dorm, where every room was a single (always a whiff of Dungeons & Dragons in the hallways), and I lived there with him, treating my own dorm room as a largish closet overseen by a roommate who borrowed my clothes.

Every night I fell asleep in D. H.'s arms, the two of us tucked into his squishy single bed. We fit only one way: him on his back and me half-draped over him, my face nestled into his chest, his arms wrapped around me. We'd wake in that same position the next morning.

Typically, we'd study until one or so—it was the kind of school where everyone studied, even the people who claimed they didn't—and then we'd strip down, do it, and lie in that single bed in the dark. We'd talk. Rather, he'd talk, and I'd listen. I absolutely loved his voice. Sort of Southern. Bet you didn't picture him from the South, did you? He hated where he was from, but there was no hate in his buttermilk voice. He spoke like the way cream swirls through coffee. No wonder [Evil Name] lapped him up. You always think a man with that kind of accent is going to be kinder, don't you?

It's killing me to talk about him like this.

He told stories about raising baby rabbits in shoeboxes. Dogs loping alongside when he rode his bike to the creek. Sprinkling salt on leeches to shrivel them off his shins. His dad teaching him how to tie knots. How his mother fried chicken for his birthday dinner each year and baked red velvet cake. (All exotic to me—the chicken, the cake, the mother.) The kids he beat up, the kids who beat him up. Moments of glory in baseball games, moments of humiliation. Eating a caramel apple and wrecking his new braces. I'm sick to think of the stories I've forgotten.

There was one favorite that I especially liked. It was D. H.'s fourteenth birthday, and his mother was sitting at the dinner table, wing in her hand, and suddenly she shrieked, "Daddy!," and all chatter cut off because she was sobbing, claiming her father—on a fishing trip an hour away—was dead. Dead.

D. H.—newly fourteen and eager to plunge into the stack of gifts; one box had to be the new turntable he wanted—expected everyone to tell his crazy mother to stop talking cuckoo, but the aunts' eyes darted as they nodded, and one aunt ran for the phone, and another wailed the way you would if you saw a dead body right then and there, and the third rushed into the kitchen to get water boiling for the macaroni and cheese the family took to funerals. All these women leaping to action before the phone call an hour later confirming the death—an aneurysm in the boat—as if his mama's one word was a done deal.

"See," he told me there in the dark, my head on his chest, ear tuned into his heartbeat. "Ghosts run in my family."

"Ghosts run in your family," I murmured.

"If I ever die, my ghost will come back to find you," he said. "I won't leave you alone on Earth without me. I would never do that."

The thought scared me—that he would come back, that he wouldn't. We were in college, but he told me this same story late at night, word for word, for years after. Each time, I made him promise, made him cross his heart. "I'll come back," he whispered in the dark, "promise." I believed him.

Each time, I thought about ghosts running through a family, their cold shapelessness passing through the gaps of hugs at Thanksgiving; weightless on the sofa during the Super Bowl, ghostly fingers reaching for kernels of popcorn; their Christmas stockings dangling next to mine, limp, empty, forgotten. I thought about a ghost settling between the two of us, and I pressed myself tighter against his chest.

Drunk driving. Only he was the drunk and the driver. I hate that, so sometimes I say heart attack or cancer. Other times I say murder victim. I never say the truth, which is that every drunk driver is loved by someone.

I didn't marry him because I inherited a fortune after my mother died. Okay, "fortune" is a fairy tale word. And it wasn't an inheritance, but more of a settlement. I never told him how much. I hated that money. It's sick to get money because someone dies. You think it might fix things, but it doesn't. It pays for college. I know, that sounds great, but there's more to the story. Another day.

The point here is that it was me who didn't want to get married. Me, not him. I let people think it was him. Maybe it was him a little. He didn't push. We were fine.

After he died, I had to rip up my will. Now what? Cats, kids, the opera, a disease? I left half to Schultz's. Hope they don't wreck the place by upscaling it; I was thinking raises for the bartenders and bigger bathrooms. The other half to—well, I'll let that be a surprise. Not my college, though.

Can you see that bit by bit I'm answering the questions you're embarrassed to ask? You're welcome. And yeah, this martini *is* damn good—didn't I tell you, didn't I tell you? You're welcome again. Have another. I am.

The last appointment with the counselor, the one that fixed us. The clock was ticking down our fifty minutes, and she suddenly said, "I don't understand why you two stay together." She sighed, clicked her ballpoint pen rapidly. There was a logo on the pen, as if she'd snitched it from a realtor or bank, which seemed cheap of her, using that kind of pen to record our angst. "I'm pretty sure you'd both be better off alone."

"You're not supposed to make those kinds of judgments," D. H. said.

"Neither of you can possibly be happy," she said. "Or happy as any normal person defines the word."

D. H. grabbed my hand. His fingers were warm.

"It's incredibly frustrating." The therapist's voice cracked. We had broken her, making her say things she shouldn't. Maybe she would yell, or threaten us, or throw one of her tasteful Chinese-style vases against the wall. (They were meant to look expensive, but I recognized them as being from one of those cheap import stores.)

"I don't know what to do with the two of you," she said. "You're beyond logic."

I blandly watched her surrender. Now that it was over with her, I felt sort of sorry. Maybe if I mentioned my retaliation affair?

"You deserve each other," she said. Finally she cried, reaching for the tissue box.

We skipped our next appointment. She didn't call to follow up. We could have reported her to whomever you report things to, but we just laughed. This was our normal. This was us. Who he said he loved didn't matter, because he couldn't leave me. It would be like gravity leaving the Earth. That counselor didn't understand and

[Evil Name] didn't either and no one did. We liked it that way. The sex that night was incredible, I distinctly remember.

I promise I'm getting to the part about the ghost. You knew there'd be a ghost, right? The only worthwhile story is a ghost story: lost past, lost youth, lost love, ancestors leaving traces of their genetic code and maybe a silver tea set.

There was a phone call. There wasn't a mother sitting upright as she passed a platter of fried chicken. There was a day where he drove to Schultz's and I didn't. I had a sore throat and a bad cold. I secretly wanted him to stay home and take care of me but didn't say so. I should have said so. I chugged NyQuil and fell asleep on the couch with the TV blasting.

There was a phone call. Accident—identify—come now. Clipped words just like the police show playing on the TV. Except on TV they knock on the door. Goddamn it. I always cry at this part. I crawled into a taxi, my mind zoned with NyQuil.

"At least no one else was hurt," someone said to me. Actually, that was not so much my concern at that exact moment.

People weren't as nice as they would have been if it had been cancer or a heart attack. I don't even remember most of what they said. I signed a bunch of papers because I told them I was his wife. You could say that's when we got married.

Someone organized a funeral, and I guess that was mostly me, helped slightly by his mother. I barely knew her. Liz-Beth, not Elizabeth. Half her friends who came up from the South had hyphens in their first names. I tried to ask her about the fried chicken, but she wasn't interested. She was thinner than she sounds in the stories, and angular and sharp, like a bad geometry problem. Wrap her in black and she would fit just fine on a New York City street. "Why didn't I know you?" I asked her. "Why didn't we visit you for holidays or something?" I'd seen her twice in my life, once when D. H.'s brother died and there was a memorial service, and once for her fiftieth birthday party, which she spent mostly in the bar next door to the restaurant where the party was. Both times she kept calling me Debbie, I don't know why. "Don't take it personally," D. H. had whispered.

"This family is embarrassingly complicated," she said. "I'll sit down and write a letter about it one of these days." (Still waiting.) His father was a no-show because they didn't know where he was. Sailing around the world, someone claimed, but someone else said in white-collar prison for embezzlement. Someone else swore he managed a coffee plantation in Brazil. Google didn't help. Imagine a life outside of Google!

Tangents. I love them. Martinis, too.

So, there was a funeral. Friends, flowers, casseroles, coworkers, hugs, Kleenex, funny stories told by sad people, men who wouldn't be caught dead in a suit wearing one anyway. You know.

At one point, I asked his mother, "Was there a ghost when he died?" I was drunk. Or, not drunk. But drinking. "Did you know the minute it happened?"

She was amused. "That old story," she said. "About my dad. I remember." She was drunk, too, or drinking. The man who came with her—attended her might be more accurate—was named Shep, as if he were a dog or a Stooge. (Yes, I know the Stooge was Shemp, but I think we need a joke here.)

I was embarrassed but I don't know why. "That old story," I repeated. Helpfully, I said it helpfully.

She said, "Yes." She was not helpful. Shep squeezed her hand.

Yes to that old story? Yes she knew the minute her son died? Yes? Just yes? Yes?

Shep shook his head. He didn't talk much, but he was quick with the liquor, and he grabbed the closest bottle, which happened to be tequila, and dumped some in my half-empty wine glass. White, so okay.

"My dad and I were—." She paused in an excruciating way. I

had a stab of sympathy for Shep and for the men who had crossed her path, including D. H. I sipped the tequila-wine mix, mouthed "thank you" to Shep. You could drive a truck through the space between the start and finish of that sentence of hers. "My dad and I existed on a wavelength," she said at long last. "We were a continuum. My son and I were—." That pause. "Not."

I held out my glass so Shep could pour me more tequila, which he gratefully did. Clearly he liked being helpful. That was probably the only type of man she tolerated, the helpful type, which was not necessarily the type her sons were.

We were at my house. The funeral after party. Lots of liquor. Someone had brought the tequila, someone trying to be helpful. Shep? Personally, I wouldn't serve tequila at a funeral, but I drank it. You know, since it was there. So, turned out it actually was helpful.

She leaned and whispered boozily into my ear, "You know what they say about those kinds of car accidents, don't you?"

I said, "You'll have to excuse me for a moment," and I walked away, giving a little wave that could mean I'll be right back or could mean the opposite.

[Evil Name] was at the funeral. She wrote her name in the condolence book in red pen. Why would someone use their own pen when there was a perfectly fine black pen provided by the funeral home? Why would she stand there, rooting around her big-ass purse for her own pen? Germaphobe? Hers is the only name written in red. She used her middle initial and kept within the lines. Her signature lacks flourish and would be easy to forge. Later, I copied it repeatedly on pieces of paper until I could replicate it. Trying to steal her soul? No, just sometimes I sign her name on petitions when people shove clipboards in my face.

She came to the house for the after party. Someone probably handed her a flyer with directions. Damn it.

She didn't hug me. She didn't come talk to me. Instead, she hovered, a shadow twitching the corner of my eye. Even when I edged into another room or walked down the hall; even when someone collapsed me into their arms, there she was, a half-step beyond my full and complete vision. She clung to the same can of Diet Coke the whole time, like she was star of a TV ad for it.

I was certain there would be people who knew she was bereaved, too. But no one hugged her that whole endless hour, and the people who spoke to her spoke small talk—"How did you know D. H.?"—and she answered back small: "We worked together at Stupid Corp. a couple of years ago." She nodded like a dummy, agreeing with observations about the weather or D. H. or the HoneyBaked ham. (A ham is God's gift to funerals.)

Okay, yes, she looked sad. Damn it. She dabbed her eyes with a napkin as she stood facing the funeral display photos lined up on a table. I hoped she might try slipping one in her gigantic purse so I could catch her. She just looked. D. H., eight years old, in his baseball uniform. Me and D. H. sprawled in a hammock. D. H. with one arm slung around his brother. A school picture of poor D. H. with a solid line of braces across his smile. Me and D. H. squinting in the Orioles dugout on a stadium tour. Suddenly I couldn't stand how she was staring at those photographs, memorizing them, so I swooped in.

"I'm about to leave," she said. Guilty voice, as if I'd caught her thinking something she shouldn't have.

"Don't go," I said. That was a surprise. I had meant to say, Good, go. Go already! Go! No one invited you.

"Cute picture," she said, pointing to D. H. in the baseball uniform.

"That was the year he played for the Drumsticks," I said. "The team name was his idea."

She laughed lightly. I couldn't tell if she knew that story. Her laugh was sort of cozy. Yet she didn't add anything, like, "I remember how the other kids called his team 'chicken,' and everyone blamed him for not winning a game all season." I would hate if she knew the things I did, HATE. Also I would like it because we could talk about him.

I said, "There's ham."

She said, "There's always ham at a funeral." She laughed again in that same stupid, cozy way.

I nodded. Secretly, I wondered what Jewish people would do, or Muslims, without ham at their funerals, how they coped.

She said, "I actually kind of like that."

"Like what?"

"That there's always ham."

I was incredibly bored of talking about ham. Is this what he was missing with me, conversations about ham? I could have gotten him back with more about ham, with ham jokes? Why did the ham cross the road? Two hams and a salami walked into a bar.

I knew she knew I knew. He told me he had told her I knew.

I wanted to scream, just open wide and SCREAM.

She opened her mouth, and damn it, I was afraid she was going to be the one screaming, not me, but her jaw hung slack. Maybe she was deciding should she say what she was going to say. When you do that, you shouldn't. You should close your mouth and shut up.

She said, "I hope it's okay if I tell you that I miss him."

Why would this be okay, ever?

I was the one allowed to miss him. Me. That picture of us in the hammock. She missed him like I did.

I said, "I know. Me too." I lifted my hand as if to pat her on the shoulder, and then I did pat her on the shoulder. A black sweater—good cashmere, not the cheap kind. I imagined his hand on her shoulder, her arm, her breast, her back, him admiring the texture of this same sweater. This sweater might be a Christmas gift from him, though he had never given me a sweater. Enough with the sweater. I folded up my arms tight in case they might spring wide to hug her. I was afraid she might ask to meet for lunch, and that if she did, I would say yes. That's how much I wanted to talk about him, that I would do it with her. So I said, "We should have lunch or something."

"Or something." Her eyes slid back to the photos. Memorizing them.

I grabbed the framed picture of D. H. in his baseball uniform, pressed it against my chest. "This is mine," I said, flipping it so the ugly frame-back faced out.

She turned and walked straight through the front door, not stopping to grab her coat, also expensive cashmere. You know what? It fit me perfectly, so I kept it and wore it. I don't know why. I don't know why anything.

Why would I remember a line like "ghosts run in my family"? When someone is dead, your memory becomes both sharper and foggier, and what you don't remember, you feel as though you have permission to make up. You realize that when you want the true story, you're going to make it up because he's not there to stop you. That's sad.

Also, to finish what Liz-Beth was insinuating: what they say is that many single car accidents aren't accidents. So what a relief that his blood alcohol level was .15. He was drunk. He was a drunk driver. No need to make anything more complicated.

Also, why blame [Evil Name], not him? I understood the truth in an uncluttered and elegant way when I was eighteen, standing outside my dorm lobby: "Then really I think you got screwed by your brother."

Funeral night, alone in the house. I kicked out the lingerers around eight o'clock. They aimed for kindness, saying, "You shouldn't be alone," and stuff. Yeah. Well, but I was. I was totally alone. He was gone. Not like two days later he'd be at the door with fancy flowers (I taught him early on that carnations do not equal an apology). Not like we could jackhammer through the problems with our counselor. This wasn't a way of gone I understood. I mean, there was my dead mother, but that was different. Worse? Never rank pain.

The lingerers had picked up big swathes of mess—food, empties, paper plates—but the place felt filthy, as if people were still hanging around, stuffing their faces. "How can you eat?" They could. The place felt so beyond dirty that the sensible solution was for me to move out, and I sprawled on the bed in the guestroom—the only room I could stand—thinking about where I could move to and the only place that made sense was the moon. I would move to the moon.

There was rain, which I hated at that moment. The day had been cloudy, threatening rain, and having that rain come, finally, at the end of this wretchedly long day, wasn't fair. Something expected actually happening seemed totally unfair.

The tequila had worked through me, carving out the deep glacier of a headache.

The guestroom had two twin beds, and I was on the one up against the far wall, flat on my back, staring at the motionless ceiling fan, crushing and kneading a feather pillow with my hands. There was a cobweb above me, and I liked how it shimmied in a nonexistent breeze. No sounds but the rain. Occasionally when I squeezed the pillow, a tiny feather floated out, and there would be that for me to stare at. It seemed this was how it was going to be, each day nothing but a series of meaningless moments drooping one after the other.

"Jesus fucking Christ," I said. It was the most satisfactory curse I knew, but I wasn't satisfied.

I was lying there, waiting, waiting for something. Waiting for him to show up. He had promised! Ghosts ran in his family! I believed in ghosts—at least now I did, now when I wanted one. His mother and that single word, "Daddy."

So I whispered, "Daddy."

Maybe you needed the fried chicken? Maybe fried chicken was a key component? Maybe KFC overflowed ghosts?

Good stories rely on repetition and pattern, usually of three things. Jokes, too. They call it the Rule of Three. That is, I say, "Jesus fucking Christ," and that's one. Then I say, "Daddy," and that's two. Then the next thing I say—number three—there's the payoff, the punch line. It's classic structure. No one messes with classic structure.

But the phone rang right then. "Jesus fucking Christ," I repeated, and my careful classic structure turned to shit.

It was his mother. Liz-Beth. "I lied," she said.

I was so surprised to hear this, just so surprised.

"No, darling, not that one, the other," she said to Shep, I assume. "Not that other, the other other."

A pause.

I knew what she lied about.

She had known about the accident. A person doesn't say something like "ghosts run in my family" if they don't.

There were muffled sounds on the phone, as if she were sliding her palm over it, the scrape of her big family heirloom ring. I wouldn't have guessed a ring like that from the stories, or maybe I would have, if someone asked. Then she was back.

She said, "I did feel something. I did know."

Another pause. She was infuriating, with all these pauses. Someone could live another life inside her silence. I thought about D. H. growing up manipulated by these pauses, the perpetual wait to hear what would come next, never an end. It was a conversational style that seemed in transit.

At least a real minute passed. I puffed out air so the cobweb above swayed. Why was there a phone in the guestroom, anyway? If the phone wasn't right here, on the wicker table by the bed, I wouldn't have answered. I wasn't about to stand up for a ringing phone ever again.

That's how long this pause was, enough time to think all that. Finally I asked, "What did you feel?"

"Oh, darling," she sighed, and I thought we were back to Shep, but it was me; suddenly I was "darling." "Something drained out of me, and I pulled the car over immediately because if I didn't stop driving, I would hurtle straight over the side of a bridge. I knew he was gone. I knew instantly, in spite of all that ugliness between us—and you don't know the half of it. . . ."

She paused. That was right. He had only told me old-time stories. When I said, "Let's go visit your mother," he'd real fast say, "I don't think so," and we wouldn't.

"I sat in my car in a Chick-fil-A parking lot, sobbing. Everything was gone," she said. "Everything was sand through my fingers, and all I could do was go home and wait for your phone call. Which came."

"But what did you feel?" I insisted. She wasn't thorough.

"Something that had been there wasn't," she said.

"How did you know?" I insisted. "How were you sure? It could have been someone else." Maybe I was hysterical. I felt hysterical, but I also felt as though I sounded very calm.

"I knew," she said.

"But how?" Okay, maybe I was screaming. Maybe I had thrown the pillow to the floor and I was screaming into the phone. Maybe my face was blotchy and hideous, seared red by anger and frustration.

Maybe she didn't notice I was screaming. In response, she sighed.

The Rule of Three. Is a story more meaningful with it? What is the best and easiest and fastest way to find some goddamn meaning?

? ? ?

"Love," she said. "I knew because of love."

"That doesn't make any fucking sense," I hissed.

I felt her shrug. I felt Shep rubbing her feet. I felt an ice cube in her glass of scotch melt one additional millimeter and tumble more deeply into the amber liquid. They were staying at the lovely and expensive Hotel Monaco, a block or two from Schultz's. I felt a lot of luggage in her room in the Hotel Monaco, a lot of expensive shoes.

"I'm sorry for you," she said. "Waiting for a ghost. Ghosts aren't real, but love is. You didn't love him enough."

Suddenly I knew exactly why we didn't go to her house for Thanksgiving. You would think someone wouldn't be mean under sad and dire circumstances, but she was.

Then there was this thought: Maybe I didn't. Maybe I didn't. What's enough? The ghost was hanging with [Evil Name] right now. I had the baseball uniform picture, but [Evil Name] loved him enough, enough and more, and more, and she got the ghost. I should have let go. I should have—. If—. How—. Why—.

Then another thought: She was lying. She was a goddamn, fucking liar. She didn't love him enough either. Jesus fucking Christ, I thought "either." What did we want, the two of us, the three of us? Scrabbling over this dead man.

I knew Liz-Beth expected me to hang up but I didn't. And there we were, breathing on the phone, our breath matching, in and out, and I think maybe she fell asleep, and it was peaceful listening to the in-out of her breath as the cobweb danced above me. I snapped off the lamp beside the bed and shut my eyes and fell asleep, and when I was startled awake late into the night, the phone was silent, and I hung it up.

There in the dark, alone, alone for the first time in my adult life—I'm talking deeply and profoundly alone, not alone in a "table-for-one on a business trip" way, but to the core, drowning in the understanding that there was no one at this exact moment, no one but me awake on this rain-strewn night—alone with my hardest thoughts, alone with the truth, and alone in that darkness, I touched my chest with my fingertips, where my heart beat deep inside me, faithfully, and there was a perfect circle of dampness soaked into my blouse—like tears—only *like* tears—that could be explained no other way—no other way whatsoever—than that he had kept his promise.

Do you believe in ghosts now? Wait. Don't answer.

There are ghosts everywhere. Actually, the building that Schultz's is in was recently bought by a convenience store chain. What could be more convenient than a corner bar, I ask you, particularly one with the best martinis in town? Nevertheless. I'll have to rip up my will again because soon Schultz's will be gone. D. H. is gone, along with those college days and that twin bed in the nerd dorm. Johnny is somewhere, but really he's gone, too. I swept away that cobweb the next day; a year later, I moved from that house to a different one. My mother is gone, or was she never here? We'll be gone too, soon enough.

The story is winding down. Check! We'll give up the booth. Time for someone else, time for their ghost stories.

Last thing, I promise. You know Terry in that Springsteen song I was telling you about? I get now that Terry is a ghost. Darling, my love; my crazy, crazy love—. Damn it. If you were here, I would explain it all to you, and the things I know that I didn't know before. I have so much to tell you.

SLUT

Nicole chose the restaurant: King Street Café in Old Town Alexandria, not too far from her house, easy parking. At the very least, she knew she'd get a good meal out of the night. She didn't ask her friends for advice because she didn't want them to know she was going on this blind date.

Ben said he'd seen the restaurant written up by the *Washington Post* and thought going there would be fun. He used the word "fun" a lot in their phone conversation, which made her nervous. "Sounds fun," he'd say, or he'd conclude a story with, "Yeah, that was a fun time." She couldn't pinpoint what it was, maybe that "fun" wasn't a very masculine word or that it wasn't very mature. Either way, she wasn't anticipating a "fun" dinner. But she had committed, and she was proud of herself for setting up the meeting for Thursday night at six o'clock—even a stealth date was a date.

A coworker, Andrea, was the only one who knew. "Trust me," she said. "You don't want to head straight into online dating. Talk about booby traps. They're 95 percent pigs out there, pigs and god-damn liars. 'Six feet tall' means 'five-eight.' Ben is a nice guy."

"Why aren't you dating him?" They were standing at the office kitchen, listening to the microwave popcorn go wild. It had to be a quick conversation because coworkers would be lured in by the aroma wafting through the heating vents.

"I did date him," Andrea said. "But it didn't work out."

"That hardly sounds promising. Why isn't he married?"

"Well. . . ." Andrea pulled open the door and grabbed the bag with her fingertips.

"Whose popcorn?" someone called from the hallway.

Andrea quickly said, "He's really good on a first date anyway. Isn't that what you said you wanted, to get that first date under your belt?"

Under your belt. She blushed and looked away; surely Andrea didn't mean anything by that. It was just a phrase.

Andrea pried open the bag, letting the popped kernels tumble into a large plastic bowl. It seemed to Nicole that the air suddenly turned greasy and heavy, that something slick coated the insides of her lungs as she breathed in. Nicole forced herself to eat some popcorn though she no longer had a taste for it.

On Thursday, she left the office early so she could go home and change for her date. She hoped to avoid Andrea, but there was Andrea stepping out of the up elevator when she was waiting to go down, and she grabbed Nicole's arm as the elevator door closed, stranding Nicole in the lobby. "You look great," Andrea said, giving her the full up-and-down appraisal.

"I do?" Nicole was confused. She wore black pants that gaped at the waist and butt, a slouchy man's white French cuff shirt with the sleeves rolled up, a heavy, silver bracelet, and leopard flats. The bracelet was Tiffany, and the flats were cute enough for twenty-five bucks at Marshall's, but the rest of the outfit was, charitably, only barely passable for office attire.

"Very what-the-hell," Andrea said. "Confident and sassy. Men love seeing women in their clothing." There was a slight pause, as if Andrea wanted to say more but decided not to.

"Actually, I was thinking I might go home to change," Nicole said.

"Thank God." She let go of Nicole's arm. "A skirt and heels. Or tight jeans and heels. Whatever you do, *heels.*" Andrea moved through the glass double doors and into the office, and Nicole pressed the elevator button again. It was wrong to keep wearing Roger's shirts, yet she felt compelled to pull one on as she got ready in the morning, even knowing it was the day of the blind date. Roger's monogram, a tiny white-on-white RKR on the left cuff, was carefully rolled up and hidden, but she supposed she wasn't fooling anyone.

Ten months ago Roger had died of a heart attack. He and Nicole had been married for six years and had recently closed on a new house after working their asses off to dent the student loans and credit card balances. They had picked out a kitten from the shelter, and they were finally ready to have a baby. Now she was back to dating. Fun. The right word after all.

When Andrea described Ben—"Brown hair; brown eyes; tall enough; very easy-going; sort of like a teddy bear, but not fat. And, I guess I have to say, maybe a tiny bit balding, but not bald."— Nicole was startled to realize that each of those adjectives could be used to describe Roger. But were Ben's eyes "brown," or were they brown like Roger's, richly deep and shimmering, appearing almost black, eyes that made you catch your breath even across the room? Andrea continued—"Nice smile, very excellent butt, no visible tattoos, no earrings though he wears some kind of cheesy string bracelet"—he better not fiddle with it, Nicole thought, she hated nervous tics on men, on anyone—"decent dresser, like someone you're not embarrassed to be with."

But, Nicole thought, but, but, but.

Oddly, Andrea said exactly what Nicole was thinking: "But he's not Roger. I know. But only Roger was Roger, right?"

It was stupid to be single again at age thirty-eight. Stupid and sad. She hated her life.

They would be meeting first in the bar of the King Street Café for a drink. The unspoken assumption was that if things went well, she and Ben could head into the restaurant for dinner. It had been at least ten years since Nicole had been on a "date," and probably what she did in her twenties wasn't "dating" anyway, so she had no idea what to expect: how to signal the transition from drink to meal, who would pay, how to escape if the conversation was awkward, what to wear that didn't look like she was trying too hard, because—she reminded herself—she wasn't trying too hard. She wasn't trying at all. Only Roger was Roger, and she was going out with this guy because she had to go out with someone eventually. Because she was thirty-eight and was hoping for a baby. Because she was thirty-eight and hadn't had sex for nearly a year. Because for a thirty-eight-year-old, she spent way too many nights slouched with the cat in her lap, watching the food shows she and Roger used to love. Because—because Roger wasn't coming back.

"Damn it," she said. Her hand had slipped, and now her mascara was smeared. She wiped off the smudge with a Q-Tip and started again, as the cat twined around her ankles. Damn it, Roger. It wasn't Roger's fault for dying, but she couldn't help but blame him: if he had tried a little harder, if he had been more considerate and less selfish, if he had—what? something, he should have done something, he should have worked harder to not die—and if he had done whatever that thing was, then she wouldn't be left here, dolling up for some random guy.

She was out the door, then paused for a moment on the top step. It was wrong. But she unlocked the door and went back in for one—only one—condom to tuck inside the zippered pocket of her purse. Slut, she thought.

Before the date, she had asked Andrea, "How did you describe me to him?" They were gathered for a conference call, and she didn't know why she asked; it almost made her nauseous to think of this guy, this Ben, hearing a vague description of her, making judgments and assumptions. Thinking maybe because her husband died she was desperate, ready to jump him on the first hello. She, personally, would never want to date someone with a dead spouse, and she mistrusted Ben for agreeing to.

The others were delayed, lingering in the hallway to suck up to the big boss, who happened to wander by. Nicole didn't bother anymore with details like sucking up; no one wanted to fire a widow, she figured.

Andrea said, "I said you were gorgeous, which you absolutely are, so shut up. Blonde hair like a shampoo commercial, very midwestern looking and wholesome but also edgy in that really interesting way."

"He'll think that means I'm a bitch," Nicole said.

"Of course," Andrea said. "You want him nervous. A little intimidation is good."

"What did he say when you told him about Roger?" Nicole asked.

"Oh." In the hallway, the big boss was striding away amid a flurry of "looking good, people," and Andrea moved to the conference table, selecting a seat across from where she normally sat, inserting the wide oak table between her and Nicole. The others drifted in, poking at the tray of doughnuts. "He doesn't know about that," Andrea added unnecessarily. "But that's better. Seriously."

Nicole rolled her eyes, but later she decided Andrea was right. Why would anyone agree to go out with a woman dragging a dead husband into the picture? Unless they felt sorry for her. No pity dates.

Wearing the expensive jeans and heels high enough to meet Andrea's approval, Nicole paused at the door to the King Street Café, pretending to read the menu posted on the outside wall, though the only words that registered were "catch of the day / market price." It was a pleasant April evening, and no one bothered with jackets as they strolled along King Street, headed to various restaurants and bars, maybe the old-fashioned movie theater, one of the ice cream shops. In the reflection off the glass menu case, Nicole watched people pass behind her: everyone was matched up into a couple. Or sometimes two couples together. Even numbers only. Nicole didn't see one woman alone, not one, and suddenly she felt self-conscious, so she abruptly yanked open the door and stepped inside.

The bar was dim with a buzz of voices, and she stood for a moment, trying to remember why she was here. It was a mistake. When she and Roger had bought the new house, they had talked about how great it would be living a five-minute drive to Old Town, to be able to eat at all these restaurants. Here she was. Roger, who loved fish, probably would have ordered the catch of the day. She would have gotten something she wouldn't cook at home: rabbit, maybe, or lamb. Or something complicated and richly seasoned. Negotiate the appetizers so they could try the two best. Share a dessert. She hated, now, going out and having to order a whole dessert to herself.

"Nicole!"

Roger. Roger's voice calling her. Her heart thumped heavily in her ears.

Not possible. She caught her breath and scanned the bar until she saw a waving arm toward the back. Again, that familiar voice, "Nicole!" and she understood immediately why she had thought of Roger: it was Roger's brother, and why had she chosen this ridiculous restaurant of all places? Never choose a place that was just written up in the *Washington Post*. Quick anger flashed through her, though anger directed at whom? Mostly at Ben—why had Ben agreed to meet here? He should have been the one to pick the place.

Several people turned to stare at her, so she lifted one arm at Wyatt, who stepped forward, away from his little group at the bar. He hurried toward her and leaned down to kiss her cheek. "I was going to call you this weekend," he said. "I've been meaning to call. We must be on the same psychic vibe because here you are."

"Here I am," she said.

"It's great to see you."

"Great to see you, too."

Their eyes met, and Nicole instantly looked away. Wyatt was the oldest of the three boys in Roger's family, a lawyer married to another lawyer. He lived in a McMansion in McLean. He was the one always arriving late to family functions, bringing better wine than anyone else brought or contributing a platter of expensive Scottish smoked salmon to a simple Fourth of July potluck, always saying, "I've been meaning to call." This past Thanksgiving, she had gone to Roger's parents' house (a mistake; she spent much of the afternoon crying in the guest bathroom and left before the pie was served, something rude and unforgiveable in her mother-in-law's book), and Wyatt and his mother got into a huge argument about making gravy, with Wyatt waving around a glossy magazine as his mother kept repeating in a stony voice, "My gravy's been good enough for the past twenty-five years." That was the last time she'd seen any of them.

There was eight years age difference between Roger and Wyatt, and they were never especially close, though Wyatt had spoken memorably at the funeral about teaching Roger how to throw a football. She remembered watching tears rise in his eyes as he spoke and how they quivered but didn't spill over. Same brown eyes as Roger. Still. She forced herself to look at them, to smile brightly.

"How's it going?" he asked.

She spoke too fast: "I'm meeting someone."

"Oh, sure," he said, and he waved his arm again, a sweeping gesture. "Don't let me hold you up."

"I mean, they're probably not here yet," she said. "You know me, always early." How carefully she had avoiding saying "he" . . . *he's probably not here yet.*

"Sure," Wyatt repeated, and he kept standing there, as if he expected something more. A confession! She remembered how he often said that silence was a negotiator's best tool. She had to break the silence:

"I don't want to keep you," she said.

"Just work friends of Lisa's." His wife. "Actually, we're waiting on her; she got trapped in a meeting and is the late one, leaving me stuck." His laugh was like a bark.

"Tell her I said hi," Nicole said.

"Tell her yourself," Wyatt said as the door opened, and he pointed. Nicole turned to face the door, but it wasn't Lisa. It was a brown-haired man of Roger's height, balding but cute—yes, a little like a teddy bear; Andrea was right—with a quick smile. Gray sweater over a white T-shirt, jeans. Not wanting to try too hard, either, Nicole thought. He stood for a moment as she stared at him, startled that he wasn't Lisa, then he strode forward with his hand out.

"Are you Nicole?" he asked.

Wyatt tilted his head, shifted his eyes from her to the man and back to her.

"Um, yes," she said, and remembered to stick out her hand. They shook; her handshake felt to her fishy and horribly sweaty, but he smiled, so maybe not.

"Ben Roberts," he said. "Good to meet you." He looked at Wyatt.

Wyatt looked at Ben.

Nicole looked at the exit sign above the door as she mumbled, "This is—this is Wyatt," and the two men silently shook hands like world leaders waiting for a translator to fill in the gaps.

Nicole couldn't guess which would be scarier, Ben's questions or Wyatt's, so she jumped in abruptly, hoping to prevent either from asking anything: "We should grab a seat," she said, and for a horrified moment it looked as though Wyatt thought she was including him as he spun around uselessly, surveying the bar. So she quickly pointed to where a couple was settling up their check and said, "There's two over there," babbling on, "I'm really dying for a good drink." Probably not the right thing to say on a date, but true. And given how rapidly Ben headed over to claim the vacated stools, possibly true for him, too.

She and Wyatt stood for a second, their arms crossed. His eyes like Roger's. That illusion that he was seeing her as Roger did when she was nothing more than his dead brother's wife.

"Say hi to Lisa," she repeated.

"Will do." He backed away, returning to the group of lawyers, but those eyes felt like something cold pressed up against her back.

"Good to see you," she called, but he didn't hear. She took in a deep breath, let it out slowly.

And there was Ben. He pushed back her bar stool so she could clamber up into it—not a graceful seating arrangement for tight jeans and heels—and said, "I got you some water."

She drank it slowly, mostly because as long as she was drinking it, she didn't have to talk or explain anything. And then the bartender approached and recommended the sidecar, the drink special of the night, and she said yes to that, and he ordered a Grey Goose and tonic.

"What's a sidecar?" he asked after a moment.

Did she want to date a man who didn't know what a sidecar was? Nicole said, "You can try mine if you'd like. Cognac, lemon juice, Cointreau. Or regular brandy instead of the cognac, which is also good and usually what you find in a bar like this one. Served up with a sugar rim. Maybe a little girly, but it's actually a classic cocktail from World War One-ish." Roger had made perfect sugar rims. She probably sounded snobby, and she struggled to think of something pleasant to say about vodka tonics.

One of Ben's eyebrows lifted, perhaps a response to her little sidecar lecture. "How do you know Andrea?" Ben asked.

It was like they were at the dud singles table at a wedding.

"Work," she said.

"Where do you—"

"That guy," she started, then stopped because the bartender set the drinks in front of them. Her martini glass glistened with a rim of sugar, and she said, "The trick is to rub a tiny chunk of lemon around the rim. Then roll the edge of the glass through sugar heaped on a plate."

"So you're kind of a sidecar connoisseur," Ben said. The eyebrow again. She couldn't tell if he was flirting or if he was annoyed. Probably annoyed. She was annoying herself.

"Look," she said. "Can we just go right to dinner?"

"Of course," he said. "Because this is going so well," and he signaled the bartender for the check. Again, she couldn't be sure: was he sarcastic-mean or sarcastic-funny? Or serious? Maybe this was a good date and she just didn't know it. Or maybe this whole thing was a terrible idea.

As she stood up—as awkward getting off the stool as she'd been climbing up onto it—she glanced down the bar and there was Wyatt, his head radiantly illuminated by a track light that seemed askew. The people he was with were talking around him, but he was silent, staring right at her, not bothering to pretend that he wasn't. He held a glass of amber liquid loosely in one hand, as if he might lift his glass to her, though that wasn't a gesture typical of him. At family gatherings, in fact, it was Roger who always proposed the toast. The youngest child, but somehow the one who wove them into a real family, she had noticed, bringing up old stories from growing up and being the first to commemorate occasions with a heartfelt toast. It wasn't a close family, but Roger had made it seem so. At that Thanksgiving there had been no toasts, until, finally, she stood up and, losing her nerve, chirped, "To the cooks!" downing her drink quickly before anyone could add more. It somehow felt like a moment of immense betrayal, but no one commented on what she had done, or even on Roger's glaring absence, at least not in her presence. As if the sound of his name would immediately avalanche into uncontrollable tears and loose, sloppy emotions.

Wyatt's eyes met hers, and she couldn't look away, until finally he turned, putting his back to her as she walked by his group of chattering lawyers—still no Lisa—followed closely by Ben, who carefully carried both drinks, as they headed to the hostess stand to get a table in the restaurant. She wasn't sure if she was supposed to say something to Wyatt, and she didn't. After she went by, she realized that Wyatt had been watching her pass in the mirror behind the bar. She looked back at Ben and smiled, her teeth feeling awkward and horsy, then turned so she wouldn't have to see if he smiled in return.

The restaurant was clattery and noisy, studiously decorated like an old-time diner with Formica and linoleum, lit a little too brightly. In one corner was an old-fashioned revolving case of various cakes and pies. She and Ben sat in a booth along the wall, facing each other, having to lean in a bit to be heard as they perused the menu and debated choices. It turned out that Ben liked to cook—perhaps that's why he'd seemed put off by her little lesson on the sidecar, he was actually annoyed at himself for not knowing what one was—and so he was happy to discuss whether she should get the asparagus with poached egg, fried oysters, or the beet salad. He didn't mention sharing, and Nicole thought it might be weird to ask, so she ordered her own appetizer—the beets—and got the bison hanger steak. He settled on chilled English pea soup and the whole roasted fish. Then she realized that her bison was the second most expensive entrée on the menu.

That worry left her mind once she recognized that with the menus whisked away, they were now on their own for conversation. Her sidecar was two-thirds gone, the sugar rim licked away, and she wanted another one, but had to be mindful that she'd have to drive herself home. Or somewhere. That condom in her purse. What was she thinking? This strange man, with his unfamiliar brown hair and brown eyes . . . she couldn't imagine herself naked in front of him. She should have worn the skirt—easier; no undressing. She blushed.

It was Roger saying, "How about over there?" But it was actually Wyatt, on the other side of the restaurant, pointing to the empty table kitty-corner from where she and Ben sat; if Wyatt and his group ended up there, she would face him directly, while Ben's back would be to them.

The hostess nodded, and the group—now including Lisa—trooped over to the empty table and settled in, chattering about traffic on 395. Wyatt positioned himself in direct view of Nicole. Lisa, her back to Nicole, apparently hadn't spotted her, and if Wyatt had mentioned her presence, Lisa surely would have said hi and come over to nose around. Wyatt gestured at his glass, looping his index finger in a tight circle that encompassed the table. Another round, she guessed. He reached for the wine list. Even as she saw him work his way through the pages of that, she felt him watching her.

She focused on Ben who poked at his drink with the stirrer straw. "So," she said.

"So."

"How do you know Andrea?" she asked, embarrassed.

"Look," he said. "I know this is awkward."

This was where she was supposed to offer a quick, easy, even untruthful explanation of Wyatt: My ex. A college crush. That horrible former boss. Two or three words, tops. Easier, instead, to natter on about the sidecar, how it was invented at Harry's Bar in Paris, how it was named for a regular who came to the bar riding in a motorcycle sidecar.

She smiled again. Her face felt brittle in the silence between them.

Finally he said, "Andrea and I were engaged, but that was in college. She broke it off. It's no big deal now—we're friends—but I'm guessing she didn't tell you that. She's weird about it, and I don't have to go into it or anything, but you should know." His face was terribly earnest, and she got the sense that Ben Roberts was a very nice guy. He would never fuck a heels-wearing, condom-carrying widow in the car in the parking garage or in a restaurant bathroom. She was disappointed to realize this, and then suddenly angry, as if he had just verbally turned her down for something she didn't even want or ask for.

From the corner of her eye, she watched Wyatt order a bottle of wine, hand the oversized menu to the waitress. She wrenched her attention back to Ben and said, "Andrea told me that you'd gone out a couple of times."

He laughed. "That's her. She's oddly secretive like that. Not fun. But still, she's great. And I'm glad we've got that in the open. I have a thing about honesty."

"Oh, me too," Nicole lied.

The big confession seemed to relax him—or could be it was the vodka—because he stopped with the Twenty Questions and started telling stories that actually were funny about teaching history at a private high school and coaching debate. She could listen and laugh at appropriate moments, ask the right questions, and seem engaged, even as she felt her mind floating free of her body, her mind watching Wyatt swirl the red liquid in the glass, then sip it with his eyes closed. He was so fucking pretentious. That's what Roger always said, when people asked about his family: "I've got one brother out in Austin, and another, the pretentious one, who lives around here, in McLean." He would laugh, but that was why Roger wanted kids so badly, to create the family he didn't have, to do it right. If Wyatt's kids were old enough for high school, they might very well attend the school where Ben taught. She tried to imagine Ben and Wyatt in a parent-teacher conference, Wyatt looming, overflowing the student desk, Ben desperate to hold his ground from the adult-size oak chair behind the teacher's desk, Wyatt listening to about one sentence before butting in to tell Ben how wrong he was about whatever he was saying. The way he'd give the classroom an eye-rolling once-over before leaving, signaling to Ben how puny this kingdom was.

She watched Wyatt throw his head back in laughter, watched him reach across the table and bop Lisa's nose with one finger, watched him point at something on the menu as the waitress stood next to him: What word on the menu had he not been comfortable pronouncing, what technique was he unfamiliar with? Veloute? Sauce soubise? Funny to think of Wyatt intimidated. He told the group a story that involved many hand movements, swinging both arms as if holding a baseball bat. Suddenly he narrowed his eyes and looked straight at her. She wanted to be casual and hold his gaze, but couldn't.

"And so then he was like, 'Hell yeah I'm from Brooklyn.'"

Ben. She looked at Ben. He seemed to sense her attention had shifted—even though she managed to laugh at this punch line—and he said, "Have you been on many blind dates?"

"Not for a while," she said. "It's . . . interesting."

He gave a half-laugh. "Usually blind dates come about because some married woman knows exactly two single people and decides it's her duty to push them together. Married people always want to drag others into their misery."

"Misery?" she asked. "Is that how you feel about marriage?"

He held up his hands in mock horror. "Oh, no, the marriage talk already! 'Is he a man who will commit? When can I get my baby?'" When she didn't laugh, he said, "I mean, of course not. It's just a joke. I'd love to be married, you know, to the right woman and be a dad. Like I told you, I was engaged before. I can be serious." He sounded defensive. "What about you?"

"I can be serious, too." No way was she going to utter Roger's name out loud. Her sad story. *I'm not supposed to be doing this,* she imagined saying, *I was all set; I had Roger.* Goddamnit. Instead, it was this, date after endless date, eating her lonely appetizer, her never-the-most-expensive entrée, swapping answers back and forth to questions like it was a test, which it was. If she'd been fifty, she could have given up, been fine with the cat and the TV. But who gives up at thirty-eight? Not Ben! Not her! She took a deep breath. "But we don't have to be serious tonight," she said. "Let's just be fun. What's your sign? Capricorn?"

She had picked at random—no, actually, she had picked Roger's sign—but it turned out that Ben was a Capricorn and he seemed to think that she had amazing insight. So there was that to talk about. Then the appetizers arrived. He didn't offer a taste of his soup. So she ate all of her beet salad, which was pretty on the plate and quite delicious. It had been mentioned in the *Post* review.

Wyatt's appetizers showed up. Beets for him, too. Probably because of the newspaper.

Ben loved to talk. At some point he said, "It's great when someone knows how to be a good listener." "Because you're a teacher," she said, but really because he liked to go on and on. He seemed content with minimal responses from her—murmurs and nods—and she felt sorry for him, for his low expectations. At least he was funny. And no rope bracelet despite the warning. He had a thing for honesty. Who could complain about any of this? At another point he said, "You know, Nicole, you're fun."

The waitress refilled the wine glasses at Wyatt's table; she wished they were having a bottle of wine, but Ben said he should have sauvignon blanc with his fish, and that she should have cab with her bison. So, the overpriced wine-by-the-glass option. Sort of like dating versus marriage, she thought, wine by the glass versus the bottle.

Wyatt stood up, his napkin falling from his lap onto the floor.

Bathroom, Nicole thought, blushing as she remembered her brief fantasy about fucking silly little schoolteacher Ben in the bathroom. But Wyatt stayed where he was, and he picked up his wine glass, tinked it with a spoon, until his table quieted, and kept tinking it until the restaurant silenced, people's heads swiveling—even Ben— tinking so the waitstaff and bussers paused, waiting one more moment until even the bar seemed still, and the only sounds were from the semi-open kitchen in back: sizzling, a beeper, someone shouting, "Fish!" Nicole couldn't see Lisa's face but she was slowly shaking her head, gesturing in a "what next" way with one hand.

"Thank you," Wyatt said in a commanding voice. "Just a wee bit of kind indulgence, please, for a special toast." He took a step back, almost knocking over his chair, and surveyed the room as people picked up wine and water glasses, confused but willing. His eyes returned to Nicole.

She felt Ben's gaze equally heavy upon her. She should have told him. She should have explained or said something. Why did she think she could escape Roger? He was dead and buried, yet it was as if he was crowding right here in the booth beside her, something she had to drag along wherever she might go.

"To my brother," Wyatt said. She expected him to sound drunk or sloppy, but his voice was perfectly controlled, as if he were accustomed to public speaking in unconventional settings, and that memory of Wyatt at the funeral, talking about throwing the football across the lawn with Roger as the autumn shadows lengthened, how Roger begged, "One more, one more"; "That was Roger," Wyatt had said then, "'enough' wasn't a word he believed in." All this a flash in Nicole's mind, as Wyatt continued now, speaking over a few titters that immediately melted away: "To my baby brother, Roger, who died too young last year, and who broke our hearts when he left us behind. To Roger, whose spirit lives on in those who loved him best. And to us, to all of us, the broken-hearted, the ones left to carry on as best we can." He lifted the glass and drank, emptying it with a single, steady motion.

Nicole found the moment surprisingly moving: an entire restaurant of strangers raising their glasses, a room united and rapt at Wyatt's words, that pocket of silence as everyone sipped meditatively, their own memory flashes, their own heartbreak. Nicole blinked, then remembered to drink from her own glass.

Oh, Roger.

She took a deep breath and looked over at Wyatt, now seated. His dinner companions were congratulatory, and Lisa extended both hands across the table, reaching out for him.

Ben twisted his head to follow Nicole's gaze.

"Okay," he said, turning back to face her. "What the hell? Just who is that guy? What's going on here?"

But Nicole was already sliding from the booth. "Hang on," she said. "I've got to go to the ladies room," and she grabbed her purse and hurried back to the bar, where the bathrooms were. Once in the bar she paused, glancing at the scene behind her: people eating and laughing, going on exactly as they were before Wyatt interrupted them. She took another deep breath, and another, but neither worked as she'd hoped. Tears welled in her eyes, overflowing, her mascara about to be wrecked for the second time tonight. The hostess was eyeing her, so she spun and hurried down the hallway to the bathrooms, two unisex rooms, neither occupied. Instead of going in, she leaned up against a small side table along the wall, and closed her eyes.

Footsteps. Please don't be Ben, she thought, and it wasn't. It was Wyatt.

"Why'd you do that?" she said.

He threw his hands up in the air. "Jesus Christ," he said, keeping his voice low but mean. "You're here on a fucking date. My brother hasn't been dead for a year. When's your next wedding?"

"Fuck you," she said.

"No, fuck you," he said, and she tried to choke back her sobs but couldn't. "Goddamnit," he said. "Stop crying."

"Then stop yelling at me," she said.

"Do you like that guy or what?"

"I just met him," she said. "He's okay. I don't know."

"Oh, Christ." Wyatt sighed, and pulled Nicole in for a hug. "I'm sorry. I just fucking can't believe he's gone."

"I know."

"Fuck."

Wyatt's arms were tight around her; he was taller than Roger, so the top of her head hit right at the base of his neck, a different place on his body than when Roger held her. She was taller than Lisa, so wouldn't it be hard to kiss someone so short, she wondered. Wyatt's chest moved under her as he breathed. Her breath slowed to match his.

Finally, she said, "I miss him so much." Wyatt's brown eyes were rimmed with tears. He hadn't cried at the funeral. He had worn sunglasses as he carried the coffin from the church, as he dropped a shovelful of dirt on top of his brother in the cemetery. She couldn't do that, couldn't even watch; she had walked away.

"I know." He wiped some of her tears with his thumb. "Your mascara," he said, pulling out a stiff white pocket square from his jacket.

She half-laughed. "Roger never noticed things like that," she said. "I could walk out without combing my hair." She carefully ran the cloth under both eyes. "Sorry to ruin this." She returned it to him, thick black smears along one edge.

He dropped the pocket square on the table, shrugged. "I have a drawer of those things," he said. "Useless shit."

She imagined a deep drawer in a mahogany chest filled with stacks of starched white pocket squares, hundreds and hundreds. The excess, the stupid excess. She'd never realized how sad Wyatt was. Arguing with his mother about gravy. She remembered Roger telling her that Wyatt used to play folk songs on the guitar when he was in high school.

"Thanks for coming back here to find me," she said. "This date isn't going very well, which I guess isn't surprising."

He shrugged. "It's different for you. I don't get another brother."

"But all I want is Roger," she said. She leaned into him again, wanting him to wrap his arms around her, which he did. She listened for the sound of his heart beating. Strong, not like Roger's. Roger and his goddamn heart attack. She gritted her teeth to keep from screaming like an animal.

"If he wasn't already dead, I could kill the guy for dying," Wyatt said.

"Exactly."

She leaned back, away from Wyatt, sliding her arms up along his chest, and thought, Kiss me.

It seemed so simple, so obvious. He had to see, too, and abruptly he did, kissing her gently at first, then long and hard and rough, tangling his hands through her hair, pulling, and there was the steady thump of his heart quickening, fast, faster, hers keeping rhythm with it, until she pushed herself away, almost panting, and she pointed to her smudgy eyes and muttered, "I should go fix this."

She stepped into one of the bathrooms but didn't snap the door lock. There was a homey-scented incense in the room, like cinnamon, and a single silk orchid in a black square pot. She stared at herself in the mirror, waiting for the knock that she knew would be coming, and when she heard it—a hard rap—she pulled the door open, and it was the two of them alone in the small room.

I AM THE WIDOW

Just like at any movie or TV funeral, his casket gets put up front, set under specially focused lighting, parenthesized by yardstick-high sprays of white gladiolus. Plump velvet kneeler in front of him, velvet curtains behind. Top half of the box open, so we can see his face. If we want to see him dead, that is, if we want to look right at death. There are plenty of people ducking their heads, twisting necks around and staring up high into the ceiling or deep down through the carpeted floor. Not me. Right off, I grab hold of his hand, entwine my fingers around his, not because that feels so great but because it unnerves the people circling me. Hell yeah. I'm grabbing a dead man's hand. I'm grabbing my dead husband's hand. Maybe I won't let go. Maybe I'm going crazy.

I'm certain I'm going crazy. I'm certain I am.

What happened was sudden. Alive—and then not. The two of us—and then a pack of family roaming around, in their suits and dark, sensible dresses, howling and clawing each other into tense hugs. A dead body sprawled on the kitchen floor—and then this dead body tucked neatly into a casket. What happened is fast. This is the worst whirling ride at a carnival you can't jump off of.

Not knowing much on planning funerals, when the professionals say, "Open casket?," I nod like I mean yes. Not knowing when there's an open casket, people read an invitation to toss a little something on in. Guess there's meaning, though a list looks pretty junky: Color photos by a lake, a postcard of the jagged Chicago skyline, pizza takeout menu, half a bottle of tequila, an old lady's rosary, a wad of clover freshly ripped from a lawn, foot-long length of red wrapping ribbon knotted in four places, wooden fraternity paddle, dog-eared paperback of *Fahrenheit 451,* brittle yellow Palm Sunday palm frond, tarnished baby spoon, crayoned drawing of a dinosaur-like creature, scuffed-up baseball, pencil sketch of a lion's head, a regular ordinary brick—come on!—an unopened package of two Twinkies, the *Let's Go Spain & Portugal* guidebook with swelled-up pages from falling in water presumably somewhere in Spain or Portugal, race bib #1458 from the Marine Corps Marathon, a bleached-out whelk, a nickel and two super-shiny pennies in a stack, smooth gray rock the size of a big toe, an acorn, Bob Marley import CD, baby food jar half-filled with sand. Four or five flap-tucked envelopes with his name in ink across the front. It's a jigsaw puzzle of a big picture of nothing. Everything all means something but the only one who maybe could explain is lying there dead.

And you'd have to say after a while that things get more than a little ridiculous, this casket as receptacle, this dump it all in mentality, because there I am holding onto his hand, when tra-la-la-ing up is some second cousin I barely met—maybe at the wedding, maybe—heaving in an old shop class project from middle school that supposedly they'd worked on together.

What's he supposed to do in the afterlife—IF THERE IS ONE, WHICH THERE ISN'T—with an old lamp base shaped like a wagon wheel, I want to know.

I put nothing in there. No note, no picture, no shop class project. I want him coming back, so I'm leaving him reasons to haunt me. I'm turning him angry enough to rise up and come after me. Damn it.

All the while I'm smiling, clinging to his hard, dead hand. They got them folded up on his chest, like insect wings, like a way no one poses in real, living life. Left hand on top, so that's the one I'm grabbing, with that malicious wedding ring, its "til death do you part" mockery. People crush into me with hugs; people pressing around me cry through a blizzard of tissues, and sobs ricochet off the walls. As long as I've got his hand, I act like I'm okay since that's what they need. I crack a joke or two, smile, smile. Everyone's so relieved to laugh, relieved that laughing is wrong but still possible. They're treating me like I'm clear cut glass. I appreciate it.

Two days of this, me clinging to that hand, rubbing my thumb along the curve of his wedding ring like I want to wear through the metal, and people dropping their shit in the casket like it's a recycle bin. I get used to it. It's the new life I've got. It's what I've got. It's something settled. It's that.

I never planned a funeral so what I forget is the part where they pack up. They've got to lock the box. Actually, I didn't forget about that part; I just never knew it. I'm, like, twenty-nine years old, so how many funerals was I not someone's kid at? How'd the box get closed? Never thought about it, but someone has to do it, it's going to be done, and someone's got to be the last one to look at him, the last one holding that hard, dead hand, the one hanging on to the end. Me.

Calm-voiced professionals infiltrate, swarm the room, though it's only two or three of them really, calmly suggesting in their calm, buttery voices that we retire to the outer lobby, that they need to prepare for transport.

Like . . . the space shuttle? *The Jetsons* and *Star Trek?* Transport? I hate words that don't mean what they mean.

It's like Noah's Ark docked out back, everyone buddying up two by two as they leave the room, the crying thick as pudding. There goes my mother with her sister; his mother—oh, she's so sad; she wants desperately to be sadder than me; I should let her win—she's draped like an eel across the arms of her husband; his two brothers, stiff-shouldered; my brother-in-law towing my sister, her spiky heels poking dots in the carpet; my dad and my uncle, the brother he didn't talk to for five years until now. His poor, sad dad standing by himself. One son comes back for him. He walks out next to his son, his body a limp, as if all the bones have been broken and put together backward. The favorite sister and her boyfriend no one likes; she's not looking me in the eye, so it's the boyfriend watching, the boyfriend's pale blue eyes, clear like flat water, the last in the room with me.

I've got his hand through all this. Don't know why. Doesn't make me feel better. But I'm afraid something will happen if I let go. They'll take him away if I let go. They'll swipe his wedding ring. ("You know they steal the jewelry," more than one person whispers in my ear.) There's a picture in my head of a bottom dresser drawer rattling with a thousand different wedding rings.

Then me. Alone.

No one comes back for me.

The one who would come back for me? Who would march me out to the Ark? I'm holding his hard, dead hand. Damn it. The professional has seen people cry like this, I'm sure. Like this, like this too, like this, this. These are endless, unforgettable minutes I won't think about again.

No one wants to touch me.

I've got to let go. I've got to, and I don't know how I do, but I do, and when I do, my own hand feels hard and dead, not part of my own body ever again.

I march myself to the outer room, to the sad stares, slam myself against the isolating wall of sympathy. Right now, I'm saddest. All I'm seeing right now are the miles of my own tears.

Then the favorite sister announces that she has a note. She has to drop it in. She forgot. She meant to. She has a note for him. This note she wrote last night. She holds up a tattered envelope, like a "who needs two" scalper. She's the youngest, the baby of the family, only twenty, nesting in the safety of being everyone's favorite, even after flunking out of the good college and then the less good college, even with the boyfriend no one likes. She wanted to be a vet, but now she works in a pet store while she figures out her life. She might be pregnant; there's that look about her of a complicated secret, and she drank club soda last night when the rest of them were at the vodka, and now this note. So hard to hate her, but with that smudgy envelope in her hand, I do. Even though she lived with us that summer, even though that summer she and I sat out nights on the moon-splashed deck with glasses of white wine, talking as if we were the sisters. Even though I never got along much with my own sister and didn't see what having a sister meant until I met his favorite sister. Even though all that.

Even though he would hate me saying in a very loud voice: "No! I have to be the last one to see him. You can't go back in there."

The outer lobby turns super-quiet. As the widow speaks . . . as the widow speaks, the lobby turns super-quiet. There are no professionals here. There are just sad people.

She's flummoxed, gripping her tattered envelope—it's pink, as if from a greeting card—and her boyfriend grabs her elbow, maybe thinking she might puddle to the ground.

I am the widow. (That word means me.)

"Okay," says the favorite sister, finally, slowly. Each syllable a hundred years long. Everyone is breath-held. "I won't," she says. "But can you please . . . ?" She stretches out her hand, giving me the envelope, which I take even though I don't want to. I don't want to go back in there; I don't want to interrupt the professionals as they prepare to transport, I don't want to have to say, "Excuse me, I am the widow, and here's one more thing to drop into that casket, one more thing that wasn't said at the right time, the right time being when he was ALIVE, one more thing that's too late to matter now because he's DEAD, and one more time I have to see him and then not see him, one more letting go to remember, one more hammer pounding this forever through my chest." Do that, say that—alone.

I swing myself through the doors, and it's okay because nothing much has happened because maybe this goes on all the time when you're a professional—maybe people come swinging back ALL THE TIME with one last thing to cram into the open casket or one last check that the wedding ring's in place. A professional snaps that calm smile back on and says, "Yes? What can we do for you?"

I look at the ceiling. I look at the floor. I tore off that hand once, I said goodbye. I'm alone.

I shake my head like I mean no. "I'm sorry," I say. The pink envelope goes right then into my purse, smashed down to the very bottom, where the lint breeds. She'll never know. I'll fish out my wallet, my keys, the sunglasses, then I'll shove this purse and everything inside down into a trash bag for the Salvation Army, where I'll also shove his suits and his T-shirts and his winter coat and his shoes and his neckties and all the rest of everything that once was his.

Let him haunt me. Let him haunt me forever, please God. It's the only prayer I've got.

ONE TRUE THING

Craft lecture, MacBride Writers' Conference,
August 10–23, 2015

Good morning. Today I'll be speaking about point of view. POV. Deciding who tells the story and how it gets told is the writer's most important decision. There are countless ways to tell the same story, as many ways as there are people in this room, and more. By offering examples of various points of view, I'll illustrate the strengths and weaknesses of these different options. Time permitting, I'll take questions afterward.

COLLECTIVE FIRST PERSON: we.

We were all young back then, or so it seemed to us. If there were old people—"old" meaning anyone older than us—at the MacBride Writers' Conference in 1996, we didn't notice. We were busy with ourselves, and no world existed beyond us, our egos, our writing, our dreams and hopes, our gossip. Some of us were on working scholarship to the conference as waiters, and some of us earned scholarships because our poetry was published in a literary journal deemed important, and some of us—though we were so, so young—had published our first book, which was the holy grail: publish a book. Those people were luckiest of all, coming to the writers' conference on a fellowship, which was the golden ticket. None of us paid. Paying was what regular people did, not us.

We were obnoxious, toting bottles of crummy red wine into dinner and toasting ourselves in loud voices, clustering at the back of the room during craft lectures to lean and whisper in each other's ears. We mocked the famous poets who taught us, their voices lilting in mind-numbing singsong as they read their famous poems. We cockteased the wrinkly, bad-bald, uber-letch fiction writers and faked shock when they assumed they would get to fuck us. In workshop, we pontificated on theories of narrative distance and rolled our eyes when the lady from Pasadena who wore the "Book Power" T-shirt raised her hand, and we sighed gustily when our teacher quoted that turd Hemingway. We organized an invitation-only séance to channel the poet James Merrill, and some of us knew tarot, and each of us, when confronting the cards, asked, "Will I be a famous writer?" and a lot of us didn't like what was revealed, though we pretended not to care and called tarot "stupid." Still, a lot of us tossed restlessly that night, not sleeping, as we pondered what we had heard, but we confided our fears in no one and guzzled coffee at breakfast to reacquire our perky sheen. We were jealous when the visiting literary agent didn't want to meet with all of us, and we were confused when the visiting photographer posed only some of us for headshots, as if they had predetermined who would "make it" and who wouldn't. We applauded crazily at our own readings, and those of us with books inscribed them effusively, weaving lavish compliments with inside jokes, swearing to remember this summer forever, as if signing high school yearbooks. We sat together at dinner, and always saved seats, and later, when it was someone else from the conference—someone who paid to be there—who wrote the *New York Times* best seller that was made into an Oscar-winning movie, we felt betrayed. It was supposed to be us.

We were ambitious. We all knew the story about the professor stumbling into the first workshop half-drunk and his sneering pronouncement to the group of twelve grad students at the table: "You know how many of you will get a book published? ONE. One of you," and hearing that, we secretly thought, "I'm the one," and then the teacher said, "If you're not thinking 'I'm the one,' you don't have the balls to make it," and we claimed this happened in our MFA program. We tossed names—Faulkner! Nabokov!—like confetti, as if their brilliance would rain down upon us, and we name-dropped professors and books we'd read and books we'd heard of and which writers wrote us letters of rec. We knew people who knew the real writers of our day: Tobias Wolff, Denis Johnson, Richard Bausch, Edwidge Danticat, Thom Jones, Tim O'Brien, Dorothy Allison, Cormac McCarthy, Mary Oliver, Mark Doty, Gary Soto. Some of us defended Sylvia Plath, and some of us defended Ted Hughes, but we all had opinions.

We slept with each other: gay-gay, hetero-hetero, gay-experi-menting. Sean and Louise. Jon and John. Jon and Paul. John and Carolynne. Carolynne and Randy. Randy and Louise. Louise and Sean again. Sean and Elena. Elena and Dimitri. Dimitri and Lou-ise. Jon and Sal. Annie and Katrina. Vanessa and Michael. Even Michael and Louise. It was possible that Louise slept with all of us, or would have if the conference hadn't ended.

It was a merry-go-round, a kaleidoscope, a whirligig, a dervishy time. Our hearts were stomped, our feelings hurt; we murmured spiteful stories about each other; we babbled the dark-of-the-night secrets we'd sworn to take to the grave; we sussed out weaknesses and exploited them, at the conference and later, last week or yes-terday. We kept in touch or we didn't, but we never forgot each other, and we hugged gaudily when our paths crossed, exclaiming how much we loved the book/poem/story/essay that had just come out, though we'd only skimmed the reviews or scrutinized the ac-knowledgments, waiting for our own name, as torrents of bitter thoughts flooded our animal brains: it should have been *our* work getting this blink of attention. Although, to be fair, we helped: we published each other in journals we edited and offered construc-tively meant insight on drafts sent to us and made necessary but noncommittal introductions to our agents and cut and pasted let-ters of rec for teaching jobs and fellowships. We were friends but we all understood ourselves to be stampeding in a giant horse race; the MacBride Writers' Conference was our starting gate.

And yet. Amid all that:

Some of us fell in love. Some of us broke off engagements to be together, and some of us filled a U-Haul with books and framed Rothko posters and a futon and drove from San Francisco to DC to be together. Some of us got married. Some of us were married for thirteen years, and then some of us who were married died suddenly when we were too young to do that sort of thing. Some of us died, or, rather, one of us did: Michael.

Ironically—or is it only coincidentally; "ironically" being one of those overused, improperly used words that we over- and improperly used back then?—this tragedy happened five weeks before some of us were scheduled to return to the MacBride Writers' Conference, invited to teach for the first time. Some of us were looking forward to delivering a craft lecture at the famous lectern, leading a workshop, reading from our newest novel, and living the life of a "famous writer" for two weeks. Our color headshot appeared in the brochure.

We could have said no. We could have stayed home. But that's not the kind of people we were.

THIRD PERSON, LIMITED: she; generally accepted as the default POV

Vanessa stood, waiting, by a large window that faced the tarmac. A fly buzzed, flinging itself against the glass, and she thought of Emily Dickinson's fly in the poem—and wondered if that would make a good joke later: "You know what would be a great name for a band of poets?" she might say. "Emily Dickinson's Fly." But the words sounded dumb in her head, as they all had lately. She hadn't written anything good in forever, and she decided last week she hated her novel in progress, so she pressed the delete key. Two hundred pages. As for the recently published novel, that sucked, too. A dour chronicle of post-apocalyptic women—again. They all sucked. How fun to be plunged now into this writing conference.

This airport was smaller than DCA in Washington, served primarily by puddle jumpers like the one she had disembarked from. Vanessa brought one large suitcase and a laptop she carried on. She barely remembered what she had thrown into the suitcase because she packed at five in the morning, in about fifteen minutes, just before the cab arrived—she wasn't sure she was coming on this trip until the last minute, changing her mind back and forth like a ball batted in a long, dull tennis match.

But here she was.

Someone driving a van was supposed to pick her up, rather, the first group of them, faculty and staff and honored visitors and scholarship waiters, all descending upon this tiny New England airport within a two-hour time frame.

The director of the conference had been sympathetic about Michael, saying she could back out, she could teach next summer instead, and it didn't matter that her photo had been in the ads. It didn't matter because no one signed up for her workshop, she wondered, or because the director wanted to be accommodating? This conversation was three weeks after Michael died, and she couldn't trust anyone. Being pitied irritated her, so she acted brusque and curt, which turned people nicer—more goddamn pity—darkening her mood. So she started keeping away from people altogether, even the virtual kind, shutting down her social networking accounts one after the other, then canceling her cell phone, deleting her blog, and cutting her landline. There was something pleasantly rebellious about dropping out. About raw silence.

That the director was being sweet made her meaner. "I'll be fine," she snapped. "I want the distraction. I want to be there."

He paused a beat too long, and she realized that he was afraid she would *be* the distraction. That she might panic or break down or change her mind at the last minute, leaving him in the lurch in some vexing way, or that she would run around bawling, making the people who paid uncomfortable. He was one of those older, manly poets, a brash, lumbering guy who would have made a bee-line for Sylvia Plath, except that Sylvia would have been bored with him in twenty minutes.

Vanessa recognized the woman with the pixie cap of red hair from the brochure, a memoirist with a book about food, not the traditional eating disorders but also not anything pleasant about food, something disturbing and splashy that got her interviewed on NPR and *The Daily Show.* Vanessa hadn't read it. Nevertheless, to drag herself out of her own stupid mind, she waved and called: "Joy?"

The woman with the red hair spun several times, as if she didn't know where her name came from, until finally she placed Vanessa. She smiled brightly, then immediately her face crumpled into sad confusion. She knows, Vanessa thought, of course everyone knows. What had she expected? She was The Widow.

Vanessa kept a grim smile attached to her own face as she walked to where Joy stood next to a potted plant. "I'm Vanessa Connally."

"Joy Ruby-Vargha." They shook hands, Joy clinging to Vanessa's too long, too tightly.

Don't you dare hug me, Vanessa thought, and when she got her hand back, she stepped back, beyond Joy's natural reach. Bitch, she added in her head, startled by this anger. Of course everyone knew the details of her sad story, every writer in America, and every writer who was coming to this conference. They pitied her, with her inconveniently dead husband.

"Congratulations on your new book," Vanessa said. "You must be excited about all the attention it's getting."

"Thanks," Joy said. Her eyes stayed lasered on Vanessa.

Vanessa said, "Yes, I'm the one whose husband died. That's me."

Joy's cheeks flushed. "I'm sorry," she said. "You must think I'm so rude."

"We can just have a normal conversation," Vanessa said. "We can just be normal. Okay?" It came out as a command.

"Sure." Joy took in a deep breath. "I've never been here. I guess I'm nervous. You hear so many stories about this conference."

"Most of them not true." Vanessa felt immediately drained by Joy's way of speaking, as if she were permitted more syllables than other people and insisted on using each one of them, even in short sentences. And then, behind Joy, she spotted another woman, potentially more draining, and she gasped slightly, but enough that Joy twisted to look.

"Louise Philips! She's amazing!" Joy babbled. "I love her work! That fearless prose, she's so brave!"

Down girl, Vanessa almost said.

Louise gripped a Styrofoam cup in one hand and tugged behind her several leopard print duffels precariously balanced on a zebra-striped hard suitcase with wheels. She was at least six feet tall and sinewy; she had been Michigan's high jump state champion, a "fun fact" she still included in her author bio. Also, it was a cliché, but her dark hair truly was a mane—it flowed and rippled and Louise constantly flung it back and flung it forward; it was as good as an extra appendage. The joke was that if Louise's head were shaved she'd be unable to speak. She and Louise had been in the same fiction workshop at the conference in 1996; at the time, Vanessa's first novel had just come out, and Louise had published a fifty-page roman à clef about her MFA instructor in the *Best American Short Stories*—reprinted from an obscure literary journal (her first publication)—that eventually was made into an HBO movie (and resulted in the professor being denied tenure). A couple of years ago, Louise married a trendy indie film star; they'd been written up in the "Vows" column of the *Times*'s "Sunday Styles." Vanessa still remembered the story Louise workshopped with the class in 1996, about a CIA spy living in a suburban neighborhood who began leaving a slimy trail when he walked, like a snail, until, after being forced to retire, he jumped off the Memorial Bridge, turning the Potomac River silver. Vanessa had written a careful critique that she considered encouraging while basically suggesting that the whole thing be scrapped. "Who do you think you are, Kafka?" she stopped herself from writing. The class pretty much ripped apart the story. But the teacher passed it to his editor at the *New Yorker,* where it was published, along with a full-page photo of Louise posing barefoot next to a dry fountain filled with autumn leaves. Right after that she got a two-book deal for a collection of stories and a novel. The novel made it to the best-seller list—at least only up to number eight and only for two weeks.

"This is ridiculous," Louise called, not explaining what was ridiculous as she expertly threaded her stack of luggage through Joy's and Vanessa's battered black suitcases and computer bags. She released the handle of her suitcase and thrust the Styrofoam cup into Joy's hand and locked Vanessa in a hug before she could react. "I was so sorry to hear," she murmured in Vanessa's ear, "and you're such a good soldier to come," the words tickling and buzzing; like Emily Dickinson's fly, Vanessa thought. She didn't even like Louise, and something in her wanted to say so, directly, putting an end to this uncomfortable sympathy.

"I heard a fly–," Vanessa said out loud, meaning only to think the words, which sounded off somehow. Louise stepped back; she appeared not to hear, though that was hardly possible. One hand remained pressed on Vanessa's arm.

Joy extended her arm for a handshake, but Louise was still staring at Vanessa and made no sign of acknowledging Joy.

"Sorrow becomes you," Louise said. "You look saintly. Beautiful."

"A dead husband isn't a *Vogue* beauty tip," Vanessa said.

Joy soldiered on: "I'm Joy Ruby-Vargha, and I loved *Where We Are When We're Lost.* I teach it to all my undergrads. Such a tour de force, that story in particular, the way you pretend to blur fact and fiction, and how you explode boundaries. So uncomfortable for the reader!"

Of course. Of everything that Louise had written, writers mentioned that book first, always. It was that title story. Inescapable. Famous, if a story can be such a thing.

"I'm going to take care of you," Louise said to Vanessa. Louise often ignored what people said. There was a well-circulated story about Louise's editor demanding she cut a three-line epilogue to the novel, and Louise added instead, ballooning the epilogue to forty pages, hardly an epilogue, though that's what it was called in the table of contents. The reviewer in the *Times* loved it.

"I don't want to be taken care of," Vanessa said.

Louise's eyes were a startling, deep blue, very dramatic with that black hair. She might be hated for those eyes alone. "You know you do." She spoke with such authority that Vanessa almost nodded.

"This cup is hot," Joy said.

"It's coffee," Louise remarked, but she didn't reach for it. Then she spoke as if Joy had asked a question: "We go way back."

"Louise knows all my secrets," Vanessa said.

Louise smiled slightly and pulled a silver flask from a side pocket of one of the leopard bags. She unscrewed the top slowly and took a quick slug.

"Sounds dangerous," Joy said, pushing herself into the conversation. She shifted the cup to her other hand, and Vanessa was amused she wouldn't simply set it on the floor. That was how everyone started: going out of their way to do exactly what Louise wanted.

"Vanessa is a notorious liar," Louise said. "All fiction writers lie, but Vanessa especially. Don't believe one word she says. I doubt her name is really Vanessa."

"Actually, Vanessa is my middle name," Vanessa said, startled that Louise would remember that tiny detail all these years later.

"What'd I tell you?" Louise took another go at her flask then capped it and tucked it into her duffel.

"Do you remember my first name?" Vanessa asked.

There was an uncomfortable silence. Vanessa didn't know what Louise was thinking, but she was remembering Louise was the one who flipped the tarot cards, telling her unhappiness would be a fog shadowing her life. Mostly she remembered Louise slept with Michael on that night he and Vanessa were feuding about whose fault it was they got lost hiking in the woods, missing the conference director's reading; people said he remarked on their absence from the podium, not jokingly calling it "career suicide." Louise had come up to her at breakfast the next morning and made a little checkmark in the air with her pinkie, then sashayed away. Michael denied and denied—"you know what she's like," and he twirled circles with his index finger around his temple—and so for years, Vanessa chose to believe him. Then she found out the whole truth when Louise published her famous story, the "tour de force" Joy had gushed over. She had called the man in the story "Michael," with quotation marks. It shouldn't have been a surprise—Louise had slept with plenty of people during those two weeks—and yet it was. Michael apologized, and she said she forgave him for the years of lying and for all the rest of it, but she knew he didn't believe her, and he was right not to. She didn't believe herself. Now he was dead.

Joy looked from one to the other and shifted the coffee to her other hand. "I don't get it," she said to Louise. "Is this one of those games?"

Louise finally turned and looked at Joy. "You're a perky little America's sweetheart, aren't you? Damn."

Joy's cheeks flushed bright pink and she sucked in her breath sharply. She set the Styrofoam cup on the floor and wiped the front and back of both hands on her skirt. Vanessa wanted to feel sorry for her, but Joy probably should hear she was too perky. And it suited Vanessa if Louise made enemies quickly.

"This should be a fun two weeks," Vanessa said, keeping her voice neutral. "So much to catch up on."

"It's terrible about Michael," Louise said. "Did I already say that?"

"You sent that gorgeous peace lily," Vanessa said. "Thank you."

An oversized, leafy eyesore Vanessa hauled to the curb. Too much responsibility, she told herself, watching through the blinds to see if neighbors might take it in. The next morning the garbage collectors swept it away.

Then Louise said, "I suppose you'll be writing about this one day. That's what we do as writers, isn't it, write about all the bad things that happen to us?"

That's what you do, Vanessa thought, that's what you did, but she smiled casually. Her face was going to collapse. What a thing to say, even for Louise, who would say anything. "Maybe," she said. "Maybe not. It just all feels pretty awful right now." She crossed her arms. "We really don't have to keep talking about it."

Louise said, "It's your one story. Like Updike and Rabbit. Roth and Zuckerman. Richard Ford and Frank Bascombe. Vanessa and Michael."

She longed to demand that Louise never speak his name again, but she concentrated on her careless smile as she said, "But it's not a story. It's what happened."

"Same thing."

"Stop it," Vanessa said sharply, the smile punctured.

Louise laughed, a silly trill. "Oh, you. You know I'm saying what's already in your head."

Vanessa's shoulders tightened as she glared at Louise. Goddamnit, Louise was right. But those thoughts shouldn't be in her head, not now, so soon—not ever. Goddamnit. She said, "Just don't say that again. It's rude and hateful."

Joy interrupted: "I think that's us," and she pointed. A girl with a sunburned nose, holding a clipboard, called and waved, coming to herd the three of them to another corner of the waiting area, where several men clustered around an elderly man in an airport wheelchair. The three women silently collected their luggage, rolling and shuffling, Louise knocking over the Styrofoam cup, which slowly bled coffee onto the carpeted floor. Vanessa couldn't be sure if this was accidental or Louise's way of leaving her mark behind, and she shivered.

NARRATIVE EXPOSITION: not a true point of view, but can provide background, especially in longer works; also useful when writing the first draft to gain insight into characters and their motivations, assuming the material is deleted later. (An inability to convey necessary information naturally through the POV character may suggest the author should reconsider POV choice.)

Vanessa Connally and Louise Phillips met at the MacBride Writers' Conference in 1996. Both women were roughly the same age—mid-twenties—and both were considered attractive, Louise in a dark, dramatic, high-maintenance way, and Vanessa in a golden, girl-next-door, let's-go-on-a-picnic way. There were some who found Vanessa to be cold, perhaps calculating. She was noticeably friendliest to people who might be in position to do her favors. She over-complimented, with an air of forced sincerity, and claimed too many things were "fabulous" to be trusted entirely.

On the other hand, Louise came across as exceedingly friendly, conversing with an array of people, from the housekeeping staff up to the visiting Nobel laureate. She was often found cozied on a porch swing or tucked into the window seat in the lobby, head bent close to her companion's, asking questions, prodding for more information, swearing the same terrible thing sort of had once happened to her. She was a wonderful confidante, so it wasn't until later that her conversational partner realized that Louise hadn't shared much of her own life as she listened to those precious secrets peeling back. It was a sick feeling much, much later to see those same secrets laced through Louise's novels or short stories. Still, she was getting her work published, and that was something.

OMNISCIENT: all-knowing, all-seeing "voice of God"; unfashionable in contemporary literature though Zadie Smith's *White Teeth* offers a welcome counterpoint.

There comes a moment when every party could tip either way, and now is that moment for this party. It's two A.M., and the food's been gone for several hours—not that there was much: two bags of honey mustard pretzels, hummus and carrots for vegetarians, and a large bag of truck stop beef jerky, presented ironically, of course, but consumed nevertheless. It's BYOB, the only kind of party the MacBride Writers' Conference throws. The skunky beer, the clutter of cheap vodka, and the single bottle of show-offy single-malt scotch are well below the halfway point; the ice is dripping into a puddle that no one thinks to mop up. Supplies are dwindling, and it's the first night, so people can claim jet lag as a legitimate excuse to retreat to bed, ignoring the truth: they're old and tired and can't party the way they imagine they used to. Or—tip the other way, and this becomes the night where The Thing That Everyone Talks About happens, The Thing that, once missed, is forever missed—an irretrievable loss no matter what other Things might arise later in the conference. No one dares miss The Thing.

And so the party tips: toward the more interesting, riskier possibilities, into the sort of party where people dribble more warm, cheap vodka into plastic cups, and the owner of the fancy scotch sees his bottle stormed by a cluster of bearded young men who don't care that he has two poetry books published by a top university press and a third coming out in October that will win the National Book Critics Circle Award.

The music from someone's iPhone pumps louder, and so does the thrum of conversation about Emily Dickinson, villanelles, the best pho in Brooklyn, what was really behind that *New York Times* hatchet job on Jonathan Franzen. (No, no—that's a joke. Even in fiction, the *New York Times* critics are incapable of giving Jonathan Franzen a hatchet job. But the fact that they won't, that Franzen seems to live comfortably in their pockets, arises in the bitter exchange between the two novelists huddled by the stone fireplace.)

A young woman shrieks, "Everybody dance," and curious gazes slide her direction, as she stumbles awkwardly through the main room, knocking into poets and playwrights, her long hair flashing and flailing until she collapses onto the overstuffed couch that has remained in that exact spot for the last twenty years.

Vanessa watches the girl while maintaining a tedious discussion about the craft cocktail scene with an eager young man. It was on that couch that she and Michael first met in 1996; there was nowhere to sit and her feet hurt, so she flopped down on his lap because he was cute.

We were that way, Louise says, sidling up to her. Louise is a sidler, and a slipper-inner of snarky comments, and a sneak. Vanessa never liked her, even back in those days when they were as young as the dancing girl who is now splashing vodka on her neck and pulse points. She had been Michael's friend, not that he liked her all that much either. He couldn't even remember why he slept with her, which made Vanessa angrier. "Don't you remember that huge fight we had in the woods?" Vanessa had asked, and he pressed his palm to his temple, said, "What woods?"

Once upon a time, Vanessa says. She introduces Louise to the man she's been talking to, calling him the wrong name—which turns out to be his dreaded brother-in-law's name—and either that's all very funny or they're all very drunk. This could be The

Thing between Vanessa and this man, calling him the name of the dreaded brother-in-law for the entire conference, each time with a laugh. He would take that, as he perceives Vanessa as higher in the writer hierarchy; he is merely a waiter-writer, and she is a faculty-writer, a real writer, a writer with books. He loves her work, he assured her earlier, striving to sound sincere, since he hasn't actually read her work but has been meaning to.

Louise says to the young man, Don't mind us, we're grumps. She barely hears herself speak; she's thinking about how thin Vanessa is, how Michael's death has turned her ethereal and mysterious, lighter somehow. Like an angel. Like a fucking angel. She hates the trite word and mentally flicks it away. Vanessa has always unnerved her. Louise isn't supposed to be here; the director invited her last-minute and she surprised herself by saying yes: only because the director begged, telling her that he needed her for backup if Vanessa flamed out. He was convinced she'd show up then run off, he told Louise, remember, she met Michael here. I remember, Louise assured him, clucking with false sympathy before agreeing to be a special guest for a big fee. The director sent her the manuscripts for the workshop Vanessa is supposed to lead, but Louise didn't mark them up, knowing nothing will keep Vanessa from her class because Vanessa relies on students to reflect her own brilliance back on herself.

Michael's death has shocked her. He was only forty-one. But in her mind he felt younger, the lanky boy she'd known, with that earnest way of grabbing your arm when he spoke about something he thought was important. It was sort of sexy. He had such dark, velvety eyes. Without those eyes, she might have stayed hands off. Or not. She was a mess back then, needing buckets of attention. Thank God for a decade of therapy. That's one of her phrases, said with a snort, indicating that it's not as though she considers herself cured.

The young man is yammering and Louise interrupts: You know what this party needs?

She is lucky—or is it skill?—to have the knack of speaking at those mysterious moments when a crowd falls into a deep and significant silence, so the entire room hears her.

She smiles deeply, thrilling in the attention and in the nervous twitches flitting across Vanessa's face. This party needs a GAME, Louise announces.

And so the party tips; so the games begin; and so our story lands upon the precipice of The Thing That Everyone Will Be Talking About. Who isn't glad to have stayed; who's worried now about cheap vodka hangovers?

SECOND PERSON: you; may be perceived as cheap gimmickry, often used in emotionally distancing experimentation with form, narrative, etc. Employ cautiously. Do not use in MFA workshop pieces.

You are not the kind of person who likes to play games. When forced, you strategize ways to lose quickly: Don't buy Monopoly property. Three-letter words in Scrabble. Slap down the cards and fold. But Louise doesn't play games where a person immediately knows how to win or lose, or even games where it's clear who has won or lost. Louise is tricky. You long to run and hide in your bed, to smile in a bemused way at the gossipy stories of tonight while immersed in the safety of tomorrow, to murmur understanding words as things sort out in the light of day, in the aftermath.

Louise likes aftermaths.

But when you turn to escape, Louise clutches your upper arm. Tightly. She's strong. "Don't go," Louise says, in that way she has. "For me? Please." Oh that masterful *please*. Is it so obvious to everyone that even now you long to please people, or obvious just to her? Or is she the one you long to please?

You nod, cursing your weakness. Already, you suspect what the game will be. No. You know.

Louise efficiently herds people into a circle, a whiff of exclusivity ruling out the fringes of the party. "It's the perfect game for writers like us," Louise says. She glances around, locking eyes, creating a bond, drawing the group more tightly together.

Like us. You wish you were one-tenth as masterful. There's her hand on your arm again, a lighter touch. You're reminded instantly of Michael but push the thought away. The group of a dozen or so rustles and whispers and titters nervously, weight shifting from leg to leg. You stand perfectly still. You will not let her sense your anxiety.

"Two lies and a truth," Louise announces. "We go around the circle, and everyone tells two lies and a truth, and we guess the one true thing."

There's a palpable sigh of disappointment tinged with relief: so, clothing will remain *on.* This game is a standby at corporate retreats, slumber parties, and awkward Thanksgiving gatherings. It's unworthy of this historic writers' conference. Nor is it worthy of Louise. But there's more here than meets the eye. For example, you've played it as two truths and a lie; trust Louise, the liar, to twist the game to her benefit.

Louise smiles, almost as if she knows what you're thinking. "People have probably played this before, so just to make it interesting, fifty bucks to anyone who beats me. Not that anyone can beat me . . . I've never lost this in my whole life."

Laughs, grumblings, smack talk; Joy rolls her eyes and shakes her head, rallying her newfound acolytes of nonfiction writers. You have no acolytes. You're still in a bubble. This game should be a piece of cake, but it won't be. You could find a strategy for losing, but you won't. You want Louise's fifty bucks. You want to beat Louise. *I've never lost this in my whole life.* A strange thing to brag about, an annoying thing to brag about.

There's the conference director, slouching across the circle from you. You expect him to smile or stage whisper or lift an eyebrow, but, like you, he remains impossibly still and impassive, as if the two of you are locked in a staring contest. You want to look away but don't because you want to win this, and do, when he drops his eyes and shifts. First you think, Michael will laugh when I tell him, and then you think, Michael is dead, Michael is dead, and those three words loop—Michael is dead—even as Louise speaks in an organizational voice, even as a doe-eyed young poet launches into a story about her father's foot getting chopped off in a combine on the Fourth of July, which you recognize as a lie. The Fourth of July sounds desperate, an obvious detail, though many think that story is the one truth, afraid to challenge a maimed father. That's a trick to winning, knowing that no one will challenge a story that's tragic. You think these things and chortle with the group even as words spin their web: Michael is dead, Michael is dead . . .

"Next!" Louise says, fanning herself with a fifty-dollar bill she's slid out of her bra. It's the man who loathes his brother-in-law, and like the doe-eyed poet, he plays too broadly, going for the laugh. His grandfather ran a still in Virginia is the truth, and the lies are that he has an identical twin brother named Elvis Rothstein and that he trained his black Lab to give blowjobs, which makes everyone groan in disgust. You're glad he's not in your workshop.

More stories—as a child, seeing Picasso sip coffee in a café in France (true); choking a pet snake by feeding it a possum (lie); playing Santa Claus in a mall (true); French-kissing George Clooney (true)—and they blur into a cry for attention; whose true stories are the wildest, the craziest—playing with an uncle's pet tiger cub; butchering a hog; traveling with Doctors Without Borders; a mother and father who were babies in the same delivery room born on the same day who met twenty years later; eating dog meat kebabs in China. You've nailed each for what it is, even with your floaty mind. No one cares about the art of the lie at this point. They insist on impressing with the truth. *See me! Look at me! Look at who*

I am! Look at who I want you to think I am! Louise has folded that fifty-dollar bill into a narrow strip wound tightly around her ring finger. She's nailing them too.

Not surprisingly, the conference director is good at this game: almost everyone believes his first lie because it is odd and simple, that he eats uncooked spaghetti noodles when he sleepwalks. He speaks persuasively about their crunch. His second lie starts out, "I grew up on a butterfly ranch," and you understand immediately that he simply relishes the idea of a butterfly ranch, but he's convincing, explaining that the butterflies were raised for wedding ceremonies, featured in bridal magazines, and so several people are fooled into thinking that's the truth. Only you and Louise and the doe-eyed poet recognize his single-sentence truth: "I'm deathly afraid of spiders." The group laughs, and he's pissed. That's the problem with revealing true truths. They make people uncomfortable. The truth should be grand and exotic, but mostly it isn't. Mostly it's uncomfortable.

Your turn. Because you're standing next to Louise, you go second to last. "Watch out," Louise says, amping up the room, "she's good." A flashy smile. The game is getting tiresome, so Louise talks faster. "But not as good as me," and she unscrolls the folded-up fifty. "All yours if you top the master."

"Number one," you say, as if Louise has not spoken. You notch your voice lower, forcing everyone to lean in close. You pull in a long breath, holding it before letting it slip away quietly. You speak: "When my husband died, exactly at the time of the car accident his voice exploded through my head, telling me how much he loved me, even though I was asleep and he was alone on a highway ten miles away."

Stiff-edged silence, as you expected. Invoking the dead husband means no one dares call that a lie, though it is. But people want to believe; it's a familiar myth they wish to be true: if it's not true, it should be. Connections to the dead are popular. The doe-eyed poet looks weepy or drunk or both. The conference director stares again in that fixed way. You suspect he's thinking, Here's the breakdown. Or maybe he's thinking, Who tells something that personal to a party of drunk strangers? Or maybe he spotted a super-scary spider. You continue:

"Number two," you say. "After he died, I had a recurring dream every night, just before dawn. Michael stands in front of me, staring into my eyes as if he's desperate to tell me something. But he can't speak, and I can't move to touch him, and he can't touch me, and I say nothing. We just stare at each other as if across an abyss, and then I wake up." Another familiar story of the bereaved. Another lie.

The doe-eyed poet sniffles, swipes her cheek. People watch their feet, rebalance their weight. The whole room seems perfectly silent, though it's not. But you would swear you hear your own heart beat, your blood pulsing through your veins, the cells inside your body multiplying and dying at a rapid pace, skin cells shedding and drifting away. You listen for a moment to Louise breathing beside you.

"Number three," you say. "Number three is this: When my husband died, I didn't tell anyone but I was relieved. He was an alcoholic, the secret kind, and he was depressed, the secret kind of that, too, and speaking honestly: I was tired of dealing with him. I was drained. We were seriously talking about splitting up, and I had privately met with a lawyer. We loved each other in the beginning and all through the middle. But at the end . . . I'd say we hadn't loved each other, really loved each other, for—not for a long time. He might have driven that pickup off the side of the road on purpose. At least he wasn't drunk. For once, the asshole wasn't drunk at the wrong time."

No no no! You do not say this, of course. You do not. You will never say this despite it being the one true thing, despite thinking of yourself in the emotionally safe and gimmicky distance of the second person. Never. What you really say is: "Number three is this: When my husband died, I lost my best friend. And the world lost a remarkable, gifted poet. I'm piecing together the book manuscript he was working on, which he called *The Ghost Child*, and I'll look to you—this community he loved—to support my efforts to carry forth his words, his true legacy to the world. We've lost Michael, but we all know his art can—and will—live on. That's what he would want."

Oh, the relief! Happy ending! With a rainbow! And a unicorn posed pertly next to the pot of gold at the end of that rainbow! This is exactly the story that everyone wants, and considerate you, giving it to them. You've turned Michael into the person they want to remember, and so what if they didn't know him? Poof, you created a new Michael. Poof, a new you, The Brave Widow. Tentative smiles ripple the group—eyes are wiped, sniffles dried—and tension dissipates like air leaking from a balloon. Michael's death felt awkward and annoying, but now that Michael is gone, replaced by a man with a half-finished poetry book, like most of the people in the room. And you're another plucky survivor of the Game of Life. This is what you have created, that Dr. Frankenstein thrill you recognize from when you were writing.

Louise does not say, "Which is the truth?" as she has after everyone else's turn. Instead, Louise announces, quite loudly, "Fuck you, you're a lying cheater."

There's a collective gasp, murmured protests, a tightening: of the circle, of crossed arms, of lips. The room turns rigid and too close. Even the excluded people stare. The director says, "Okay, Louise, okay," as if speaking to a child. His eyes fix on her. "I think . . . ," but his voice trails off as if he isn't sure what he thinks, what anyone could or should think.

You extend one flat, upraised palm—kind of a Jesus gesture of forgiveness, a Brave Widow moment—but what you say is, "I'll take that fifty bucks, thank you," and there's another collective gasp. You wonder who is more hated right now, you or Louise, and you don't care. You gave them the stories they wanted; does it matter why? She smirks, setting the money in your hand. The bill is slightly sticky. You don't need fifty dollars; you've been told that the check for thirty thousand dollars of life insurance finally will be wire transferred to your bank on Monday.

"No one's ever beat me," she says.

"Meet the new boss," you say. You like feeling cocky.

Louise yanks you into an uncomfortable, showy hug meant to suggest more rainbows and unicorns, and you're brash: "Go, Louise. Your turn now." A few vague murmurs are enough to encourage her, so she steps back, gathering in a deep breath: "Okay. First, I ate acorns when I was a kid. My mom and I gathered them from the neighbor's yard, and then she roasted them in the oven and ran them through the blender into powder and baked bread. Actually delicious."

"They're poisonous," whispers the man with the bad brother-in-law, Mr. Blowjob Dog. The know-it-all. Acorns are not poisonous for people, and you guess this story is true. You remember a chapter in one of Louise's novels where a little boy eats acorns because he's afraid to go to the grocery store with his mother. You immediately Googled "acorns poisonous" because you wanted to catch Louise being wrong.

Louise says, "Next, is that my cat was on David Letterman's 'Stupid Pet Tricks' because I taught her how to crack open eggs." Everyone should know that's true because she links to the YouTube clip on her website.

"Finally," Louise says, "the last thing is that ages ago, back when I was at this conference the first time in 1996, I didn't have my diaphragm one night and I got pregnant by Vanessa's dead husband Michael—though he wasn't her husband then and she didn't know and he didn't know until later—and I told him I got an abortion but I didn't really. I had a little girl, and after two weeks, I hated being a mom, I couldn't deal with a baby, and so a really nice couple adopted her and a little while later, I got an 'inheritance' of twelve thousand dollars that paid for me to move to New York. That's where my story, 'Where We Are When We're Lost,' came from— not from the dream I had while dozing on the Metro in Paris on my way to Jim Morrison's grave, like I say in the interviews."

No no no! No, she doesn't really say that. But she could. This is true. Michael told you. Michael was the man who was "Michael" in the story. This is true, and Michael told you nine years after you got married, eighteen years after you got together, which adds up to four years ago when you found out. Recent, still. You had read Louise's famous story in the *New Yorker*. "Look," you said, "the man is named 'Michael,'" and, "Look," he said, "there's something I have to tell you." The two of you were eating tuna salad when he said this, and you gagged. You saw her finger cutting the air, that check mark. You don't eat tuna salad anymore. Louise knows you know this. You never thought the money was true and neither did Michael, but maybe it is, maybe that's how disgusting Louise might be.

No no no!

She really *does* say this. She really does say this, and everyone laughs in a horrified way because she says it in a fast, pleading voice like a little kid repeating a fabulously dirty joke she doesn't get. Everyone laughs because they have all read her famous story, they have read the interviews about the famous story: the story about the story. Now there is this story on top of those stories. This new story cannot also be true.

But when they look at you not laughing, they fall silent, confused and nervous, like sheep being herded toward a cliff by a malevolent border collie. There are too many stories, suddenly. Suddenly no one knows what story to believe. The director opens his mouth as if he wants to say something but once again doesn't know what to say, or maybe he wants to puke. But you can't worry about him.

You scrunch up the fifty dollar bill into a tiny wad and hold on tightly. There are several things you could do right now. Laugh. You could choose to laugh.

"Which is the truth?" Louise demands of the group.

You choose to throw that wadded up bill in Louise's face and then spin and push your way through the party, hurrying into the dark night outside as people call your name. You hear pity, and you run from it. You hear the truth.

INTERIOR MONOLOGUE: fully inhabiting one mind and its thought processes; often erroneously viewed as interchangeable with "stream of consciousness"; use sparingly, if at all.

Don't look at the clock, don't, don't. Christ. 4:12. Goddamn doctor, one more refill would've been okay. Over-the-counter crap. *The Ghost Child.* Melodramatic title. Like her titles are anything, "Where We Are When We're Lost." Pillow smell, like a wet Band-Aid. A fly—a moth at night. If Emily wrote the poem at night, would've been "a moth fluttered." Fluttered—buzzed—buzzed—fluttered. *Buzzed,* yes. Oh, Emily. If he hadn't found her. If we had our own baby. If. Told him not to look. Michael is dead, Michael is dead. *The Ghost Child,* and the real ghost child, Emily, named for her grandmother, not the poet. Not everyone thinks about poets. He found her. Michael found his baby, found Emily. "Where We Are When We're Lost." Where we fucking are is standing in front of a tiny fucking gravestone in Portland. That shortcut growing up, cutting through the cemetery to walk to Mercer pool summers in Iowa, baby graves along the fence. Don't walk on those, tiptoe over. Tiny. Lonely. Sad. We shut up, squabbles silenced. Picking dandelions to arrange on the sad baby graves. What those parents thought, a dozen dried-up dandelions on their kid's grave. Sure, they visit years later, forever, now, still. Their child. Emily. A name Michael would pick if he were asked, if he had known. "Emily." Father to a dead child. No wonder he. Supposed to be a teenager, cheerleader, mean girl, nerd, slut, drama queen, jock, smarty-pants—his eyes, that gap-toothed smile. Who believes in heaven? If he listened to me . . . don't look, I said, I said, don't look don't don't, no . . . no. If he didn't want to make it right. If he hadn't told me. If Louise. If. Damn it, who thinks a kid is dead? (And who is relieved when she is, relieved?) Eight years old, and a tiny gravestone. Michael is dead. I didn't wish for that. (That, or for her to be—) Just—maybe, just— (Yes, you did.) Holy Mary, Mother of God, pray for us sinners, us fucking sinners like me, now and at the hour of our death, amen. Shit. (Sinners and suicides go to hell and cannot be buried in consecrated ground.) The clock—don't look. There's a clock in every book someone said. Okay, here's my clock. Here's the ticking. "HURRY UP PLEASE ITS TIME." Eliot. [*sic*] In your own fucking head you think, "[*sic*]" because you know the line exactly. Goddamnit. Always the writing, always words. Just once to escape! (Fuck.) Agent all, *keep notes,* she'll shop the memoir. *The Ghost Wife.* Didion was a best-seller, Joyce Carol Oates excerpted in the *New Yorker*—no. No. No. Shouldn't. Never wish for it. (But you did.) Never wish for anything. (You did.) Except sleep. It's okay to wish for sleep (I'm a fucking sinner. Fuck.) (Everything could have been different.) If.

FIRST PERSON: I; primarily used in conjunction with a unique voice or the "unreliable narrator"; beginning writers should avoid this POV as its simplicity is deceptive.

That next morning I hunched in a corner of the dining hall, my hand curled around a cup of bad coffee, and people got the idea and left me alone. Louise didn't show for breakfast, not when I was there anyway, which was fine by me. With nothing scheduled until the welcome reception before dinner—the students would be arriving throughout the day—I wandered outside to an Adirondack chair in a sunny field overlooking the pond. With a book in one hand, my computer in the other, I cultivated an aura of "writer at work," ready to stave off anyone who approached. What a joke; I hated every word I wrote the past four years, even the published ones. Delete, delete. My computer was mostly a bookmark of cute cats. But for a good long while, I sat undisturbed, airport shuttle vans and cars coming and going amid a pleasant blur of distant commotion: crunching gravel, the bang of the main hall's screen door, grunts of luggage shepherded about, jokes and greetings, hugs and handshakes, laughter. It was the sort of scene where it was easy to imagine Michael emerging. "Hey you," he would say, not buying my "writer at work" pose, knowing I was anxious for the right company. "Hey you," I'd say back, but then what? We were barely speaking in the end, fuck you about as likely as hey you.

The field—tinged golden already in August—was infused by sunlight. Grasses bent and whispered in an invisible breeze. I resolved not to drink tonight, or not to drink more than one drink. Dragonflies flitted and darted, their wings latching glints of light. I tried to think only of the things in front of me. Ripples on the pond. A group of attractive young men on the far side, bare-chested, smoking and lazing on a scrap of smooth shoreline. Something unmoving on the close bank that could be a turtle or a stump.

Sometime after lunch (I didn't go; I barely ate anymore—only when people were watching), the director joined me, lugging over the chair that I had dragged ten yards away from mine. He wore shorts with too many pockets and a light blue windbreaker that had a damp-looking stain down the front. He sat down and slapped both his thighs. His legs seemed extraordinarily hairy. He pulled a slim paperback out of one of his many pockets and opened it widely, cracking the spine a bit.

He wasn't actually reading—but then neither was I. We sat for a minute or two, staring blankly at our books, and finally he said, "I hope being here isn't too hard for you."

"It's not."

He said, "You shouldn't mind Louise."

"I don't," I said.

"You know," he said, "I was in love with her."

"We're not playing the game anymore," I said, trying to laugh and failing utterly. "But I suppose that sounds like the truth." It wasn't exactly a secret that Louise always had a string of men, so this wasn't a surprise.

"I guess you remember that was about a year after my second wife died."

Suicide, I remembered. So sad. There was a line in my book that I kept staring at for no reason: "Forty-three years old, and the war occurred half a lifetime ago, and yet the remembering makes it now." *The Things They Carried*. Tim O'Brien. The words felt like a different language, but one I understood slightly, like something once studied in high school. Michael meant to read this book because I told him he would like it. Now I was rereading it as if to compensate.

"Michael was a good man."

"He was," I said.

"Though it's never that simple, is it?" he said. "'A good man.' Whatever that means."

"What you call someone when he's dead."

He grunted, maybe in agreement, maybe not. "That's what I'm hoping. But I don't know."

"Of course you are," I said—a reflex, the expected reassurance, the E-Z suck up to the man who hired me to teach at the conference. "Here, I'll say it when you're alive: you're a damn good man." Once I heard myself, I was ashamed; my voice sounded artificial, like too sweet flavor syrup.

His eyes were fixed steadily on the open page of his book. Poetry. I saw short lines and white space. I wondered if the words on a page of poetry felt lonelier than the words in a novel. Or maybe they felt more precious. I could think about that all day, hours of only that in my mind so as not to think about anything else.

Finally, he said, "You met here, didn't you?"

I nodded again. I felt sweaty and nervous and I suddenly had to pee. There was pressure to decipher a hidden meaning in his words, a message he intended that I couldn't hear. I crossed my legs, uncrossed them. Nothing was comfortable.

"And we all played Louise's game," he said. "That night in 1996. Remember? Michael spooked everyone by describing his uncle's exorcism. Remember that? We all knew he was bullshitting, but what a great story. The eyes rolling like pitted olives in a drunk's martini. Remember?"

"Did we?" I said. "Did he say that? Sounds like him."

"And you told us——." He paused, flipped his book for a quick glance at the back cover, then continued: "You told us your mother committed suicide when you were six. You woke up and she was in your bed."

"You've got quite the memory."

"A lie, you said."

"Of course it was, all of it." I pressed one finger to the bridge of my nose, wondering if I should have put on sunscreen—not that I had any.

"But I think you were telling the truth," the director said. "I'm pretty sure you were."

I laughed. I swear there was an echo. "Then you were the only one," I said.

"And Michael," he said.

"Michael," I repeated.

"He also thought it was true. That's what I remember."

I studied his face, pretending I wasn't. A gleam cut through his eyes that might have been only a tricky bit of light. "Why would you say that?" I tried laughing again. "Why would you say that now?"

"The hardest thing when they're gone," he started. A long pause. I wondered if he would finish. Just when I was about to ask him, he continued: "The hardest thing when they're gone is that they never actually leave. I loved her," he said. "I really loved her," and he stood up, shoved his book in his pocket and wandered away.

As I listened to his footsteps crush the grass, I realized that I didn't know if the her was Louise or the wife who had committed suicide or both or even someone else.

My mood was disjointed after that, his words running through my head like a toy train circling a single track. Yet I continued to sit, as if waiting for something more, until the light started to settle, and it was time to head back and get ready for the cocktail party.

When I returned to my room to change into whichever baggy black dress I had dropped into my suitcase at five in the morning (only yesterday!), there was a folded note thumbtacked to my door that I yanked free. I didn't have to read it to know who it was from, so I crumpled it—like the fifty dollar bill—and, setting down my computer and book, I turned the knob, but there was a slight cough, and then there was Louise, rounding a corner in the hallway. "Going to aim that at me?" she asked, keeping her voice light.

"I like your skirt," I said quickly. I didn't—a zebra print; too short, too tight, and too expensive, for here, for her—but it was the sort of thing one might wear wanting attention, so I played along. Plus, she had scared the shit out of me, showing up abruptly. I wondered if she'd staked herself out, waiting.

"This old thing?" she said. Ironically, sardonically, sarcastically. I was never one for adverbs tagging dialogue—red penning them in my students' work—but her voice had an edge that wasn't easy to define. When unable to define things, I threw words at the problem. Mockingly, acerbically, derisively. Scornfully, disdainfully, contemptuously. That's about it without clicking on the thesaurus function.

"Yes," I said. "That old thing."

She seemed startled, then rallied and said, "Did you read it?" She pointed at the note. Her fingernails were painted blood red, a different color than they'd been yesterday, and looked professionally done. Had she spent the day getting a manicure?

I smoothed the note and read out loud: "I loved him too— many of us did, you know. Yours is the greatest loss, but we've all lost something special. xo Lou-Lou," which is what we had called her in 1996, or maybe it was what she had called herself. I couldn't remember, only that seeing it there on paper made my stomach lurch, and I balled up the note again.

Two women emerged from a room at the end of the hall— scarves, shawls, jangling bracelets, striped tights—and they walked past us, jingling and clicking—one wore spurs on her cowboy boots, and the other was in tap shoes. Everyone was an overly studied individual here. *Look at who I want you to think I am!* It was exhausting. I was exhausted.

Once they were out of earshot, Louise shook back her big wad of hair. "You know, I didn't know what happened to that baby. I never wanted to know." She sounded angry. "Giving her up was the hardest thing I ever did, and the worst thing. The worst thing I've done in my life."

That famous story, "Where We Are When We're Lost," was about a woman giving up a baby ("Michael's" baby) for adoption and secretly taking money. A more realistic style than Louise was known for, it filled twenty-five *New Yorker* pages. There were letters to the editor about it, which there never were about the stories, and it made the list for the forthcoming *Norton Anthology of Short Fiction*. Students of the future would write papers and wrestle with MLA citations for Louise's story. Everyone read it. I read it. Michael read it. "Michael." When Michael told me about Louise, he said, "I didn't know there was a real baby. I would have done something. I would have done right. Do you think maybe it's not too late?" I suppose that's being "a good man." I was the one who told him—well, to stay out of it. That weren't our lives fine just the way they were, already complicated enough? That diving into all that would open us to the darkest kind of pain.

"I told him not to involve you," I said. "To stay out of the whole thing, actually. And I'm sure her parents didn't think that your giving her up was 'the worst thing in your life.' I'm sure her parents loved her." I had almost accidentally said, Loved her *to death*.

My door was half open, and I could see inside to my unmade bed, the rumpled sheets, the pillow that smelled so much like a wet Band-Aid that I squirted expensive French perfume on it when I couldn't sleep. The room looked shadowy and quiet.

"Anyway," I said. "Last night. That was wrong. Maybe that was the worst thing you ever did."

"They didn't believe a word of it," she said. "They knew the cat thing was true, which it was. So they just think I'm a bitch."

"You shouldn't have said it, not even to be a bitch," I said.

"It's a game," she said. "Everyone was lying all over the place. Like you."

"Why do you play it?"

She shrugged. "What people lie about is revealing." She looked me straight in the eye and paused. *Like you.* I steeled myself. But she said, "The father wasn't Michael. It was—" Here she named the director of the conference. That year we were all there, that year we met, was his first as the director of the famous writers' conference. "He doesn't know." She sighed. "I swear to you. I swear."

It was as if my whole body abruptly gaped, every soft spot exposed: No one would lie about such a thing. Only a liar. "I don't believe you," I said softly.

"I don't believe me either most of the time." She looked unhappy. She looked as though she might be thinking about crying, which was different than actually crying, of course.

I couldn't believe her. Believing her would change everything. But really, believing her would change nothing:

Michael? Still dead.

Emily? Still dead.

If what she said now was true, what would be different? Would it be the director's heart crushed to learn that his unknown daughter was buried in a tiny grave on a hillside in Portland? Would it be the director plummeting through a dark and dangerous sorrow, wallowing in emptiness, drinking, shopping gun shows? Would he stop writing, putting down two lines in a year? Would his wife wish him dead? Would he die? Would the director die because of Louise's careless words? This ghost child would never be his; the ghost child stayed all mine, and the guilt. Louise's words didn't matter one iota. I hoped all of that was packed into the furious stare I gave Louise, but of course it wasn't. It couldn't possibly be.

I could choose not to believe Louise, but I would wonder. I would doubt.

Drifting through the open window at the end of the hallway: excited voices, footsteps on gravel, a whoop. Writers and wannabe writers gathering for the party, for gossip, name-dropping, sucking up, for the stories and the booze and the boozy truth.

"What you did is . . . a sin," I said. Not the right word, but there was no right word.

"Then I guess this is confession," she said.

"I'll never forgive you," I said. "Or myself."

"Write about it."

"I said stop saying that. We're talking about a real, dead person," I said, "someone who was alive but now isn't. Not some character in one of your idiotic *New Yorker* stories." Childishly, I threw the note at her but missed, and it sailed beyond her shoulder, hitting the wall before dropping to the floor. She bent and picked it up, slipped it into the waistband of her tiny skirt, an action that both irritated me and made me sad.

After a moment, I said, "I'm not like you." Now I was about to cry. I took in a long breath. I wasn't like her. I didn't want to write about this. I didn't know how I could tell this story or why I would.

She was calm. "Writers don't choose their material. It comes to them."

Something our workshop teacher had drilled into us back in 1996. Something I parroted to my own students, in interviews about writing, in conversation, even at the party last night. *As one of my writing teachers once said, writers don't choose their material. It comes to them. . . .*

Louise said, "Bet you've written up some notes."

I shook my head no, and she smirked at my transparent lie. She said, "I know what happened is for real, which is horrible and I'm so sorry. But also, it's a story. It simply is. What happens—no matter how painful—it's material for people like us. You know that. You chose it when you became a writer."

I shook my head again, harder, like an obstinate child.

"Suit yourself. But if you're not careful, I'll tell the story," Louise said. She spoke lightly, but a chill zipped my spine. She would.

Louise turned, then turned back, studying me as if memorizing my face in a peculiar way. Then she said, "Michael knew. When he contacted me about wanting to find her, I told him he wasn't the father. I told him who was. I think I would know when I've got a diaphragm in and when I don't. So Michael knew what the truth was. He just refused to believe it. He wanted that girl, because—." She suddenly looked up at the ceiling. Her neck was luminously pale and didn't seem to belong to the rest of her body.

"Finish," I demanded. "Because what?"

"Because," she said. "I don't need to say it."

"Because I didn't want one." I spoke clearly but couldn't finish. "Because . . ."

She looked me full on with shimmering eyes. "Oh, Vanessa," she whispered. "No, no. Not that, not about that. I'm sorry."

"Don't you pity me," I said. "Or hug me. I don't even like you.

I never did." I poked one foot at my computer case, tipping it over. I thought of those two hundred pages I'd deleted, how very easy it had been. All those books of mine about post-apocalyptic women, each one sneakily and only about my mother, and however many words I dumped on the page she didn't come back to explain herself.

Louise tugged at the hem of her zebra skirt. "I know," she said. "We're too much the same. Like God made us and threw us together, with Her crazy sense of humor."

There was a silence between us that lasted forever.

I lifted my computer case, jostling the strap up onto my shoulder, settled the book against the crook of my arm. Looking like that, I could have been any bright-eyed MFA student.

"The truth is overrated," I said, suddenly believing the statement utterly.

She said, "At least maybe try to get paid more than fifty bucks for it."

Retreat. I walked through the door to my room and pushed it shut behind me. I knew she was expecting me to slam it, so I closed it quietly and gently. The unexpected action is preferable, the surprising yet inevitable ending. Something else that teacher taught us in 1996.

DOCUMENT: Not a classic point of view but a useful technique on occasion; examples include letters, a diary, or directly addressing the reader in speech. A means of playing with form or bending conventional rules of narrative.

Excerpt of transcript:
MacBride Writers' Conference schedule, Wednesday
9:00 A.M.–10:30 A.M.
Creative nonfiction craft lecture:
"The Perfect Imperfection of Memory"

Joy Ruby-Vargha, author of *The Food Diaries*
The Goodwin Theatre

Good morning. What an honor for me to open the conference with the very first craft talk. Wow! This is totally that thing you dream about when you're hunched on a ratty couch in your studio apartment, eating ramen noodles for the sixth day in a row, getting email rejections from literary journals you've never heard of, haha.

I chose as my topic the imperfection of memory, and before we dive into the examples of the text—which I hope you all read!—I want to talk for a minute about writing in general, sort of to set the tone for the rest of my lecture. I like to describe myself as a "writer of stories," which means that even though I write memoir—real stories from my real life—I recognize that what I write is shaped and shifted by my mind. It's not the absolute truth. The absolute truth doesn't exist. We have only our own individual truths, and even though we might swear in a court of law on a Bible that we're telling the absolute truth, we're limited to telling only the truth we know.

One reason we can't get to that absolute truth is because the act of telling the story changes the story. Once I write the words on the page, that's when the truth changes from "what happened" to "what happened *in the story.*" "The story" exists separately, alongside the actual event. And "the story" is ultimately more powerful than the event itself. Yes.

Crazy, right? But human brains are hardwired for stories and narrative. On the handout, you'll see links to recent studies in neuroscience about that, and a book I totally recommend, *The Storytelling Animal.* Very exciting stuff.

So while we want to remain true to our best memory of the events, once you write down that you were wearing a red dress, that red dress imprints on the mind, so much so that if you come across a photo and discover you were actually wearing a blue skirt and white blouse, you'll resist. The story puts you in a red dress. The story is what you believe, not the photo. And the story—the act of telling—has transformed your blue skirt into a red dress.

Haha—I probably should have worn a red dress today! But I bet that if you were to think of this talk years from now—not that you have to, haha—it just may be that you'll remember me in a red dress. And if you do, you'll be proving my point exactly: story creates truth. Truth is powerless before the story.

And who tells stories? We do. Writers. That's what we do. Create the truth, even when we're making shit up. I love my job, I do!

Picasso said, "Art is the lie that tells the truth." It's where we create our lives—first by living them, and second by telling others what happened, writers do, yes, but even people making dinner conversation by talking about what happened today at their boring jobs. They're shaping their lives via story; they're turning their lives into art. Story can make the unbearable bearable; it can deliver the message that dares not be spoken directly. That's what fairy tales were before Disney got hold of them, you know, stories to explain those dark undercurrents roiling the subconscious: I wish Mommy was dead, I want to fuck Daddy. God, could I go on about the role of fairy tales. But back to my main point:

Writing something down, speaking, telling the story—that subversive act of trying to capture time—that alters what has happened. You all heard of those famous studies about how observing something influences the observed object, right? It's on the handout. So I'm saying that whatever truth there was to our story is lost once we put the words on paper.

But I stand here as a memoirist, as a goddess of "this

really happened," to say, *so what?* We've lost the truth, but we've gained the story. And, seriously, for an artist, that's barely a trade-off. The story is what there is, and the story is what remains. The story becomes the truth, and the story is the only thing that has half a chance of outlasting us. The story matters. The story. You and I—each of us in this room—like it or not, we're the walking dead the minute we're born, marching lockstep toward our own ends. But the word. Art. The story. That shit outlasts us all.

Don't laugh, don't be all "ironic" and "I live in Brooklyn."

Orpheus returned from the underworld and my God, he had a hell of a tale to tell—we're still telling it, aren't we? And so do you have a hell of a tale to tell. So do all of us. That's why we're writers. To shape our lives into stories. To take what happened and make it matter. To find the words to create the myth, yes, and to find the words to create the truth. All we have to do, as they say, is open up a vein.

OBJECTIVE: an absence of point of view, perfect neutrality as if a camera is watching and recording the events as they unfold; see Ernest Hemingway's "Hills like White Elephants."

The woman in a wide-brimmed hat and oversized sunglasses sits alone, in an Adirondack chair in a field of long meadow grass. The sun is on the verge of setting and the clouds in the sky are tinged pink and purple. A small pond ripples steadily, evenly. The woman picks up her black pen and opens a small, leather-bound notebook. She chews on the pen cap with her left molars. Then she places the tip of the pen on the first line of the first page of the empty notebook. She begins to write, seldom lifting her pen off the paper. The page fills with words.

Golden light spills carelessly, illuminating some of the grasses into vibrant green, leaving others locked in shadow. Wind picks up, rustling and bending the grass tips, and she writes faster, the pen sinking more deeply into the paper, the ballpoint scratching slightly.

She flips over the page and does not write on the back, but continues at the top of a fresh, white piece of paper. She keeps writing, she keeps writing.

When the sun is low and her arms prickle with goose bumps, she turns back the pages she's written until she gets to the first page and at the top she prints "The Ghost Child" in strong, firm letters and underlines it once, twice.

She does not write down her name, and there is no one here to speak it, so in the objective point of view, with the camera's eye, it is not possible to know who this woman is. It is only a woman, writing a story.

Okay, so I wanted to leave time for your questions, but we're running over. Probably the main thing to remember about point of view—if you remember one thing from this lecture—is that the story belongs to the voice telling it. That's where the control is. If you're the one telling the story, the story is yours. Control is yours. Like having the keys to the car. So it's simple: always be the one *telling* the story.

Because you all know what happens next: Along come the readers, with their interpretations and symbols and opinions and assumptions and questions needing answers. They really fuck it up for us.

SOMEONE IN NEBRASKA

You have finally met someone—live and in person—who has seen the white light at the end of the tunnel. She's a bartender in a small town in Nebraska who had a heart attack when she was forty. "They run in my family," she says, as if that might be an obvious thing to understand about her. She knows everyone in the bar, everyone except you. You're the stranger. You must like being the stranger wherever you go. That's why you go to so many different places.

"I was clinically dead for twenty-five minutes," she tells you. Others in the bar listen, but clearly they've heard the story, the minute by minute. Only you don't know, although you know the end: there she is, standing in front of you, bringing you a Bud whenever you ask for one.

She's forty-two now, but the kind of forty-two that's surprising, as if she should be younger. There's a bottle of Lubriderm hand lotion on the bar, next to the Jack Daniels. Maybe you should try that brand on your own skin.

It still surprises you, what all can be learned about people in the short bursts of conversation that punctuate a bar. "So, are you from around here?" (knowing you're not) is enough to start. You always let them ask first. You don't want to push your way in. You were taught not to push. Dallas, the bartender, has told you she was named for the city though she's never been there. "Someday, maybe," she says, but it sounds like she doesn't care anymore about getting to Dallas or not, not the way she once used to. You think

142

about telling her it's not such a great city—sweaty, sprawling, excessive—but you keep your trap shut. "Those cheerleaders are pretty enough," she says, "but I'm suspecting they're kinda dumb, kinda pathetic." She shakes her head. Those poor, dumb, pathetic Dallas Cowboy cheerleaders. The way she talks, the way she conveys an opinion convinces you also to feel sorry for them.

"Damn helicopter ride to Omaha was seventy thousand bucks," she says. "Not that I remember a lick of it."

How did she know, you ask, that it was a heart attack? You've seen the public service announcement ads scroll by during whatever heart health month is; women often don't recognize the signs. Women are trained for pain. (This is something Dallas announced earlier, during a quick skirmish of the sexes sparked by some men who didn't properly push in their barstools as they stood up to leave.)

"You know," she says, conspiratorially. "For real, I'd rather give birth again, take on that torture than feel another heart attack. It was squeezing and pushing all up through my back, and my hands crunched up like devil claws." She demonstrates, palms up, fingers locked in a gnarly, arthritic pose, then shakes them loose. "I yelled at my dad—he was living with me at the time—I screamed up the stairs, 'I think I'm having a fucking heart attack, goddamn it,' and he jumped on the phone quick. My mother had her first when she was thirty-two, so I got that it was borrowed time for me, especially since I smoked back then. At the hospital here, there was my doctor, the one I took my kids to, and I looked up at him and told him there was a booger in his nose and then said, 'Don't let me die,' and I was out. Out and clinically dead for twenty-five minutes they told me. They saved my life, waiting for the helicopter. And all that pounding they did on me, not one of my ribs cracked, which was cool. They knew their CPR shit for real."

Someone wants a stack of lottery poppers. Someone else needs a refill on Jack and ginger. Someone yells that the john needs more t.p. and the whole bar finds that hilarious. Dallas handles all these situations. You sip your beer. Your hand shakes the tiniest bit, not so anyone would notice but you.

You guess that Dallas wouldn't lie about this. To the cops, maybe, about a joint in the car not being hers, but not about something of this magnitude. Anyway, she doesn't know about your husband and his heart attack. You don't go around telling people because it only confuses them. Thirty-seven-year-olds aren't supposed to die, especially not from heart attacks. You're too young to be who you are: a widow.

Dallas returns to her spot behind the bar and jumps back into her story: "So I was out. And I swear to you I saw the bright white light, just like they say, glowing at the end of a tunnel, shining like a Christmas tree. Right in the middle, there was my big sister surrounded by that white light, her face whole and peaceful, looking like she did before the car crash, just beautiful. Like an angel. I couldn't stop staring. She was the one out of us lucky enough to take like Mom and her side—everyone else, including me, got Dad all the way, and he's a pit bull. Not Janie. She held four red roses across one arm, like she was prom queen, and the sweetest little smile on her face, like that painting, whatsit, you know the one: mysterious but calm. You'd never see a smile like that in real life. I'm walking right for her, aching to hug her, but she straight-arms those roses, like to stop me, like a wall, and says, 'You gotta go back. It's not your time, Cookie,' which was what they called me when I was just little, and I was all, 'No,' not that arguing at her when she was alive did any good, so why think I could because she was dead? 'They need you back home,' she says, and that's for sure, those three boys of mine are hell-raisers, and God knows I gotta yank their chains every day. But my sister looked so still and so damn pretty. The light was bright, but not like sunlight—it was soft—and the smell . . . that's how I knew it was real. Every drug I ever did, every hallucination or whatever under the influence of everything (and I do mean everything), out of all that, nothing ever smelled. But this did, heaven did: it smelled fresh, like cement after a good summer rain. It just was . . . the most amazing smell I've ever smelled. I can't describe it really."

She pauses, twists at the waist, putting her shoulder and triceps in view, so you see a tattoo of four roses twining up the back of her arm. "We each got the same one on my birthday," Dallas says. "On our arms. Three days before that wreck on 29. I would've stayed to be with her. But she said to go back. Then there was my kid going, 'Mom? I love you.'"

You're supposed to say something, but nothing you've seen or read or thought in your life prepared you for this moment of hearing this story. You've heard on TV variations of the "white light" before, but a story is more believable when someone stands in front of you in a bar in Nebraska, and when you want—desperately—to believe it. When you want it to be true. Wow, you say, feeling stupid, and to complete the stupid feeling you repeat the single, stupid word: Wow.

She gives her head a quick shake, shattering the mood. "It's just something that happened to me," she says. "Two years ago already."

"Two years?" someone down the bar leans forward to ask.

Dallas nods. "And eight years since Janie passed," she says. "Time sure fucking flies."

"Now that you're back to life," someone else says, "grab me another Bud Light. Or is that a Bud White Light?"

But no one laughs. Indeed, bars are never actually quiet, but this one is for the spare moment where Dallas leans against the counter, tilts her head so she's gazing up at the pressed tin ceiling, a tiny grimace fluttering her lips. You know that look. The lost sister, the one who wasn't sent back, the one who was, the one who sits here. The, *why, why?* You never stop pretending that question might get answered, but by who? Your brain insists there is no answer.

And yet. Things align. Surely things align.

This place isn't Brooklyn, her story isn't on a cable talk show, it's not her night off; you are sitting here alone, it is beer and not scotch, the carved graffiti in the wooden bar does misspell "asshole." It's not two years ago, or eight years ago, or ten years ago that morning you found him on the kitchen floor, it's now.

You want to thank her for the story. You want to tell her about your dead husband and his heart attack and how there wasn't a happy ending, unless this, right now, is a happy ending of sorts, ten years later: that maybe you will believe the picture in your mind. Him seeing that white light. His grandmother, his childhood *busia,* reaching out, enfolding him in a hug. Her whisper in Polish, "I've been waiting for you," and he understands exactly though he never spoke Polish. You want Dallas to know how much it means to know—to *know*—that someone flesh and blood, someone in Nebraska, has seen heaven and believes in it and that heaven smells nice. You hope that's true. You hope heaven smells like pizza.

You don't say any of these things, or any of the things you wish you knew how to say, and there are many of those. Dallas lets her fingers rest lightly on the beer tap, eyes snapping to the door as it whooshes open. "Another?" she asks.

But it's time to go. You push over a twenty, a big tip on a five-dollar tab. Maybe now she'll remember you, too.

WHAT I COULD BUY

What I could buy with the insurance money they gave me when you died:

One Ferrari, red or black, assuming V-8 instead of V-12, assuming premium gas, assuming insurance, assuming no major breakdowns or repairs, assuming no superlong driving trips, assuming street parking, assuming ironic fuzzy dice to dangle off rearview mirror. Or:

Four separate world cruises, assuming 107 days at sea, assuming *Queen Mary 2* on the Cunard Line, assuming supplement for a single room, assuming balcony, assuming one glass of wine per night, assuming no more than twelve land excursions as arranged by the cruise ship personnel, assuming winning at the casino, assuming Internet access, assuming laundry service. Or:

Two years at Harvard Business School, assuming acceptance, assuming Cambridge sublet, assuming books and fees, assuming ramen noodles and pizza for most dinners, assuming public transportation, assuming roommate, assuming no significant social life. Or:

One thousand water buffalo as purchased through Heifer International to help one thousand families in the Philippines become self-sufficient, assuming the charity is legitimate, assuming 75 percent of donations are used for the program mission as stated in the most recent annual report, assuming Charity Navigator ranking of three out of four stars and 55.66 out of 70 is correct and considered worthy of financial support. Or:

Seven in-ground swimming pools, assuming no diving boards. Or:

Two shares of Berkshire Hathaway, assuming no sales commissions, assuming modern market volatility. Or:

One-third of a moderate vacation home in Rehoboth Beach, Delaware, assuming water but not ocean frontage, assuming parking for two cars, assuming three bedrooms and two bathrooms plus outdoor shower, assuming eat-in kitchen, assuming built-in bunk beds, assuming deck refinished by sellers, assuming hurricane insurance. Or:

410 nights at the Fairmont San Francisco, assuming room tax rate of 15 percent, assuming room service breakfasts, assuming five-dollar daily tip for housekeeping, assuming free shoeshine, assuming no luggage storage, assuming one lost umbrella, assuming one stolen bathrobe, assuming no valet parking. Or:

3,333 sweaters, assuming 100 percent cashmere, assuming post-Christmas sale at the mall, assuming one coupon for 15 percent off entire purchase, assuming sale items not excluded, assuming assortment of colors and styles. Or:

One Patek Philippe ladies watch, assuming platinum, assuming moon phases subdial, assuming water resistant to thirty meters, assuming purchase in a state where sales tax is no more than 5 percent. Or:

8,928 breakfasts, assuming 1,785 packages of bacon, assuming twelve ounces, assuming thick cut, 744 dozen organic grocery store eggs, 1,339 cartons of orange juice, and 595 pounds of coffee from Starbucks, assuming black coffee with no cream or sugar. Or:

8,000 bottles of Johnnie Walker Red, assuming mixers necessary, or 1,250 bottles of Johnnie Walker Blue, assuming served neat, assuming different friends to appreciate each. Or:

1,086 massages at the spa, assuming 20 percent tip, assuming free sauna, assuming free parking, assuming eighty minutes, assuming aromatherapy, assuming one post-massage product purchase every other visit. Or:

Eighty-four purebred Labrador puppies, assuming two annual vet visits per puppy, assuming Iams dog food, assuming responsible breeders and no puppy mills or pet stores, assuming one chew toy per month, assuming leashes and collars. Or:

11,904 movie tickets, assuming six-dollar buckets of popcorn, assuming five-dollar Diet Cokes, assuming four-dollar boxes of Junior Mints, assuming equal alternation between popcorn and Junior Mints, assuming the concession stand never runs out of Junior Mints. Or:

71,428 packs of cigarettes, assuming purchased in North Carolina or Virginia, assuming never purchased in New York City, assuming Camels. Or:

100,401 boxes of tissues, assuming Puff's Plus Lotion brand, assuming decorative boxes, assuming an assortment of designs. Or:

1,851 sunrise hot air balloon rides, assuming the premium package with the bottle of champagne and breakfast croissants, assuming commemorative flight certificate, assuming souvenir photo. Or:

Sixty-five Super Bowl tickets, assuming reputable ticket broker, assuming lower level end zone, assuming frequent flyer plane ticket to city, assuming round trip taxi to game, assuming three beers at stadium, assuming one hot dog, assuming two night's stay at Hampton Inn. Or:

252,525 tubes of Chapstick, assuming strawberry flavor. Or:

291,763 tulip bulbs, assuming delivery for fall planting, assuming no reprise of the 1637 Dutch tulip mania, assuming long-stemmed red and yellow, assuming half the bulbs will be eaten by squirrels before spring. Or:

62,656 frozen Stouffer's dinners, assuming none are on sale, assuming no coupons, assuming no tuna casserole. Or:

10,879,000 pieces of paper, assuming white, assuming twenty-four pound, assuming ninety-four brightness, assuming laser printer quality, assuming delivery. And:

Assuming this money isn't tainted, assuming this much money is about right for what a human life is worth, assuming I don't drive off a bridge in my grief and my guilt, assuming I can live with myself, assuming I can live. Assuming a lot.

TRUTH-TELLING FOR ADULTS

When I read out loud to the class, I'm way too fast, though I try to speak slowly. But the words take over:

"One Monday, I was driving to work through the usual bad traffic on Route 1 in Crystal City. In the grassy median a Latino man cradled a Weedwacker in the curve of his arms, holding it loose and low, at his hips, his weight shifted onto one leg. The slouch; the baggy pants and boots and dark, straight hair; the slack but affectionate grip on the machinery—this was the silhouette of any of the three men who robbed us at gunpoint in Guatemala, on our honeymoon in 19—. You wanted me to love traveling the world the way you did, so you handpicked countries to introduce me to, looking for good food, interesting history, pretty landscape, colorful crafts—and safety—and in 19—, you choose Guatemala.

"Now, nearly twenty years later, the photos blend and blur— Mayan ruins, marketplaces, wooden doors, bright flowers, secret courtyards, churches—but not that night in Antigua, the popular tourist city, when we walked from our small inn to a well-known restaurant on the square. We were seated up front, close to the open air, amid scattered tables of Americans, all older and better dressed—couples who looked as though they owned houses with enough rooms so one was 'the sun room'—and we sorted through the Spanish words on the menu, *churrasquito, chuleta, pepián,* amid the leisurely swirl of the dark-haired waiters carrying sweating drinks on silver trays. Something imperceptible shifted; I noticed it the way a dog will suddenly stare hard at a closed door. The waiters slid through the shadows at the far end of the restaurant as three men sauntered in, M16 assault rifles slung at their hips, loose and easy, the way a man on a street median in suburban Washington, DC, might hold a Weedwacker. 'Money, money, money,' the three men chanted in singsong, so that it took a moment to understand we were all being robbed at gunpoint.

"Who was I? No world traveler. But I leaned forward to let my baggy sweater and the tablecloth conceal the black fanny pack strapped frontward on my waist. With one quick thumb, I spun my ring so its small diamond faced my palm and I rearranged my left hand under my right. *You* were the world traveler, *you* were the one who handled situations. I only thought about my wedding ring.

"A gunman strolled to our table, as if he carried a violin to play or roses for sale, not a gun, and you pulled Guatemalan bills from your pocket, careful and methodical; you slowly unstrapped your Timex watch and let it dangle as the gunman delicately cupped it. A pause. Our gunman's attention flickered, listening to his cohorts at another table, and I captured your left hand under my right, covering your wedding ring.

"But two tables away tension thickened as a hulking American brayed, 'Is this a joke? Is this a joke?' as the men demanded his knuckle-size gold ring, his flashy, not Timex watch—'Give it to him,' his wife urged; *give it to him,* I thought—but he kept insisting, 'I'm an American, I'm an American,' and the guns, the guns steadied, but finally, the ring was pocketed and the watch and a tremendous wad of cash, and abruptly, yet without rushing, the three men ambled into the plaza, dispersing into darkness, and the waiters reappeared, carrying plates of food on silver trays, which they set before us: *pollo en crema, chuletas fascinante, arroz.* 'Are you calling the police?' the American brayed. 'What kind of joke is this?'

"We jumped up, you and I, grabbing hands, and ran through deserted streets back to our inn, tumbling through the thick wooden door into the walled courtyard, where we told ourselves we were safe, we were lucky. Later, much later, 'I'm an American,' we mimicked, when we felt safe for real, back in America, 'what kind of joke is this?' We told our story at parties.

"That man with the Weedwacker, that casual slouch—those men, that trip, you. I drive Route 1 to work every day, every day, and now, every day both memories confront me: the ghost of the man with the Weedwacker and because of him, there—superimposed in this unexpected place, on an unremarkable median—stands one more ghost of you."

I finish reading my piece, and the class stirs, dropping pens, slurping lattes, straightening posture. (Apparently no one wants to be mistaken for a slouching gunman.) We're in a class I secretly call "Memoir for Dummies," though the official name is more poetic, referring to a line from Emily Dickinson that no one else in the class seems to recognize: "Tell It Slant: Memoir and Truth-Telling for Adults." The teacher is an intense, and intensely thin, thirtyish woman with waves of dark hair that she curtains over her face while we read our assignments, like sending semaphore signals: hair draping one eye = good; hair shoved back with one hand = irritation; hair flailing wildly = beware. At the start of each class, she stacks five Triscuits next to her water bottle and nibbles each down to an edge; at the midway break, she drops five Triscuit rims in the garbage can.

The class was advertised in a cheap paper catalog that came in the mail: $350 for six meetings. We're at meeting number two, reading aloud from an in-class exercise: *write about fear.* "What if we're too afraid to write?" asked the man with the shaved head who everyone realized would be nonstop annoying back in week one.

The teacher, Jinx (not her real name, I'm guessing), said, "Use it. That's exactly the kind of fear that's honest."

Well, I don't much like thinking about fear, whether honest or dishonest, but no refunds, so I scribbled out my something. The rule is that you can pass on reading out loud once during the six classes, and I already passed during week one, which suggests that maybe I do know something about fear.

This is the first writing I've read out loud to anyone, ever. The class lunges at my words like they're red meat, which is a cliché that would draw Jinx's ire and a curtain of swishing hair. There's no focus, someone says, and someone else thinks I might be racist because I used "Latino" instead of "Hispanic" (or maybe the other way around; I got confused), and the man with the shaved head pontificates about point of view for five minutes before Jinx shuts him up, and the lady who is always knitting says that she must have liked something about my essay because she dropped a stitch. Jinx nibbles a Triscuit. Then she says, "Are you being honest?"

I nod. "That was how it all happened," I say.

"That doesn't equate to being honest."

The man with the shaved head snorts. His "writing about fear" assignment was about his sailboat tipping over in the Potomac, and I'm positive he made up the whole thing. He's too impatient to be a sailor. I can tell that he'll never pass on reading, that he wants everyone in the world to know everything about him.

"Okay," I say. "I guess you're right." I tend to agree with people. Doing so makes them like me. I'm lucky I don't live under a totalitarian regime because I would be agreeing that yes, my neighbors probably are spies, now that you mention it.

She says, "There's a difference between honesty and truth." She pauses until we write that down in our notebooks or type it onto our keyboards. Then she says, "That, and the tension between the two, is what we're here to explore."

A young man sits directly across from me; before class starts, we drag our desks into a circle, and last week and this, he's across from me. He's about twenty-five or so and generally quiet, writing in a battered spiral notebook with a photo of the "Welcome Back, Kotter" cast on the cover (with Travolta), using one of those old-time Bic pens that click down four different colors. Did he find those things in his grandmother's attic? I want to tell him that "Welcome Back, Kotter" was my favorite show in grade school, but I don't want to come off as an official old lady, or like his grandmother. Anyway, he watches me during this exchange, half-listening to Jinx, and then he tilts his hand up off his desk and flashes me thumbs-up so fast it's like the gesture's not there. It's nice. He seems like a nice boy. (If I'm worried about sounding like his grandmother, well, now I do.)

The truth is, I liked this boy immediately when I saw him last week, across the circle from me, and I like him even more right now. I like him a lot. He looks exactly like my husband who died fifteen years ago, like my husband looked when he was the same age, which is the age when we got married. It's my husband I'm writing about in this class, and—if I were being honest (damn Jinx), I would admit that—truthfully—I'm writing about this boy too, this new ghost of Y, my husband.

If I were being honest, I would type out his name, wouldn't I?

If I were being honest, I might have not lied about his wedding ring: the man in Guatemala took it. Just a gold band, easily replaced at a mall jewelry store. Not even engraved with initials or a date. But still. The new ring never felt right. It's funny, the things you don't want a roomful of strangers to know, and one of them is that my dead husband was buried wearing an imposter wedding ring.

The class is three hours long—which seems excessive for a cheap-catalog community class; exactly how much do they pay Jinx to sit with us for three hours?—so we get a break halfway through, which is when Jinx stacks up Round Two of her Triscuits. The twelve of us pile and cluster at the door like a herd of wildebeest, then funnel through and stampede down a poorly lit hallway where college posters are tacked to the walls—we meet in an alternative high school on the edge of the bad side of our suburb—and once the hallway splits, vending machines are to the left and bathrooms to the right. I let the man with the shaved head dictate my direction: whichever branch he takes, I go opposite, and so tonight I end up at the vending machines. There are other classes, also breaking, and people clot the machines, jostling to slide their dollar bills, so I stay back about twenty feet, leaning against the wall next to a confusing bank of garbage bins—paper, waste, metal, glass, plastic (someone has helpfully Magic Markered "puke here" across the waste bin). It's just candy, I want to shout at the swarming mob.

The young man who looks like my dead husband sidles up, standing close enough that I imagine I hear him breathe, and that our breaths catch up and match. He's got on a long underwear shirt, which looks like something Y wore when we met in college in Chicago, and a generically plaid, untucked flannel shirt loose over it. It's more than the same shirt as Y: it's the same dusty-blonde hair, rumpled and lank; the same dimple in his chin, an embarrassment to Y, with girls fussing over it, and guys calling him "butt-chin," as in, "you still dating butt-chin?" my brother asked that first year. It's the wide-set, dark eyes, virtually without pupils, unless you look closely, unless you catch them glittering in firelight, and when you stare into them, they expand into utter blackness. It's broad hands and short fingernails and delicate wrists and a peachy shade of skin and slashing eyebrows and eyelashes long enough to curl and a wide face shaped like the kind of pumpkin that makes a smiling jack-o'-lantern, and it's the smile: warm and loopy, but with a slight downturn at each corner, creating a tinge of sadness, so that when Y smiled, I always wanted to hug him. It's that smile. The young man turns it on me right then, that smile. I want to hug him, so I focus on standing perfectly still.

"It's just candy," he says.

I agree. "Yeah."

I'm not good at writing dialogue, for myself or for others, and knowing that, I steer away from it in Jinx's assignments. Nobody speaks. Ever. That's my kind of world.

"Though I could go for a Snickers," he says.

Y's favorite.

"Dinner," he says. "You know, the peanuts are protein."

Afraid I might launch into a lecture about poor nutrition, I press my lips together. I must look like a troll. It would be better if I learned how to write dialogue. I let my body relax, just the tiniest bit. I still want to hug him. He hasn't read his work out loud yet. For some reason, Jinx has exempted him from her rule, maybe because he looks capable of saying, "Forget it then," before walking out, when the rest of us only nod mutely when Jinx points and says, "Go."

It's like Jinx's voice fills my head—"go"—and I do: "You look like someone I know."

"Yeah?"

Now I don't know what to say next. I parrot, "Yeah," and maybe I sound aggressive. Or afraid. (*Write about fear.* This.)

He easily fills the pause with half a laugh. "Man, that good, huh? What'd that guy do to you?" Another laugh.

He died, I think, when he wasn't supposed to. I say, "Nothing. Just a really long time ago." Translation: I'm old. Translation: And weird. Translation: Better stay away.

But he sticks out his hand and gives me his name, which is a derivation of Y's very common, yet very specific, name.

"You longed to read everything, to know everything. You weren't fussy or elitist; you'd read the back of a cereal box and turn that into conversation: 'What's riboflavin again?' You picked up the *Weekly World News* at the 7–11, laughing at articles about women giving birth to half-human, half-mole babies, quoting interviews with doctors who autopsied space aliens in Roswell. You kept file folders of newspaper clippings about dozens of pertinent topics and could locate any article you needed in minutes. You were totally and deeply in love with knowledge, and with ideas, and with me, maybe prioritized like that. Early on, I read books you insisted I read: V. S. Naipul, Graham Greene, *Atlas Shrugged*. I couldn't keep up with your recommendations, your panoramic mind.

"You were a political idealist, an intellectual; you cared passionately. Not a marcher or a protester, but a thinker, a ponderer. I'm guessing you wouldn't be impressed by politics now, the hammering 'I'm right, you're wrong' and the constant spin.

"Back then, a year out of college, you interned at a political think tank. I visualized big-brained fish flitting through cubicles under cool fluorescent light. You read and researched, citing facts and statistics and relevant studies and quotations to prove and disprove what the Important Thinkers who were the bosses cared about; you drafted op-eds to be published in newspapers and magazines under the names of the Important Thinkers. Occasionally you were allowed to publish your own op-ed, and there was your name printed in the *Christian Science Monitor* or the *Orange County Register,* papers that may no longer exist. Sometimes you got paid. We always needed money, but it wasn't the money for you, it was the ideas.

"After you died, after Google was invented (imagine! you never knew Google)—after Google was invented, sometimes I Googled your name when I was lonely, and one time an article you had written popped up, your name and an impassioned plea about cultural imperialism. What was wrong with a McDonald's in Santiago, you wrote, if people got jobs as well as the Big Macs they craved? How can the French government pass laws banning American gangster movies from the multiplex in Paris; will doing so bring a renaissance of French New Wave cinema? An old, forgotten worry: Mickey Mouse taking over the world.

"On my computer were your words, young and naïve and idealistic, arranged exactly the way you had arranged them when you were alive. I remembered that while drafting this piece you needed a punchy ending, the call for action, and I was on the floor, twirling a feather for our playful young black cat to chase, and I said, 'Let their wallets decide,' and you gasped at my perfect suggestion, and I was impressed that you were impressed by me. All these years later, those words written in 19—glowing on my laptop: your byline, my punchy ending; your words lingering, haunting me, a ghost of you forever here; what you thought, what you said, what you imagined was important. Your words outlasting you.

"And an author's bio: *Y is a research associate at X, a think tank based in Washington, DC. He has a master's in international business from Z. Publications include etc.* Is. Has. Present tense. On the Internet, you're alive.

"But I email the publication: Y is dead, I write, therefore the bio should be updated accordingly to be factual. To be correct. I press 'send,' and you die again. Not for the first time I regret the inescapability of being a responsible person.

"I miss you."

Class Three. Jinx looks at her phone constantly, for the time or waiting for a text. She thinks we won't notice, but we do. Three people don't show, so we're down in numbers, which Jinx pretends is okay—"More time for discussion!"—but I imagine she takes such things personally. She shouldn't care: no refunds. This policy is very clear on the registration form.

Even in our diminished circle, the young man ends up directly across from me.

"Did the writer go far enough?" Jinx asks about my piece, which I've read too fast out loud.

The class debates me and my life as if I'm not sitting there, as if I'm a baboon plucking lice off a friend's bright red butt. Some think I go too far, comments that send Jinx's hair flying back in fury, but most think I don't go far enough. "I'm uncertain about that last sentence," someone says. "But that's the heart of it," says the lady who is always knitting. The man with the shaved head treats us to a loony political rant while Jinx dips into her email, pretending she isn't, before reeling him in with a curt, "We're here to talk about the words on the page. The words on the page." The way she recites that line makes me visualize it tattooed across someone's shoulder. "Do the words on the page show us that the writer is honest?" Jinx asks.

I'm in court, up on unspecified fraud charges. The class is working too hard because I could pleasantly agree that, yes, I am a fraud, that I'm not the least bit honest. But the writer being discussed isn't allowed to speak. I'm supposed to sit there, scribbling notes like a moron. But I'm doodling.

To be specific, I'm writing Y's name and my name and crossing out the letters that are the same, in that way girls did back when I was a girl. Count off with the remaining letters: love, hate, friendship, marriage. Where you end—the last letter—is the relationship you'll have with your beloved. Back then we included middle names, or initials, or even nicknames, to get what we wanted. Already I know that Y and I match "love" with my middle name and his middle initial or "marriage" with his middle name but not mine. I shouldn't be doing this in class; I should listen to the smart comments about my at-home assignment: *write about a terrible mistake.*

The young man with Y's name flops his head down hard onto his folded arms. I don't know what that means.

The class is distracted momentarily because someone questions when Google was invented.

I want to figure out my memories about Y; I want them organized in computer files: MistakeAssignment.docx and such. Pertinent topics. It's not like I think about Y all the time. No. Not until Jinx presses me for Truth and Honesty.

Not until I see the man who looks like Y sitting across from me. I want to hug him. Or, I want him to hug me, I want his arms to be that right sort of wiry, his grasp leaving me almost breathless. It seems possible that I may have a worse terrible mistake to write about next time Jinx teaches "Tell It Slant."

The young man with Y's name lifts his head and says, "She's on to something."

"The writer," Jinx prompts. We're supposed to refer to The Writer, separating ourselves from this personal material. "Say 'The Writer,' not 'she.'"

He repeats, "She's on to something. She should keep at it. She should just keep going."

"We never say 'should' to The Writer," Jinx snips.

Oh, yes. I'm totally, completely, utterly captivated by this young man! I might be a little in love, or even a lot.

Did I mention that I married a perfectly wonderful man two years ago? This perfectly wonderful man, this lovely man—The Writer will call him R—asked to read my assignment, and I told him the teacher made us promise not to share our work until after the class's critique. This lovely man believed me. He even said, "That makes sense," though it doesn't, because what I told him was totally, completely, utterly a lie.

He looks at me, this young man who looks like Y, looks at me straight and hard as Y used to look at me straight and hard, and I'm expecting Y's words: "Ignore the bullshit." This boy doesn't say that because that would be too crazy, right, too much coincidence, so instead, he says, "Truth, it dazzles gradually, you know?"

The man with the shaved head obnoxiously goes, "Huh?"

Jinx nods. "Not quite Emily Dickinson, but close enough and so the last word," and she calls for break, lunging for her phone as we herd through the door and down the hallway. I end up in the direction of the bathrooms but keep heading down the hall, to a door propped open with a cinder block that leads to a metal fire escape, the old-fashioned, slightly dangerous, clangy kind. I step out onto it. It's early spring, and clocks sprung forward on Sunday, and there's novelty to this light and airiness. Out past the parking lot, a skinny, flowering tree is about to burst, as if it's been waiting all winter, doubting through that freakish February blizzard that the world would turn to spring again, and now that it has, now that it has.

Well. I silently root for the little white tree alone on the edge of the parking lot.

"Nice night." It's the young man with Y's name in the doorway behind me, framed and silhouetted, as he scrunches both sleeves of his long underwear shirt up to his elbows. I move two steps, an unspoken invitation, my feet noisy and awkward—as if I'm someone who might fall—and he slips out onto the fire escape and stands next to me. He grasps both hands onto the iron railing, flexes his body backward as if pulling at an oar. This is the first time I've seen his bare forearms.

"You didn't read," I say.

He shakes his head. "Not this time. Next week."

"It's such a personal class," I say. "I don't know why I didn't expect that."

"My dad says writing is nothing but cheap therapy."

"He sounds like a jerk," I say, which I shouldn't have, but he laughs. His laugh is expressive, like a saxophone late at night.

"You're right about that."

"Three hundred fifty dollars for the class," I say. "That's only like two or three therapy sessions. Depending on if you're seeing a city therapist or one in the suburbs."

His saxophone laugh. "You're funny," he says.

"Do you want to be a writer for real?" I ask.

"I guess," he says, all casual in a dead-serious way.

"I admire that," I say. "I think writing's hard."

"Someone said that writing is hard, but that for some people *not* writing is what's harder."

"You're the some people," I say.

"So are you," he says.

I shake my head and watch his hands, wrapped around the iron rail. I wish I could touch one, just once, just brush my fingertip along his knuckles. I fold my arms around myself quickly, hoping I won't be stupid.

"You are," he insists. "You have a story. You're not like those other bozos. That guy with the shaved head."

My turn to laugh. My laugh sounds like an ailing foghorn, but it's a little late to revise a new laugh for myself.

He says, "What a great laugh. It's bold."

"Bold" is a nice word to hear. Maybe I'll use it in my next assignment. Maybe I'll use it now:

"I'd love to read your work," I say, boldly. "For critique, or just so I can tell you that you're a genius."

"I'm no genius," he says. "That's for sure."

"Life is so hard if there isn't that one person who thinks you're a genius," I say, which is what Y used to say, which is who Y was to me, which is who I was to Y. "I could be that person. I mean, since it doesn't sound like your dad is doing that for you. That's all I mean, that's all."

There's a silence that might be awkward or that might be meaningful; it's hard to tell. Fifty-fifty.

I take it as the latter.

His hands are so close. I just want to. As if you're still here; as if we're still twenty-three, twenty-four, twenty-five. I listen to my heart beating.

I peer over the rail. Broken glass, a scattering of dry leaves. "Long way down."

He straightens and leans over, way farther than I have, and flings forward both arms. "Romeo, Romeo," he falsettos.

We laugh, then shamble back to class.

It was the former. *The former.* I knew that all along.

"A September afternoon. I took the metro to your group house on Capitol Hill. I had lived in Washington for a year, and in August, I went to my first Bruce Springsteen concert—the Born in the U.S.A. Tour—invited by a male friend who wanted to be more than a friend but knew he never would be. He had camped out in line overnight to get tickets in the second row. The Cap Centre. Watching Bruce explode into 'Born to Run,' pointing directly at me when he sang, 'tramps like us,' told me in a single moment that I wanted passion in my life. I needed to be bold. I was twenty-three and I might as well have been fifty-three, saving old bread wrappers and shuffling outside in my slippers and robe every morning to bring in the *Washington Post*.

"You had moved to DC for your internship, and we had known each other in college, and the plan was to go to lunch and hang out for the afternoon. You didn't call it a date. I wore an old T-shirt and ratty jeans. We had worked together in a grungy takeout pizza restaurant where everyone always showed up in their sloppiest clothes. You lacked direction. You wore battered work boots I scorned for being hideous. You fought with your father, who phoned the pizza restaurant late at night, during cleanup, and your face turned grim. 'Uh-huh,' you repeated in a monotone, 'uh-huh, uh-huh.'

"I got confused by the quadrants on Capitol Hill, not understanding that 500 A Street SE is nowhere near 500 A Street NE. You were perched on the brick steps outside, about to leave when I trudged up forty-five minutes late. Hot, muggy. My face all pink, all sweat. You scoffed at my old clothes the way I had scoffed at your boots. You wore a clean T-shirt, clean jeans: no frayed seams, no holes. Chuck Taylor high-tops, black with red laces. We hugged. It had been two years since we'd seen each other. You had found enough direction to leave our college town to go teach English in Japan. Back then, everyone without direction went to teach English in Japan.

"Lunch was at a Greek restaurant you knew. We split the check.

I ordered grape leaves—*dolmades*—which I had never eaten before, and I admired the tight, tidy rolls lined up across the plate. We walked to the National Gallery, talking about music and restaurants and people we had both known who were doing interesting and not so interesting things. Tramps like us, I thought.

"Picasso and Braque, a special exhibit I had already seen earlier in the summer, with a different man who also wanted to be more than friends—but with you, the paintings were refreshed—fractured guitars, chunked-up women, violins. You read each plaque and stared hard, wanting to see how the artist saw. (Later, I joked that this was the only art museum visit you initiated.)

"Outside, we bought red, white, and blue popsicles at a truck parked at the curb of Pennsylvania Avenue. We sat on a low cement ledge outside the museum, letting our tongues stain purple, letting tourists in fanny packs and tennis shoes blur by, and you suddenly asked what I was looking for in a man. I had a list to reel through. All girls back then had checklists for focus, to keep from wasting time on guys who didn't match our exacting criteria. I reeled through my list: funny, confident, smart, kind, must love Springsteen, and the rest, down to favorite pizza toppings and not a morning person. You smiled, the edges of your teeth sky blue. 'Good luck finding all that,' you said.

"I said, 'I think I'm describing you.' My realization and those words came at the same time, and you said, 'Yep,' leaning in to kiss me.

"Oh, wow, I thought, wow, oh, wow. Like seeing Springsteen from the second row, his finger pointing at me. What my life was missing was passion. Was you.

"The Greek restaurant is closed; the truck that sells popsicles sells sushi now; the Picassos and the Braques hang on other walls; our group houses have disbanded, the men and women now in their forties and fifties, in the suburbs. Yes, Springsteen still tours, but Clarence is dead.

"I can write all these things—these stories and these words—

and I can tell the truth or I can tell it slant but you're not here to read what I've written. To add a detail, to tell me I got it all wrong or remind me what I missed, or to laugh. You're not here to say, 'I remember those days and how we were and us.' You're not here to say, 'I remember *you*. I remember who *you* were back then.'

"And so it turns out that what I've been writing about all along has been myself.

"How embarrassing."

Write about love. The man with the shaved head reads about his dog. The woman who knits reads about the birth of her twin grand-daughters. Jinx smiles through everyone's critique, her hair tame and calm, the phone silently tucked into her purse, unnecessary. It's as if a storm has sailed far out to sea. We like everything that everyone wrote and find much to admire in what The Writer has accomplished with the words on the page.

The young man with Y's name does not sit directly across from me. He plops down in the desk next to a young Indian woman with olive skin and waves of dark hair like a cape all the way down her back. She wears thin gold bracelets that tinkle when she talks with her hands, which she often does; she's beautiful and expressive and makes smart comments. She is twenty-two, twenty-three, twenty-four. Her voice is soft, and the group falls silent when she speaks or reads, leaning close to catch each word. Even the man with the shaved head sets aside his Starbucks to listen. Her essay is about a tree that she watched through a bedroom window of the house in India where her grandmother lives, where she visited every summer when she was growing up, and how the tree moved and whispered to her, how she felt the tree understood her sadness about her lost father, and how when she is sad now, late at night, she closes her eyes and feels her hand pressing against the rough bark of that tree.

When she finishes reading, a tear drops from her eye and falls onto the Formica top of the desk. I watch the young man with Y's name staring hard at it; I feel him wanting to reach for that tear, to swipe it away with his finger.

He won't today. Not now, not here. But he will: he'll hold her when she cries, and she'll hold him; there will be times ahead when he might be the cause of her tears, or when her words make him curse in frustration. They will travel to India, where he will see the tree for himself, this tree that has brought them together. They will grow old together, or expect that they will, promising "till death do us part." He is bold, this young man with Y's name, he is funny, confident, smart, kind. Possibly he loves Springsteen, possibly he's not a morning person.

As it should be. Definitely, all is as it should be, and I have no choice but to believe that.

Because something exists entirely inside your own mind doesn't mean that the end of it isn't painful.

I read my piece about the playful black cat that I loved.

Jinx asks, "Has The Writer achieved honesty?"

The man with the shaved head nods, and so does the lady who is always knitting. So does everyone. They like the story about my cat.

"Quick break," Jinx says, sweeping the crumbly edges of her Triscuits off the desk and into the palm of her hand, and we scatter.

I will never show these assignments to the lovely man who is my husband. I will never write a book. I will never know the difference between truth and honesty, and I will never, never understand why you died.

And I will not return to "Tell It Slant," after the break, or ever.

CHAPTER TEN: AN INDEX OF FOOD (DRAFT)

My publisher is making me write this "index of food." My editor has politely but definitively informed me that I should think about including lists in my book. Readers aren't interested in long blocks of text, she tells me, not in this 140-character world. A gust of a sigh before she adds, Everyone knows that readers want short and snappy.

My agent agrees. She confesses to me a horror of short stories that stretch to fifteen pages and novels that tiptoe too far into the two hundreds.

My husband agrees. He reads my work in progress from time to time but usually starts snoring five pages in. His excuse is that he works hard in a stressful job, but what if it *is* a short and snappy world now?

Maybe think about adding a dog, my editor suggests. Books sell big when there are dogs, and also any connection with a celebrity helps.

First, I don't like dogs (but please keep reading!). Second, my connections with celebrities are obscure, vague connections to obscure, vague celebrities, like seeing Julia Louis-Dreyfus in a student production in college during our freshman year. (She was quite good.) But can I really capitalize on that? Ha—I guess so, because here I am squeezing in a celebrity, and upfront, too! (*Author's note: No offense, Julia—you win Emmys, so clearly I'm using poetic license in referring to you as "obscure and vague," but I think we both know your name isn't the biggest headline on the checkout magazine rack. Still, I hope you'll overlook this pathetic name-dropping should we ever cross paths.)*

So, How about recipes instead? I ask my editor. I've got recipes.

Done to death, she groans, don't you want your book to *sell?*

Do I?

Of course. Of course I do.

And because I want my book to *sell,* here then is a list of the food mentioned in my book. Not content, but an easy-peasy *list* of content. Here is what they tell me readers want:

Pizza, pages 38, 40, 98, 146–47, 164–65, 187, 209, 211.

- ◆ *"If I could eat only one food for the rest of my life, I choose pizza."*
- ◆ *"Bad pizza is at least edible, but bad Chinese food and bad barbecue are just baaad."*

In my real life, these are my two biggest pizza proverbs, so of course I have to put pizza in my book.

And of course I would include pizza in a book that's about you.

(About you, how? Novel? Stories? Memoir? Yes and no. I grandiosely like to claim it's the truth of you with an overlay of fiction.

Call it a novel, my agent says, novels are what *sell.* Don't even mention stories.

Okay—this *novel* about you. This novel.)

Pizza was more than your favorite food, it was your passion. You wanted to open a pizza restaurant someday—you saved recipes and subscribed to *Pizza Today* magazine (pizzatoday.com; motto: "the most powerful marketing tool in the pizza industry"). During college you worked part-time in a small, family-owned pizzeria, learning the tricks of Chicago pizza, and after graduation, you went full-time, making hundreds of pizzas each night—not manager, not assistant manager, just a guy who dreamed of opening his own Chicago-style pizza place somewhere beachy. Pi Guy was one possible name I remember you bounced around; "no one likes math," I had cautioned.

Your father pinballed between embarrassment and horror, exasperation and fury. He didn't tell his friends what you did. His friends' kids were getting jobs at Merrill Lynch after college (this was the 1980s, when all anyone wanted was to work in finance). Not you. You were about making pizza—rolling dough; slathering on sauce; cheese by the handful; pinching sausage from a bulk slab and arranging the dots in concentric circles on small, medium, larges, on thin crust and deep dish; sliding pizzas into the oven and back out. Four years of college tuition for this, was the question buzzing your dad's head.

You loved your life—cooking pizzas until midnight, highlighting and reading stacks of books back home in your basement apartment with the cheap rent, sleeping in to noon. You didn't own a tie. You walked to work. All you wanted was this life, forever.

We met at this pizza restaurant. We fell in love later, but this is where we met. The "us" of us started with pizza.

You know, it really wasn't my dream to be married to a guy who made pizzas all day long. So you chose me, also pleasing your dad in the process.

I'm sorry.

Bacon, page 149.

Who doesn't love bacon? Bacon is perpetually trending, so of course I threw it in.

When I cooked bacon for you, I microwaved it on a special plastic tray, swathing it in layers of paper towels—like half a roll—to soak up the grease. Much healthier cooked that way: fewer calories, less fat.

Now, I fry bacon in a frying pan. No paper towels. Grease everywhere. It tastes a whole hell of a lot better.

I'm sorry.

Watermelon, pages 9, 57.

You had a singular way of eating watermelon with a knife and no fork, and a vocabulary you invented, calling that deep red middle section the "fillet," and so what did I do? I snagged these unique and quirky details about you—details that capture the essence of who you were, defining you in the most charming and individual way possible, a way that would make a girl utterly fall in love with you—and I used them as a plot point here on page 12. I also threw them in randomly on page 84 because that paragraph needed something.

I'm sorry.

HoneyBaked ham, pages 71–72.

I put out ham after your funeral, but it wasn't HoneyBaked®, with the registered trademark symbol. It came from the deli counter at the grocery store. It was only an okay ham. People ate it because people don't fuss after funerals.

I'm sorry.

Malted milk balls, pages 9–10.

The candy you craved. Now and then I bought those big, fake milk cartons of Whoppers at the drugstore as a surprise for you. I was in charge of errands and shopping because you worked full-time and I only worked part-time, so it was up to me to buy the special treats, to decide which treats to buy, and, well, I don't like Whoppers all that much (plus, they're caloric, 190 calories in 18 Whoppers, not to mention 35 percent of one's daily saturated fat), so the treats I mostly bought were peanut M&M's, also unhealthy, I admit—220 calories in a quarter cup and 23 percent daily saturated fat—but peanut M&M's happen to be *my* favorite candy.

I'm sorry.

Snickers bars, page 157.

Another candy you liked. Also, the name of your beloved childhood dog. I've used stories of this dog before, in other books I've written,* not only here in this current work.

You and your father got teary when you spoke of Snickers, a collie. She was the best dog ever, you would say in unison, nodding your heads in unison. You disagreed about dozens of things, but never this, that Snickers was the best dog ever.

As noted, Snickers is a dog mentioned in a previous novel, and I'm also bringing her up here in "Index of Food" because, well, she's a dog. I've never owned a dog and I expect I never will and I'm talking now about dogs in general and Snickers the remarkable wonder dog in particular because my editor assured me that dogs *sell,* and now that I've gone on about this dog (who undoubtedly even I would have liked), it's not farfetched to imagine putting a pretty collie on the cover to try to sell more books.

I want to sell more books.

I'm sorry.

---

*See Leslie Pietrzyk, *A Year and a Day* (New York: William Morrow, 2004), 226–27: "and he got a collie for his tenth birthday that he named Snickers, after the candy bar; Snickers still lived with his mom and dad in Muscatine. 'Great dog,' he told me. 'She'd love you.'"

Guatemalan food, pages 151–52.

I admit that I consulted the Internet to get the exact dishes listed in the book, including: *churrasquito, chuleta, pepian,* or, translated, steak, pork chops, and some sort of native Guatemalan dish that won't translate but stays a Spanish word that looks authentic on the page and will be fun to read aloud: *pepian, pepian.* Say it. (Sadly, I don't know how to make my computer put the accent mark above the "a." Maybe the copy editor can handle this?)

You and I went to Guatemala for vacation once, but I have no idea if we ate pepian.

I'll assume so. I'll start telling people we did. Now, that I reflect back, I actually think we did. Yes—we did. Definitely. I remember. I definitely, distinctly remember—for sure. We ate pepian at that restaurant with the hand-woven turquoise tablecloths and the old, hunched-over waiter who said to me in English, "You are soaked with youth of Lauren Bacall," when he meant I looked like her. Remember? The restaurant next to that gray stone church we tiptoed into after lunch, where we sat in the cool air, whispering about God and the universe as hopeful votives flickered and the sun pierced the blue-and-red stained-glass windows, scattering colorful shards of light up our bare arms. Remember that church?

Of course you don't because I made it up, and the restaurant, too. That's how easy it is to forget things. That's how ridiculously *easy* it is to fill the enormous gaps of what I've forgotten that I never, never should have forgotten but did.

I'm sorry.

The Majestic Café, see King Street Café (asparagus with poached egg, fried oysters, beet salad, bison hanger steak, chilled English pea soup, whole roasted fish), pages 79, 82, 83–97.

King Street Café in the book, but in real life it's The Majestic Café, on King Street in the Old Town neighborhood of Alexandria, Virginia (703–837–9117, majesticcafe.com; you'll probably need a reservation—request a booth).

It wasn't even open when you were alive—or was it? I can't remember. I could figure that out, because of course I know the exact date you died in 1997, and The Majestic is in a historic building, located in a town that values historical. (George Washington slept here for real.) There's a tab on the restaurant's website labeled "The Old Majestic" so clicking on it would tell me everything about the original restaurant in its pre–World War Two life—when it opened, when it closed—and about its resurrection: the new, modern restaurant and what year it reopened. Was that a year when you were alive? I don't click because I don't actually want to know. I go there often—Saturday night maybe, dress up a little maybe, makeup. It's one of my favorite local restaurants, only ten minutes from my new house and twenty minutes from our old house.

Yes, there's a new house now.

I'm sorry.

Pie, pages 28, 85, 89, 201.

I like pie. Some of this book is about me, right? That's okay, isn't it? Or am I just being selfish? I'm probably being selfish.

I'm sorry.

Booze (to include: Crown Royal and Coke, 7&7, Jack and ginger, Johnnie Walker Red, Johnnie Walker Blue, Drambuie, Tanqueray martini, tequila, white wine, scotch, scotch and a splash of soda, white wine, sidecar, Grey Goose and tonic, gin and tonic, cheap vodka, vodka tonic, cognac, Cointreau, brandy, a bottle of

wine, vodka, Frangelico, sauvignon blanc, cabernet,
a bottle of wine, Chianti, a bottle of wine, drinks at
Morton's, cabernet, champagne, sparkling wine, pinot
grigio, rosé, prosecco, sake, a pitcher of gin martinis, a
bottle of cabernet, bourbon, Jack Daniels, craft cocktails,
crummy red wine, and a bottle of show-offy single-malt
scotch), pages TK.

Forty-three items are listed under this single catchall of "booze"
because, as the writer, I'm only human and I can't possibly dredge
up separate anecdotes to cover each sip and every slug of liquor
consumed in the course of this book. Mea culpa. I understand that
I'm basically a failure as a writer for not even trying, and that a
better writer would at least divide the entry into subentries, i.e.,
"Booze, wine" and "Booze, mixed drinks."

You know what's funny is that you didn't even drink all that
much. And when you did drink, it was beer. You didn't like wine,
and you really, really didn't like hard liquor, the real stuff. Your parents drank an impressive amount, but not you. Back then I had a
margarita if someone else was buying, not much more.

But beer. You did drink beer. You died just as microbrews were
getting popular. For sure you would have loved the multitude of
regional beers out there now, all so easy to find online or in grocery
stores, and you would have been pleased at the respect beer has
earned in the foodie world, with flights and beer pairings at certain big city restaurants. Craft beers, people call them. I bet even
your dad drinks a craft beer now and then, though he was a firm
Heineken snob on the few occasions he strayed from Chivas.

You know how many times beer is mentioned in my book?

Zero.

Crap. (*Q: Too late to add section with beer?? I'll email new pages
by COB tomorrow.*)

Anyway, so where did all this hard liquor and wine come from, I wonder?

I'm sorry.

Cornflakes, pages 199–200, 206.

And then here are Kellogg's Corn Flakes, which happen to be something I would very much like to forget. I haven't bought them since. Or eaten them.

When I came back from the ER—alone, alone, alone—there was your cereal bowl on the kitchen table, centered on the plastic placemat with the lemons on the border. The skim milk in the bowl was warm and filmy, the cereal a mess of sludge, the spoon handle poking up like a broken ship's mast.

One droplet of milk on the plastic placemat that had dribbled off your spoon. Or your mouth.

I pushed everything into the garbage—spoon, bowl, milk, soggy cereal, placemat, the half-full box of cornflakes on the counter that no one had put away.

Also, I threw away the pieces of the light blue terrycloth robe the paramedics had slashed off your body as they repeatedly tried to shock your heart into beating while I sat on the too soft bed in the guestroom, shuffled there by a middle-aged cop distracting me from the grim beeps and grunts with his chatter about the weather, which I don't remember at all except that it was stupidly sunny. And the sky was stupidly blue.

I wanted to be in the kitchen with you. I know that keeping me out of the kitchen was standard procedure; I know that I wouldn't like seeing what was happening in the kitchen if I had been in there, that distant, helpless professionalism at work. I would have screamed for them to try harder, to try again, more, more, no, no. No! I would have grabbed someone by the throat. I would have punched someone. I would have fallen onto my knees and howled.

I know the cop was doing his job. I know one shouldn't disobey a cop.

I know, I know, I know.

I know.

I'm sorry.

Coffee, pages 64, 69, 105, 112–13, 115, 121, 128, 149, 183, 193, 211.

I'm drafting this index of food in a neighborhood coffee shop. Like The Majestic, this coffee shop is ten minutes from my new house and twenty minutes from our old house. It's a beloved spot in this neighborhood, and though it had opened before you died, you never came here.

We didn't drink coffee. We didn't even own a coffee maker. When your parents visited, your dad drove two blocks to the 7–11 every morning because he and your mom were desperate for fast and immediate coffee. We didn't understand how important coffee could be to some people, the caffeine of it, yes, but mostly the routine, the "I always start my day with a cup and read the sports section" of it. The "I'm just not myself until that first cup" of it.

Now, I'm a social coffee drinker—no caffeine required, no morning coffee habits ingrained. But it's only here in this neighborhood coffee shop—with the mismatched thrift store chairs and the bulletin board overlapped with pictures of lost and found cats and houses to rent and buy with and without off-street parking—it's only here, away from my routine, away from my cluttered writing desk and my new house and my new life—it's only while sitting here at this table scattered with scone crumbs, writing by hand on the unlined pages of a gift journal printed with inspirational quotes by famous women, drinking an iced skim decaf latte with a plastic straw—it's only here, amid strangers who don't know me or care who I am, sitting amid strangers consumed by their own fascinating lives and their own litany of sorrows and joys and secrets—it's only here, sitting alone, muffled in the white noise of people and the background keyboards of The Doors, then Bread, then someone snapping off "Baby I'm A Want You" mid-lyric and laughing, it's only here, only here—

—apparently it's only here where I find myself able to write about you. Only in this place.

(I'm almost finished.)

I'm sorry.

Mexican food (guacamole made tableside; stacked cheese enchiladas drenched in red chile sauce; an entire basket of chips; virgin margarita; chilequiles; tamales; menudo; that restaurant in Nogales), pages TK.

We lived in Arizona for two and a half years when you were in graduate school, so we ate a lot of Mexican food. I entered the state disliking avocados and I left with definite, irreversible opinions on the right way to make guacamole. I also pried from a tiny restaurant in Kearney, Arizona, their supersecret salsa recipe, which was the best salsa I have (still) ever eaten. They gave it to me only after I promised never to divulge how to make it.

We all, all of us, promise a lot of things.

Like not to include recipes in a book.

So here's the recipe, which remains in its original form, handwritten on the back of a credit card receipt from a bookstore in Tempe dragged out of the bottom of my purse, and which I keep tucked in the pages of *The Joy of Cooking:* One large can tomatoes (drained), 8–10 chile tepins, 4–6 green onions, 1 medium white onion, 2–3 cloves of garlic, a handful of cilantro, a tablespoon or so of white vinegar, a pinch of dried oregano, salt, pepper. Run it all through the blender to the desired consistency.

Chile tepins—dried, red, the size of blueberries, potent—are the secret ingredient because they're not usually found in a regular grocery store. Don't accept chile pequins, which seem similar and are easier to find—not after I've told you specifically and clearly what the secret is to this salsa. Don't screw up this perfect recipe over one tiny thing just because it's a little bit hard.

Okay, so I broke my promise to my editor, and I broke my promise to La Cantina in Kearney, Arizona, and I broke my promise to you. I should not have kissed that man that one night when I was out of town. I should not have done more than kiss him.

I'm sorry.

Burke's (Schultz's in the book, the way I think of it in my real life, because you called it cute that I perpetually forgot "Burke's," a name that felt wrong, and remembered instead "Schultz's," a name that was exactly right), pages 54–55, 58–59, 66, 68, 77–78.

Maryland seafood: oyster stew, crabcakes, steamed shrimp. German food: schnitzel and sauerbraten. Old-fashioned, lost in time options: chopped steak, chef salad, cottage cheese diet plate.

You found this place up in Baltimore. You loved food, you loved to eat, you loved finding secret spots and the homiest, diviest place for lunch wherever you were. The building that might have been shut down a couple of times by the health department but which had the absolute best something: pulled pork, doughnuts, fried clams, tamales, oyster po'boys, pecan pie, corned beef, pierogi. You taught me what to look for—pickups AND Cadillacs lining the barbecue parking lot; "family owned since 1946" printed in the yellow pages ad in the motel room phone book; odd hours and early closing; fried chicken with a parenthesized note to allow thirty to forty minutes to prepare—so I've found great food using your tricks in the years since you died. (Though the Internet makes the search much easier now: chowhound.com, roadfood.com.)

I still go to the places you discovered, including Schultz's.

Sometimes I take people with me, and sometimes they start calling it Schultz's just the way I do, and sometimes these people and I have very intense and private conversations in the booths lining the wall in the bar, and sometimes these intense and private conversations go on at the same booth where I sat with you, eating all those bowls of spicy steamed shrimp.

Sometimes these people are men.

Sometimes—one time, really—I marry these people. Sometimes I love them—him, really.

Always, I love him.

And you.

They say that being able to hold two contradictory ideas in our head at the same time is what separates us from the apes.

Maybe.

If so, then this:

You died.

I . . . didn't.

THE CIRCLE

The church door was locked, so the group stood in the May evening, a cluster of seven women and one man, none of them saying much of anything beyond murmurs about what time it might be, and that surely someone would come soon to let them in. It was a Lutheran church, or maybe Methodist—one of those churches that blurred a bit for not being imposingly Catholic like the churches she had known growing up in Chicago. This was a church that was more like a school: functional, not worshipful, nothing to inspire. That was okay. Impossible to imagine she would feel inspired ever again.

The church was located in Virginia, off a Beltway exit she had never taken—Little River Turnpike, which was a charming, old-fashioned name for a road, though the buildings and houses along it were like everywhere else—and not too far from the Beltway. Standing silently, she heard the distant drone of traffic.

She worried that she would be the youngest one. She worried that she would be the oldest one, though the man was surely older than she was; he had to be in his late forties. Still. People sometimes looked old when they weren't.

She was thirty-five, turning thirty-six in September, and couldn't wait to not be thirty-five. Like being a child, caring intensely about a birthday.

Across the cluster stood a woman with shoulder-length, wispy, white-blond hair—not colored but naturally that way—and the blue eyes a country singer might have. The woman's arms were

pressed rigid against her sides, perfectly straight and stiff, as if someone had told her not to let them move, not even a little bit. Her
cheeks were pink, as if from the sun or wind, a natural pink. There
was a trick she had learned from her mother, "Find one person in a
group who you could be friends with. That settles the butterflies."

Her. The white-blonde woman.

But picking the white-blonde woman didn't mean she would
smile, or go talk to her, or do anything but stand in this shapeless,
formless clump, waiting for the person who was supposed to come
and unlock the door for them, the person who was going to show
them what to do, the leader they would follow.

Ruth Feinstein is a social worker who specializes in grief and
grieving. When the newscasters report that grief counselors are
available to students in a school tragedy or to office workers following a shooting, Ruth might be one of them. "How can you
do that?" people ask at parties when she tells them what her job
is. "It's so depressing," they announce, as if they somehow *know*
Ruth's life, and on and on they go, about how sad it would be to
be around sad people talking sadly about sad things. Finally, there's
the point where Ruth always says, "What's sad to me is people who
cut themselves off from feeling. That's what's sad to me," and she
stares in a lingering way, making clear the unspoken conclusion to
the sentence: That's what's sad to me—*assholes like you.*

She's the one with the key to the church, and she's running late
now, at seven thirty, because five fifteen was the only time her doctor could squeeze her in, and when they work that hard to squeeze
you in, it isn't because they're anxious to give you good news. So
she leaves her office early to drive all the way out to the doctor
in Reston—rush hour traffic is hell times two—and once she gets
there, she parks the car and sits in it, hands staying dutifully on
the wheel in the proper position. It's one of those office complexes
that's trying too hard, with a fountain, tidy red brick walkways

lined with shrubbery, and flowering trees arranged in the parking lot medians. Even through rolled-up windows, Ruth hears a mockingbird singing madly, a wild riot of notes, including some that sound like a car-remote door lock, and on and on the bird goes, working the scales, spinning repeatedly through its repertoire, and finally Ruth backs out of the parking space and drives to a New Mexican restaurant she and her ex-husband liked when they lived out here. She orders guacamole made tableside—"that's enough for two," the waitress warns; "I know," Ruth says—and stacked cheese enchiladas drenched in fiery, musky, bloodred chile sauce. She eats all of it—including an entire basket of chips—and compromises only with a virgin margarita instead of the real thing. Then she heads to the church to lead the inaugural meeting of this iteration of the young widow support group she has organized.

That's why she's running late.

The group silently passed through the glass door and into the church basement. The room was what she would have described if anyone ever asked, What kind of room would a support group meet in? Drab, large, as shapeless as something with four walls could be, so that while the room was rectangular, the boundaries felt ill-defined. Alternating between stuffy and chilly. Windows high up on the walls, offering squeaks of light but no view. Fluorescent lighting with a slight buzz. An unplugged coffee maker on a long table covered with a plastic, red-checked tablecloth with dark brown burn circles where someone had set down something hot. It was a room where sad people collected, people with vast problems. She stared at a wall calendar with a picture of a European castle, wondering why something seemed off, and finally realized she was looking at last month's dates.

They unfolded white plastic chairs and arranged them into a rough circle. It would have been better to sit around a table, she thought, with somewhere to put the hands, a protective barrier.

Sitting in a folding chair across from the woman with the white-blonde hair, the two of them might as well be buck naked.

The man was already crying. Not loudly, but soft, seeping whimpers, as if he were a dog having the worst possible dreams, a dog dreaming of a world without other dogs. She had Kleenex in her purse—surely they all did—but she was afraid to offer it to him. It seemed he was imagining that no one noticed his tears, and she didn't want to point out how visible they were.

There were moments of awkward silence, of scraping the chairs on the linoleum tiles to get situated, a couple of people rustling in their bags to turn off their phones, the slowing whimpers of the man. She inhaled deeply. This was a good time to stand up and leave; she could announce she was going to the ladies' room and moments later, she could be safely in her car.

"I'm Ruth Feinstein," Ruth said, and she explained that she was employed by Fairfax County and was responsible for leading work-shops and facilitating support groups for people grieving varieties of losses. "Like this one tonight, the young widow group," she said, speaking casually, as if it were nothing, and the more traditional groups: older widows, children who have lost parents, parents who have lost children, even people who have lost pets—*pets who have lost people?* she couldn't help but wonder, and maybe a half-smile flickered along her lips because the white-blonde woman raised one eyebrow at her and also half-smiled, possibly thinking the same thing.

"People helping each other through shared experience," Ruth continued. "What I have found to be the greatest benefit of support groups is that here you'll meet and interact with others who share similar experiences. Look around you. These people understand better than anyone else out there in the world what you're going through right now." Ruth paused as the words settled, then looked around the room, significantly, looking at each of them one by one.

She didn't like that abrupt gaze, its sudden intimacy adding a new layer of responsibility to rest upon her, like ash after a volcano. She didn't want to help anyone. She wanted—no, needed—desperately needed—help. What if she told them that yesterday she didn't get out of bed except to pee, and then only reluctantly, going so far as to wonder whether she might order a bedpan online and how soon it would arrive? That she hadn't opened the blinds in the den since the day he died nine weeks ago? That she threw away— entirely away—ran through the shredder—the season tickets to the Washington Nationals baseball games—and what if she mentioned that the tickets were seven rows behind the home dugout? What if she mentioned those things? Would that excuse her from helping others? Would Ruth's gaze skim past her? Or, God forbid, would someone say something worse? Was anything worse than what she had been through? What was worse? She wanted to be the worst. She wanted to win at being worst. It was all she had to cling to: I suffered, she thought, I suffered the *most.*

Ruth said, "I think it would be a good idea to say our names and then the name of our spouse or partner. Then tell us a little bit about how that person died and when." Ruth was stocky and solid, in her late forties maybe, but she had a wild mass of black hair that cascaded halfway down her back in a stream of ringlets; straight hair might be the current fashion, but Ruth's hair was gloriously curly and glossy, and from the way she tilted her head from time to time, it seemed evident that she loved her fabulous head of hair, too. Even in this bad light, it shifted into a blue-black sheen that was mesmerizing. It was confident hair.

The man went first, because he was sitting to Ruth's right. He was Tom, and his wife died two months ago from ovarian cancer. A sympathetic ripple moved through the circle. "I'm a mess," he said. "I've lost all my credit cards twice already, and I know that has nothing to do with anything, but I can't focus." More murmurs, more sympathy. "My daughter left last week for study abroad in Italy, and I'm the shittiest dad in the world for knowing she should go have fun in Europe because that's what her mom would want, but then I gotta say, what about me? I want her back home with me, but I can't say that. But why doesn't she know? Shouldn't she know I need her here?"

He went on for another few minutes, talking and crying and sniffling, dragging his sleeve across his face, his nose turning red, the words muddled and virtually without sense. Of course, none of it made sense, right; why they were here? Because their husbands had died. Because they were young widows. "Widow," a word that was wrong to begin with, and then "young" tacked onto it, emphasizing how very and totally wrong this was.

She was thirty-five and her life was over, almost as much as her husband's was. Maybe she would rather have died. If the choice were offered, she would not recommend being the one left behind.

The woman with the white-blonde hair was next. "Hi, everyone," she said, with a twangy accent. "I'm Jayne with a *Y,* and I moved here about six months ago, and my boyfriend Sam drowned in the Potomac River out at Great Falls when he was trying to rescue a little boy who'd fallen in and who also drowned." There was a long, lingering sigh of sadness. The story had been in the newspapers, and the local news channels led with it for several days. There had been follow-up stories about how many people drowned each year in the Potomac River, the dangerous, swirling currents.

Jayne said, "That was April 7. A Saturday. A really beautiful, perfect, sunny Saturday."

Were you there? she wondered but didn't dare ask. With him? Watching? Which was worse—to be there, tearing along the riverbank screaming for help, or to be running errands at Home Depot, imagining that he was going to love the stone birdbath you picked out, planning what you were going to cook for dinner that night, which bottle of wine to open?

Other people spoke—a lawyer whose husband dropped dead of a heart attack while playing racquetball, and someone whose husband died of lung cancer, and a man hit by a car while on vacation, and an ex-husband who had been bipolar and killed himself. The names blurred, the widows and their men—Doug-Josie-Sarah-Philip-Eman—one long name, one long string of loss and sadness. There was so much sadness that she imagined herself drowning in it, as if in the Potomac, dangerous currents sucking her under. Why would anyone want to win? There was one woman whose husband had died two years ago, and she exploded into tears the moment she said his name and couldn't stop crying while she talked. Through it all, Ruth with her fabulous hair, was calm and serene, nodding gently, as if nothing she heard surprised or shocked or hurt her. She was immune to sadness. No doubt Ruth, leader of all her groups, knew the story that would win.

When it was her turn, she said, "Andrew had a heart attack one day at breakfast. He was thirty-seven and had been in perfect health." That explained nothing. Those were "just the facts, ma'am," the "what happened" of what happened, the barest outline of the emptiness inside her. "Nine weeks ago," she added. Nine weeks, nine innings to a baseball game, married nine years, nine people in this room right now, nine thirty in the morning when he died, nine minutes for the stupid ambulance to pull into the driveway of the ER, nine people who spoke at the wake, nine, nine. Like the man's lost credit cards, that had to mean something. Otherwise—what?

Don't think about that, the false hope of that empty, useless word: otherwise.

Or its hand-in-hand cousin: If. If only.

After the meeting, the group—minus Ruth—went out to Pizza Hut, which wouldn't be her choice, ever, of where to eat, but she went along, maneuvering herself into the spot across the table from Jayne. "Where did you move here from?" she asked Jayne after the orders had been placed—pepperoni and onion, and veggie. She and Jayne were the only ones to get Chianti; it was iced tea and

Diet Coke for the others. The waitress looked annoyed to have such a large group and had preemptively warned that there would be no separate checks. Tom offered to pay for everyone, which either was extremely nice or extremely show-offy.

"Columbia, South Carolina," Jayne said. "Teaching biology at Midlands Tech. It's a community college."

They talked about details like that for a while—siblings, South Carolina, biology, where Jayne lived now, how Jayne liked DC—but all the while, she was thinking that she didn't know anyone else who taught biology or who thought about the presence of biology in the world in any particular way. We wouldn't have met, she thought, we wouldn't have crossed paths except for this one irrevocable fact, this single word our lives boiled down to, widow. Our carts might have been in the same aisle at Safeway, and we just would have walked on, grabbing our carton of milk, our apples. We wouldn't have known.

As if her mind was being read, a woman kitty-corner butted in to say, "I think they should go back to the days when widows wore black so everyone would know. I hate when I'm having a bad day and someone's mean to me. If I were wearing black, I really think people would be nicer. I know I would be, now. Now that I know."

Widow. She looked at this woman, admired her bravery for speaking the word out loud. She planned never to do that.

At the far end of the long table, the two-year woman was sobbing and shredding her napkin, dropping the tiny bits into her water glass.

Jayne's blue eyes followed, seeing the same thing. "I won't stand it if I'm like that two years from now," she said quietly. She picked up her wine glass, swirled the liquid around before finishing it off.

The black-clothes woman said, "She's a mess," but then she laughed. "Probably we all are, just in different ways. Like, when I look at Doug's tuxedo, I just lose it. A guy buys a tuxedo and the plan is to wear it for years and years. This thing's practically brand new, and now what? I donated sweaters and T-shirts, but it's wrong to get rid of this stupid tux."

She nodded. There was a tux zipped up in a garment bag in her closet that she planned to keep forever, that she planned to cram into the trashcan the minute she got home tonight. They were all a mess. She was as messy as any of them.

The waitress brought another glass of water for the two-year woman.

Jayne said, "It's boggling how much stuff one person accumulates, how many things. Now, I've got his collection of antique cameras."

This is something she has thought many times—staring in the closet, staring at the bookshelves, staring at the photographs on the walls—but there was comfort in hearing her thoughts in Jayne's South Carolina twang.

"His suits were also really nice," the black-clothes woman said. "Made to order. How'm I supposed to find a 44-short guy to give them to?"

Jayne shook her head mournfully, and the black-clothes woman brayed out a laugh that was also a cough that was supposed to cover a tiny choking sob: "Guess what I really mean is how'm I going to find another 44-short guy? How'm I going to find someone else to wear those damn suits?"

Like dogs barking, she thought, or babies crying in church; one started, and the rest jumped into the chorus of howls. By the end of the night, each of them had cried several times and laughed several times and said, "I know exactly what you mean," over and over. She and Jayne exchanged cards and promised to get together, and the black-clothes woman also handed each of them her card. Her name was Suellen, which seemed like the least likely name this woman would have, and that made it easier to feel fond of her.

Ruth Feinstein is on the treadmill, and she hates the treadmill.

Because she hates the treadmill so much, she only works out in the early morning because that's when her friend Charlotte works out, and the only thing that makes the thought of thirty minutes on the treadmill palatable is thirty minutes spent talking to Charlotte. The two women met almost twenty years ago in a group house in the Adams Morgan section of DC. After losing touch for a while, they reunited—surprisingly—four or five years ago, in the waiting room for the DMV, each with complicated, car-related paperwork that couldn't be handled online. The tortoise pace of the DMV gave the women time to navigate apologies to each other, made easier when they realized neither remembered exactly what bad thing had transpired between them all those years ago. Then they blew off the rest of the day with a long, late lunch and a bottle of wine. This health club has been chosen because it's equidistant from their condos.

"I've got someone for you," Charlotte says, breathless from walking with the incline.

"Not this," Ruth says.

"I met him at a networking thing two days ago," Charlotte says. "You should have come with me." She's always going to networking things, always wanting to drag Ruth along.

"Grieving people find me," Ruth says. "I don't have to network for them. My job's very safe."

"Nothing's safe," Charlotte says. "But this guy is perfect for you."

"He's a six-foot-one, gorgeous Jewish doctor with a beach house and no mother issues?" As soon as the words are out, Ruth knows she shouldn't have said "doctor." So she quickly adds, "I don't know, maybe. Tell me more about him," with *tell me more about him* being the only words that might possibly stave off Charlotte's inevitable questions.

"Well," Charlotte says. "He has a boat. So think about watching July Fourth fireworks on the Mall from his boat. But how come you never told me what the doctor said?"

Ruth is a licensed MSW who almost became a practicing thera-pist before deciding to make grief work her specialty. She knows very well that it's hurtful to lie to her friend. "The doctor didn't say anything." So not exactly a lie.

There's a pause, and Ruth hopes it's the exertion of the treadmill that's silencing Charlotte. Ruth asks, "What's the guy's name?" and when Charlotte doesn't answer, Ruth says, "Better not be Stuart. That's a loser name."

Charlotte flips off the machine, grabs for a towel. "Your grand-mother died of breast cancer. Your aunt. They saved your mother because they caught it in time. What are you doing?"

Ruth looks forward, keeps walking at her brisk pace, one foot in front of the other.

"Did you even have the biopsy? How come you don't have stitches or something?"

"*Minimally* invasive breast biopsy," Ruth parrots. "*Minimally* invasive." Haha. Who came up with that one? Who knew the word "minimally" could be such a knee-slapper?

"Am I going to have to call Noah?"

Ruth's ex-husband. She can only imagine what he will do or say. It shouldn't be the case—not after how he treated her—but she's still a little bit in love with him. Yes, she thinks, that's exactly what you're going to have to do, call Noah, but she says, "Don't be ridiculous. Whatever you do, don't drag him into this. I'm calling the doctor first thing today. The minute the office opens."

"Or I could call your mother," Charlotte says.

"I'd like to see that," Ruth says. "She'll eat you alive."

"Then promise."

Ruth promises. Upon demand, Ruth even crosses her heart, right there in the health club at six fifty in the morning. Then she spends the rest of the day doing everything except calling the doctor.

Something about the young widow group the other night has

disturbed Ruth. Not the woman who, for whatever reason, hadn't done any grief work in two years and who's still about as gaping wound raw as the day it happened. Not the woman who talked about moving to Florida the second her house sold so she can forget everything. All that's normal. People ramble through grief at their own pace—tiptoes to raging bulls—and Ruth does not judge. It's not a race.

No, what Ruth finds disturbing is the steady gnaw of anger as she listened to the widows speak that first night. She's been tired lately, maybe, or about to get her period. Maybe that ill-advised Mexican meal. But today, home after work, after not calling the doctor, she realizes why: those bitches are alive, and she is dying.

She hates them for it, even as she hates herself for hating them, even as she knows she is supposed to be open to feeling. "Stay with the emotion," is her mantra, and that's why she can admit to herself—if not to anyone else, not even Charlotte—that she is still a little bit in love with Noah. But this. She can't admit this—even though, sort of, apparently, she just has. And exactly what is it she has admitted? That she is angry at the young widows? Or that she's dying?

She was meeting Jayne and Suellen at the mall at Pentagon City. She didn't like malls, and neither did Jayne, but Suellen did, and shopping together seemed like something to do on a Saturday afternoon, to keep her doing something. The three of them had met for drinks (too many) downtown last Friday after work, which had seemed slightly illicit, the three of them sitting in the bar at Morton's along with lawyers and lobbyists, as if they were normal women sipping cabernet at a Friday happy hour. Instead of flirting or dishing office gossip, they talked wills and insurance and paperwork. Possibly an eavesdropper might have mistaken them as lawyers, until Jayne said, "Well, I don't care. He's dead, and there's no law that says I have to pay off those credit card bills." Her boyfriend had no will, and so everything—technically—went to his parents, who blamed Jayne for dragging their son up north where he drowned, though, actually, he was the one who had dragged her up north. "They raised him," Jayne said, "making him think being a hero is ever any kind of a good idea. It's a stupid fucking bad idea if you ask me." They laughed at that, the cabernet taking effect, the freedom to say whatever the hell they wanted—to blame their stupid men for their stupid deaths—and when they got puzzled looks from the men and women in suits, who cared?

She was early—as she typically was—and Jayne was next and then Suellen. And there they were, standing at the coffee café in the concourse outside Nordstrom, and Jayne said, "I haven't gone shopping with girls since maybe high school."

"Probably works the same way," Suellen said. "Look at clothes, buy clothes, return clothes two days later." Suellen always spoke as quickly as possible, so no one would beat her to the same words. She was the youngest of the young widow group, only thirty-one, and she had been engaged to Doug for a month. They had expected that he would wear that new tux in their wedding, which they had started planning. Doug had been eleven years older than Suellen; they'd met by hooking up at a weekend business conference, but then were seated next to each other on the plane home, which sat on the tarmac for two hours, delayed: "forced to talk," Suellen said. Unfortunately, Doug had been married, but that ended quickly, though messily. Suellen was one of those people who seemed destined to thrash her way through a lot of entanglements. There was a raw edginess to her, so it was easy to believe Suellen when that night at Morton's she told them she struggled to keep female friends, even growing up.

"I'm a biology teacher," Jayne said. "It's not like I need clothes."

"Retail therapy is good for everyone," Suellen said. "Even biology teachers."

It turned out that Suellen had a personal shopper at Nordstrom and had made an appointment for the three of them to try on evening wear and cocktail dresses. "Who doesn't like looking at themselves in pretty dresses?" Suellen said, leading them through a glass door at the back of the store and into a hushed salon decorated in muted tones, cast in flattering light. The personal shopper was a tiny Asian woman named Mei who radiated cheerfulness and poured them each a small flute of not bad champagne that they sipped nervously. ("Told you," Suellen whispered. "This is how to do it, ladies.")

She felt Mei's cool eyes skim her body, appraising her, and while she knew the assessment was professional—considering dresses; possible shapes, colors, cuts, lines—it had been nine weeks since anyone had regarded her body with such frank interest, and she blushed under the blatant scrutiny. Her body had become now nothing more than a pile of flesh, dully maintaining its various functions, the way a refrigerator hums in a dark kitchen.

Mei had already set aside some dresses for Suellen to try on, but Suellen refused to peek until each of them had a pile, so off went Mei.

"I should have worn my good underwear," Jayne said.

"Yeah, because what are you saving it for now?" she asked.

They laughed. It was these comments that no one else would think were funny that they laughed hardest at. As if there was something to prove that could only be proved by laughter.

"Really," Suellen said. "I'm so spending as much money as I want to on whatever I want to. It's not like I'm saving up for kids' college funds any time soon. Mei is going to earn a big old commission today, that's for sure." Suellen lifted her champagne flute. "Here's to the good underwear."

They toasted. It was nice to feel a glimmer of a buzz on a Saturday morning, to luxuriate while someone took care of them, a professional devoted to making them feel pretty. She told the others what she was thinking, adding, "I guess in a terrible way she's like our prostitute," and they all laughed again, and she thrilled to the sense that no one else on Earth would understand what she meant.

Eventually, Mei returned with an armload of dresses, each color richer than the last, plum, turquoise, fuchsia, orange, ruby red. It was as if Mei had been privy to Suellen's comment the other night about wearing black and was determined to remind them that there were still colors in the universe, that there were two parts to "young widow" and one of the parts was "young." Jayne, the oldest of the three, was only forty, which might mean sixty more years ahead.

They tried on the sparkling dresses, keeping up a conversation with Mei about the imaginary dress-up event they were all attending at the Willard Hotel, a birthday party for a rich friend who lived now in New York City, but whose parents were too frail to travel. She had been in a number of Broadway shows, and the chef at the Willard was a buddy of hers, and there was going to be a ten course tasting menu—"so nothing too tight!" Jayne joked. "I'm not skipping even one of those courses."

Throughout the whirlwind of sequins and mesh and beads, Mei moved among them, adjusting a ruched waist, tugging a strap, stepping back to admire—"very fabulous"—or "maybe try another" when she sensed discomfort—insisting Jayne show off more cleavage; dashing out for tiny sparkly bags, impossible stilettos, and blingy costume jewelry; keeping up a running patter on the mythical birthday party; pouring a second, a third glass of champagne.

The shimmery silver dress, the strappy shoes she would never imagine wearing . . . she breathed differently, as if she hadn't properly filled her lungs for a long time, until now, and Jayne wriggled into the turquoise taffeta sheath for the third time, and Suellen posed on the pedestal at the three way mirror, admiring her butt in the tight peacock blue. And then Mei asked, "How do you three know each other?"

Silence for the tiniest moment, half a moment, the amount of time it would take for an apple to drop from a tree and thud onto the ground, for Cinderella's shoe not to fit, and she couldn't breathe anymore, not in the shimmery silver dress, not at all.

To break the silence, Jayne said, "How much is this dress?" and when Mei flipped the tag to show her, Jayne turned to let herself be unzipped. The ratchet seemed to echo, seemed to sound to her like the undoing of someone's heart—when, say, it stopped working suddenly one morning over breakfast, or when it shattered into a thousand dangerous shards.

Suellen said, "It feels like we've known each other for a long time, doesn't it?" and Mei nodded, too eagerly, too enthusiastically.

"I know what's next," Mei said, that whorish cheerfulness swinging down like a hammer. "What about a dress for your wedding, Suellen? Or did you decide to go traditional after all? I have a friend in bridal at Saks in the Tysons Galleria who you'd love."

Suellen bought the tiny purse and a dress that she whispered she would return to another Nordstrom. No one else bought anything. She had a headache for the rest of the day, meaning the champagne—sparkling wine, actually—was cheap and overly sweet. She had shared countless bottles of champagne with him over the years and never once got a headache. That night she lay in bed, flipping through their wedding album, beginning to end, end back to beginning, over and over. What was the point of saving that wedding dress, professionally preserved in a special box? Why had she been trying on a shimmery silver dress that he would never see her wear?

The group meets every other week, and Ruth doesn't allow herself to be late for the second meeting. There are two new women plus a new man, and the woman who wanted to move to Florida doesn't show, so maybe she has up and done it and is sitting on a beach in Miami right now, forgetting her life back here. The hard thing to learn is not to think about them after they go. There are a few Ruth might wonder about, especially among the teens who have lost a parent, but for most of the grievers, Ruth silently wishes them well on their journey and then turns her attention to their replacements. In these short-term groups, Ruth purposely tries not to remember anyone's name from meeting to meeting.

The doctor's office has stopped calling, but she signs for a certified letter that she throws away. A lawyer's recommendation, no doubt. She has been notified, blah, blah, not our fault she didn't come in, not our fault the stupid fool died. Blah, blah.

The man from last time, Tom, is talking again about how he wants his daughter to come home from study abroad in Italy. He needs her, he says—whines, it seems to Ruth, though she shouldn't think such things. The daughter wouldn't let him drive her to Dulles. "'You'll just cry at the airport, Dad,' she told me," Tom whines. "Of course I'm going to cry. I'm crying talking about it." He claws for a Kleenex then looks at Ruth, needing an answer.

She says, "That's a lot of loss to deal with all at once. First your wife, and now your daughter."

The rest of the group nods. Ruth has used her wise voice, so they assume she's wise, when, in fact, she's only repeating what the man has said, using better words. That's what she does: reword things they already know.

My husband is dead. *That's a tremendous loss.*

I'm sad and scared and confused. *Those are powerful feelings.*

This is unfair. *It is unfair.*

I'm angry. *Hell, yeah.*

I'm dying of cancer. *You're dying of cancer.*

Charlotte is on a business trip, but Ruth goes to the health club at 6:30 anyway, and cranks up the incline. Noah called last night while she was at the young widow group and left a message demanding her to call him, that it was urgent. "It's about Jiggs," he said. The cat. She lost custody of the cat in the divorce, though

Jiggs sometimes visits when Noah is traveling. She knows the cat is fine. That cat will live forever; it's fifteen years old and as spry as a ferret, with nine lives to rely on.

Noah is still programmed in her phone.

"Jesus Christ," he sputters. "What the hell time is it?"

"Six thirty," Ruth puffs. There's a no phones rule, but the twentysomethings yammer on phones constantly, so she supposes she can, too. In case the cat really is sick.

"Ruth, shit. I mean, fucking fuck."

Noah is always liberal with the cuss words. In another life, he must have been a sailor. In this life, he's a procurement officer. And, now, he's gay. She cheated on him, just a stupid one-time thing, frustration with their lack of communication, and when she confessed, hoping to forge a pathway to the new beginning they needed, he confessed that he was finally being true to himself and admitting he was gay. It was a moment a therapist might dream of; a wife not so much.

"Up and at 'em, tiger," she says.

He groans. "Something about a doctor," he says. "Why aren't you taking better care of yourself?"

Why aren't *you* taking care of me? she thinks.

"They can cure it," he says. "Doctors will make you better. It's not some automatic death sentence. . . ." More in that vein—not one word about the cat, of course—but what lingers after Ruth hangs up is a refrain in her head, in rhythm with her feet pounding the machine: *you* take care of me, *you, you* take care of me. If the words were in a song, it would be the saddest song in the world.

The third meeting. Mostly it's embarrassingly easy for Ruth not to think about what's going on in her body—*denial ain't just a river in Egypt, haha*—but here, the messy circle of young widows always reminds her of that first meeting, the one she was uncharacteristically late for, and that skipped appointment at the doctor's office.

Here, in the church basement, she listens to the sad stories unfold like an old-fashioned line of identical, linked paper dolls, as she feels her cancer plow furrows up and down the inside of her body. She thinks of her cancer as breathlessly efficient and thorough—not like a toddler run amok with a butcher's knife, but like a Nazi, the worst Nazi there could be: calm, cool, organized, patient. Hitler times two, times infinity. The precision. She imagines her cancer goose-stepping through her body.

The quiet one is talking. She usually doesn't say much, and Ruth hasn't seen her cry, though sometimes her eyes get a glassy, pre-crying sheen. She's pretty, but in a shy way, as if it's embarrassing to her to be considered attractive. Today, though, she's shown up in a sleeveless, leopard print blouse. It looks expensive, bought at a boutique rather than a teen store, definitely not tawdry, but the blouse also looks confused, as if it landed on the wrong body and is puzzled to be here, on this woman, at this meeting, the center of attention, all eyes watching as she talks. Her husband is the one who died at breakfast. Cornflakes—she mentions the cornflakes every time, as if they are important. People latch onto details, Ruth thinks.

The cornflakes woman says, "I guess I'm confused about all this stuff of his. How much I should throw away or what, though I have to say, I moved some of my clothes to his side of the closet pretty fast, like maybe even the day after the funeral."

There are titters and smiles. That's another thing Ruth has noticed about this cornflakes woman, that she is quick to go for the joke. Deflection. Stay with the feeling, Ruth thinks half-heartedly, but does she really care? There are jokes about breast cancer: *Hey, at least this double mastectomy means that men will look me in the eye now, haha.*

The cornflakes woman crosses her arms tightly against her chest, either because she's about to say something revealing or because the leopard print blouse isn't warm enough as the air conditioner kicks into full gear. She continues: "All his books are organized in this special way. One bookshelf for his absolute favorite books. Another for his absolute favorite books about Africa. I look at those shelves and cry, but if they were gone, I'd miss them. Am I supposed to box up the books and keep them for the rest of my life? Someone will just throw them away when I'm dead, right? I mean, no one but me cares about these books, and the way they're arranged and the order they're in and how it was his hand pushing each book into its exact spot on the shelf. There's his notes scribbled inside, and sometimes yellow Post-its fall out, with to-do lists in his tiny writing of places to eat and things to read and, and—" Tears glide down her cheeks, and she makes no move to wipe them away, as if she's afraid to touch them.

Stay with the feeling, Ruth thinks. Stay, cornflakes woman, stay. You're doing good work here. She is surprised at how touched she is; she hasn't expected much from this woman, has pegged her as one to drop out early.

Her friend rests a hand on the woman's bare arm.

The cornflakes woman takes a deep breath: "Those books are him. That collection of books that he assembled, it's like that's the story of his whole life, just right there. Not even the story. The life. The life is right there. It's in front of me, right in front of me, and yet . . ." She makes an angry little exhalation. "I can't explain what I mean."

"Like, how could all this be gone," Tom says. "How could it just be . . . gone?"

In the thickening silence, the rumble of the air conditioner feels rude. The faces of the group turn toward Ruth, who sits in the same icy blast that they do. She will say something wise. Instead, she finds herself sobbing harsh, frightening tears wrenched from some deep darkness, and she leans forward, letting her hair curtain her face as she sobs. She senses the paralyzing terror of the members of the group. This is a thing that isn't supposed to happen. Ruth has never made this mistake before.

There's a flash of clarity in Ruth's head: I'm only human, she thinks.

In July she invited Jayne and Suellen to her house for drinks and dinner. It seemed like a brave thing to do. She hoped maybe they could sit in the screened-in porch and not have to be too long inside the house, staring at his things and at the empty space where his things had been. It was silly; only she knew what was no longer there. The watercolor his parents gave them was no longer on the far wall. Lined up along that bookcase used to be the rocks they had picked up in Cape Cod while on their honeymoon—she liked the smooth, he preferred jagged. The champagne corks used to be in that basket until she dumped them into a shoebox that she shoved under the guest bed. He had taught her how to open champagne properly: "twist the bottle," he said, "never the cork," and though she was angry with him more days than not, looking to rebel against his every remembered word, she had to agree: twisting the cork led to a mess.

She stirred up a pitcher of gin martinis, and though it was too hot to sit outside, Jayne and Suellen followed her to the porch without complaint. Dinner was Caesar salad, steak on the grill, sautéed wild mushrooms from the farmer's market, green beans, and homemade peach pie now cooling on a wire rack. A bottle of cabernet. It was an intentionally manly meal, food women living alone might not cook.

They had unconsciously created a flow to their get-togethers. First they caught up with daily life—what happened to the awful admin she was supposed to fire; how Jayne's bathroom renovation was coming along; how to keep Suellen's visiting father busy and was the tourist tour of the White House worthwhile—and then they covered issues of general interest—movies to recommend, books that were good—followed by gossip about the group—did Ruth color her hair; jokes about setting up support group bingo with the constancy of Tom's crying, the two-year woman shredding Kleenex, and Ruth's, "How does that make you feel?"—and then, finally, what they had been waiting for, with the steaks now on the plate—perfectly cooked; she had also learned that from him—and the talk could turn to the missing men.

None of them had children, and that was all at once harder and easier . . . *discuss.*

Should Jayne call Doug's mother on her birthday the way he used to . . . *discuss.*

Was Suellen a terrible person for flirting shamelessly with the new guy at her office, since she admitted to loathing his personality but liking that he didn't know what had happened to her because he was new? "Someone must have told him," Jayne said. "You know what offices are like." *Discuss.*

She had something they had not spoken of before. She had known about it for a couple of weeks, but she hadn't mentioned it. Remember when she was going through all those books?

They nodded.

Cicadas buzzed. Jayne sliced her steak into squares. There were fireflies suddenly. The red glow of the coals out on the patio, and the scent of burnt fat. Moths crawling up the screens, attracted to the candlelight within the porch. Someone remoting a car door. Maybe even a star or two penetrating the urban wall of lights. The quiet danger of calm.

She had been going through all those books, and she had found a small leather book with no words written on the spine, so she pulled it out to see what it was: a diary of sorts, a journal of sporadic entries.

"He kept it on the shelf?" Suellen asked. "He didn't hide it?"

"There were so many books," she said. "And it was pushed way back. You'd never see it, unless you knew it was there. Unless you were going through every single book."

"Did you read it?" Jayne asked.

"Throw it away," Suellen said. They spoke simultaneously, the words loud in the dark.

Yes, she had read it. She had taken it to bed immediately, leaving piles of the real books teetering everywhere, and she read each page. His handwriting was quite clear, especially for a man. Actually, their handwriting looked alike. Early on, his mother mistook one of her notes for a final letter from her son and called, angry and sad. She stayed up past midnight, reading and rereading the journal.

"Well?" Suellen asked. Everyone had put down their knives. All the steak had been eaten.

She said, "It was something he took with him on business travel, so there'd be entries for those days, and then maybe a month with nothing. So very erratic, you know? But reading what he'd written. It was like hearing his voice."

Jayne let out her breath in a swift gust. "So a good thing?" Jayne ventured.

When she didn't speak right away, Suellen did: "He didn't—?" Suellen asked.

"No," she said. "He didn't cheat on me. Or if he did, he was smart enough not to write about it." Her half-smile, nervous, making the other two nervous, so they laughed lightly.

"That's super-dumb," Suellen said. "Dear Diary, Today I fucked a waitress I picked up." And then they did laugh for real.

"He was impatient and felt trapped," she said. "He said I was needy. And demanding. And it took so much out of him sometimes just to get through the day with me. I complained about stupid things. I was moody."

"Stop," Jayne said. "You're none of those things."

"I'm all of those things," she said. "He's right. I was a terrible wife to him."

Discuss.

People just let off steam, Jayne said, pointing to the example of the group, where people said some pretty shitty things about their spouses sometimes. Suellen wanted to snatch up the journal and throw it away immediately. "Where is it?" she demanded. "At least lock it up so you don't read it and obsess." Don't let his mom ever get hold of it, Jayne advised, "she'll use it as evidence that you weren't good enough for him."

"It's not the whole story," Suellen said. "It's the story of one day, out of how many?"

"Married nine years, together thirteen," she said. "But more than one day actually. He started it a couple years ago."

"You know what I mean. It's a pinprick in the universe," Suellen said. "In the whole great sky."

The night felt like velvet brushing against her skin.

"He loved you," Jayne said. "They loved us."

"They loved us," Suellen said.

She let them talk it all away from her, until the journal was just another confusing thing in a sea of confusing things. He loved her. He loved her, and it turned out that loving her was also confusing, but he did it anyway. He loved her anyway.

It's the heart of summer vacation weather, when everyone heads to their beach rental or their friend's beach house. Charlotte has invited Ruth for a long weekend at her parents' place in Rehoboth. "Do you good to relax," Charlotte tells her. Charlotte has stopped asking about the doctor, stopped volunteering to take her to appointments, stopped telling her about friends who either are or know specialists, stopped forwarding various medical links that Ruth deletes, stopped with the worried and frightened eyes. Now Charlotte's eyes are furious. Charlotte will not be able to last much longer. This beach weekend is—Ruth assumes—Charlotte's last-ditch effort to rescue Ruth.

Ruth knows she should go—to the beach, to the doctor. She should be a courageous example; she should be the kind of person of whom it's murmured, "She was brave through the end"; she should be a pink ribbon-wearing inspiration. Instead, she thinks of herself as an inspiration to those who give up. Where is their leader?

The young widows complain that well-meaning friends, relatives, and—yes—strangers constantly bray variations of this refrain: "If that happened to me, I'd fall apart. I don't know how you're doing it. I couldn't get through the day." The sentiment is neither helpful nor comforting to the young widows, implying that they're not sad enough, or suggesting there's an alternative to getting through the day when the most painful thing the young widows have to figure out is that there is no alternative. If there was an alternative, they would take it in a heartbeat, in a New York minute, faster than a speeding bullet. They would not choose this, this ENDLESS ALL CAPITAL LETTERS PAIN, but no one gets a choice. There's no choice. And you too, Well-Meaning Friend, smug and happy and alive, you'd do the same thing, you really, truly would. Yes.

It has been Ruth's experience that the young widows don't mention suicide. There are children, families making a fuss, the discipline of paperwork: there are reasons to live even in pain. When they're in this group, they're still in crisis, still afraid. They haven't found anger yet, especially not the women. This doesn't mean suicide doesn't happen. She worries about Tom.

Ruth tells Charlotte that she can't miss the young widows group. She'll head up early Saturday morning and stay overnight. On Sunday, she'll hit the outlet mall for tax-free shopping, then drive home. She promises. Charlotte will have to up her game and work quickly with this schedule.

Tom is missing, but the rest of what Ruth considers the core group has come, along with one new woman who Ruth spoke to on the phone; Ruth invited her to the meeting but is surprised the woman actually shows up. She had seemed iffy. They start by going around the circle. The people who have been coming since the beginning are brief and matter-of-fact, though their facts are still sad. *My husband's name is X, and he died because Y, and that happened Z months ago.* The women tell their stories without tears. The women laugh when the cornflakes woman jokes that her husband died on a Sunday because he didn't want to mow the lawn that afternoon. The two-year woman shreds Kleenexes, but that's all.

The new woman sits next to Ruth, staring at her own feet, which are lined up next to each other, touching. She wears battered blue and yellow striped espadrilles, the kind you might buy on vacation in a sunny country. She doesn't have a purse, just a bulky keychain loaded with keys and club cards that she clutches tightly in one hand.

When it's her turn, the room falls silent. The new woman keeps staring at her feet. It's as if she's in a trance and finally Ruth has to say, "Did you want to tell us your name?" in her most gentle voice, the voice saved for skittish animals.

The new woman starts. "I'm sorry," she says in a quivery whisper, and the others lean forward. No one will dare suggest that she speak up. "My name is Elizabeth and my husband Bill died two weeks ago. He was thirty-six." She pauses, and glances up from her shoes as if to measure the effect her words are having. The group looks back at her, with wary compassion. This woman is unpredictable, this woman might be trouble. Ruth feels each of them thinking exactly that. "He had colon cancer," she continues in her whisper-thin voice. "We found out earlier this summer, when we were in France, having this really great time—our first big vacation away from the kids—and it was the day we were going to the Eiffel Tower. But he woke up that morning with awful stomach cramps—we thought it was the fancy food, and he said he'd be fine, and he took Pepto. But we were waiting in this really long line of thousands of people, and he was sweating and clammy and could barely stand, grabbing the rail, and all I could think was being trapped at the top of the Eiffel Tower with him sick, so I dragged him out of line and we found some people who helped us get to the hospital, and my God. There were all these tests and everyone speaking French and trying to help but the words you need to know most aren't in a French–English dictionary. People were nice, but I thought if I could just get him back home, everything would be okay—his dad's a doctor and knows all kinds of people—and there I was all by myself in France."

She pauses. As she's been speaking, her voice has grown stronger. Tears are streaming down her face, and her mouth screws up before she hunches over and breaks into sobs. Someone nudges over the Kleenex box, and she grabs a tissue that she wads up and pushes against her mouth, then she reaches for another that she presses to her eyes. The big ring of keys balances in her lap. "I'm sorry," she says. Her shoulders shake as she cries. "I can't stop crying," she chokes out. "I'm so sorry."

The group is silent.

Ruth watches them without appearing to. They are shaken. They remember this raw grief, this pain, this intensity, the freshness of being lost down in the very bottom of that trench. They remember being there themselves. And now—likely for the first time—now, they suddenly realize that they are no longer all the way down there. Maybe they don't know exactly where they are, but it's somewhere else. Several of them shift in their chairs, perhaps embarrassed, or perhaps ashamed that they didn't break into tears when telling their own stories—but Ruth suspects that for these women this realization will bring mostly relief. Wherever they are on this journey, it's not where the Eiffel Tower woman is. Time has been at work already. Scab is an ugly word, as is scar, so Ruth uses sediment, evoking layers, evoking rock formations, evoking the forward inevitability of time.

They're in a fragile place, this group of young widows, and have only barely clawed their way to here. The Eiffel Tower woman's tiny voice calls to them from some distant, terrible place. They can't look back, not now.

So Ruth knows that many of them will not return for the last meeting. Two-year woman and maybe Tom, Eiffel Tower woman and some of the others who joined midstream. But the rest will discover an unfortunate scheduling conflict: an out-of-town visitor that same night or tickets to a concert. It doesn't matter. Ruth will show up at the church basement in two weeks, as scheduled, but she already considers tonight the final meeting of this young widow support group.

She was driving down the George Washington Parkway with her sunroof open, admiring shimmers of light dissolve across the Potomac River.

She was sitting in the screened-in porch at twilight, watching fireflies flicker off the grass, too many to count, reading their secret language.

She found the first thick caterpillar, striped yellow and black, munching the butterfly weed.

She saw a shooting star. She had never before seen a shooting star in the Virginia suburbs, and she glanced up at the right time to make her wish. She knew no one else would wish for the same thing. She understood that this wish would never come true but also that she would never stop wishing it.

She watched crisscrossed airplane contrails melt into a blue sky from where she lay one Saturday, in a hammock, the lawn freshly mown, the scent of cut grass and the crisp hint of autumn mingling in the air. She thought she might rent a cabin in the mountains for a week or two. She'd never done anything like that, taken a vacation by herself, and she had always thought she might like to. She would do it this fall, now.

Ruth is driving to the beach. Not that time; it rained that weekend, and she canceled, and then put off another time. But Charlotte will not allow her to cancel again or put off. Charlotte is insistent on the phone, her voice twisting Ruth's arm, and Ruth lets her. "I'll be there," she says.

"Labor Day," Charlotte says.

"I never liked that one," Ruth says. "The end of summer."

"Yes, the end of summer."

There's scads of traffic, but Ruth doesn't mind. It seems interesting to be doing something that everyone else is doing, to be traveling on a popular path. She's excited to be at the beach—Dolle's salt water taffy! Grotto Pizza! Thrasher's Fries!—and though Charlotte doesn't know it yet, Ruth will let her win. Ruth has known all along that there is no alternative.

She has this feeling—she is going to die—and she must stay with it. She, who teaches people how to live after their great sadnesses. She will die. If not from this, though this seems likely, but if not—another time. Some time. Yes.

She will die, and there will be people to mourn her and people to talk about who she was, people to tell stories and miss her, and people to love her—to love the memory of her, the precious memory of her—until the day *they* die. She has lived, and now, too soon, she will die.

Too soon.

That's what the young widows all say when they share their stories in the circle: Too soon. It is always too soon.

PRESENT TENSE

He knew I was a writer when he married me. He knew I write about everything, eventually. That I write about everything eventually.

That I *would* finish this book.

We're walking side by side; it's March, frozen, windy; the empty beach might as well belong to us. Thick gray sky, gray surf. With each wave, sea foam hisses and laces, sliding up and back along the sand, white bits fluttering free. The gray horizon doesn't frame, only blurs.

Too cold to hold hands; we hunch in pockets, under hats, deep within now vertical collars. My cheeks feel scraped of skin. After twenty easy minutes away from the boardwalk, with wind ramming our backs, now we've turned.

"I never noticed seagulls have polka dots on their tails," he says, pointing to a bird lingering on the sand, at the sweep of the last wave.

"Me neither," I say. The wind slaps our words.

The gull dances from us; then, resigned, it heaves itself into the wind, careening, zigzagging. We stop, circle our backs to the wind, and watch. For a moment the gull stops, suspended, before getting caught and carried away.

"The spots are on the edges of the wings," I observe. "Not the tail. The tail is white."

He says, "I like it the other way. Polka-dotted."

"Me too."

We walk backward a step or two, then turn, continuing on, heads down. The shells are only shards and fragments, most hued white, and plentiful enough to invite carelessness; they're common—clams, oysters, scallops.

From time to time, we cross the tangle of our own footprints, those that haven't yet been washed away. My step is deep and rough: boots chopping sand, divots under each heel. These tracks look sad to me, or scared. Anxious. His step stays flat and exactly even.

He's not a beach person, so this weekend celebration is for me, to make me happy. A reward for all that writing. We ate a dozen oysters each. Browsed the bookstore and bought hardcovers. Shared beach pizza and French fries with vinegar. Cosied on the same side of a booth and listened to a not bad bar band called Freezer Burn. Salt water taffy waits in the car, one box for us, two for folks in the office. Caramel corn.

Everyone else is driving home already, stopping at the outlet malls, gulping McDonald's coffee, dreading traffic. He wants to be doing those things—to be driving home—but I want this last walk on the beach.

In front of us, suddenly, is a heart etched into the sand, a heart the size of a picture window.

RYAN

LOVES

ASHLEY

scrawls across the inside, each word its own line. We both stop.

This heart wasn't here when we passed this point before. Was it? The lettering is thin and precise, and I picture a boy's bare finger pushing through the cold, damp sand, a girl posing for a photograph on her phone. Laughter. A kiss, another. This wind forgotten.

On a sunny day we might bend down and draw our own beach

heart and write our silly names in the sand. But now we're older, wiser—we aren't those people, Ryan and Ashley. It's okay, I tell myself.

"That won't last," he says, "that's so . . . ," but his voice ebbs.

The sand, the waves, the ocean, the crashing waves, the shifting sand, the endless ocean. Love and life and death.

There are no new metaphors at the beach. All we can do when we write about the beach is report what we saw, so I report that I saw a heart in the sand; I report that Ryan loves Ashley.

Or omit. We can omit things: the bloated seagull with the twisted wing; the tattered Ziploc weighted with dog shit; the decaying horseshoe crab, washed ashore and pecked apart; Styrofoam crumbs rolling off the waves and the empty soda bottles. We choose what to report.

"Nothing lasts," he says. He is facing out, staring at all that water.

The first husband, the first wife. Their invisible footprints pressed into the sand alongside ours.

Stop it. Stare at the horizon. Stop thinking, because every beach metaphor is a cliché, even when the heart in the sand is real, even when I see it with my own eyes, even when Ryan and Ashley truly love each other, even when my first husband died when he was thirty-seven, even when he fits neatly into a beach metaphor where nothing lasts, where waves endlessly smooth the sand, where shell fragments get swept back into the sea, where no wave is the final one.

I will cry if he kneels to draw his heart in the sand. I will sob.

We both know what we're talking about here.

All weekend I've held my breath for him to ask me, for him to say it: "Would you ever write a book about me? Do you love me enough to write a whole book about me? Do you love me that much, as much as him? Do you love me as much as you loved him?"

No.

No, he does not ask that. He does not ask that. He does not draw a heart with his bare finger. He doesn't need to ask those questions—or to hear my answer—he doesn't need to see our names written in the sand. He can stand and stare straight at the endless ocean in this moment and be unafraid.

And that, that is always the first thing on the list of the things I love about him—about you, Steve, about you.

ACKNOWLEDGMENTS

So much gratitude!

First, I'm extraordinarily grateful to Drue Heinz, the University of Pittsburgh Press, and contest judge Jill McCorkle. It's an unbelievable honor (and thrill) to see my book and my name listed with the Drue Heinz Literature Prize winners.

Portions of this book were written and revised at the Virginia Center for Creative Arts, the Kimmel Harding Nelson Center for the Arts, and the Hambidge Center. I am so appreciative of that lovely gift of time, space, and place. Also offering time, space, and place was Anna March, who lent me her beach apartment for two fabulous weeks of writing.

I'm lucky to have a smart community of writers to share with, lean upon, and learn from. As this book progressed, many people read pages and/or offered advice, insight, and clarity during much confusion. I'm especially indebted to: Marlin Barton, Sandra Beasley, Susan Coll, Dan Elish, Rachel Hall, Beth Kephart, Dylan Landis, Carolyn Parkhurst, Charlotte Safavi, Clay Snellgrove, Amy Stolls, Susan Tekulve, Paula Whyman, and Mary Kay Zuravleff. I'm thankful for the support of director Rick Mulkey, my teaching colleagues, and the graduate students at the Converse College Low-Residency MFA Program, where I first shared several of these stories in public readings. I'm grateful to S. M. Shrake and Story League in Washington, DC, for giving me the opportunity to attempt live storytelling, with a piece that eventually led to "One Art." And how I love my neighborhood prompt group, always ready with an encouraging word . . . these people never fail to remind me that writing is also joyful!

My thanks to the journals in which many of these stories were first published, and to their hard-working editors: *Cimarron Review, The Collagist, Gettysburg Review, Hobart, Potomac Review, Shenandoah, The Sun,* and *r.kv.r.y.* And my ongoing appreciation to Converse College for selecting "Ten Things" for the Julia Peterkin Award in 2003.

Under the awkward catchall of "special thanks," I would like to acknowledge my parents, who filled my life with books from the beginning, and the world's most supportive sister. Thanks to Gerry Romano, Cynthia Weldon, and Veronica Grogan, for their abundant enthusiasm. I am grateful to have met Sandy Spidell when I did. And I will forever treasure the Rauth family.

Finally, gratitude and love to Steve Ello, for believing in the written word, for believing in me, and, always, for trusting that there *are* second acts.